A FLY HAS A HUNDRED EYES

A FLY HAS A HUNDRED EYES

AILEEN G. BARON

Academy Chicago Publishers

Published in 2002 by
Academy Chicago Publishers
363 West Erie Street
Chicago, Illinois 60610

Printed in the U.S.A.

**Library of Congress Cataloging-in-Publication Data
on file with the publisher**

To
DAVID, BOB, ERIC AND JIMMY

LATER, LILY WOULD REMEMBER the early morning quiet, the shuttered shops in the narrow lanes of the Old City. She would remember that few people were in the streets—bearded Hassidim in fur-trimmed hats and prayer shawls over long black cloaks returning from morning prayer at the Wailing Wall, an occasional shopkeeper sweeping worn cobbles still damp with dew.

She would remember the empty bazaar, remember that the peddler who usually sold round Greek bread from his cart near Jaffa Gate was gone.

She would remember the crowd of young Arabs, their heads covered with checkered black and white *kefiyas*, waiting in the shade of the Grand New Hotel, leaning against the façade, sitting on window ledges near the entrance; remember them crowded under Jaffa Gate in a space barely wide enough to drive through with a cart, standing beneath the medieval arohoo and crenellated ramparts, faces glum, arms crossed against their chests, rifles slung across their backs, revolvers jammed into their belts. One wore a Bedouin knife, its tin scabbard encrusted with bright bits of broken glass.

Only their eyes moved as they watched her pass. Lily remembered holding her breath, pushing her way through, feeling their body heat, snaking this way and that to avoid touching the damp sweat on their clothing. No one stepped out of her way.

She would remember the bright Jerusalem air, fresh with the smell of pines and coffee and the faint tang of sheep from the fields near the city wall; the empty fruit market, usually crowded with loaded camels and donkey carts and turbaned *fellahin* unloading produce, deserted and silent. Vendor's stalls, looking like boarded shops on a forlorn winter boardwalk, shut; cabs and carriages gone from the taxi stand.

She would remember the pool at the YMCA, warm as tea and green with algae, and the ladies gliding slowly through the water, wearing shower caps and corsets under their bathing suits, scooping water onto their ample bosoms, gathering to gossip at the shallow end. She would remember swimming around them with steady strokes, her legs kicking rhythmically, and the terrible tempered Mrs. Klein, blowing like a whale, ordering Lily to stop splashing. A tiny lady holding onto the side of the pool and dunking herself up and down like a tea bag nodded in agreement; Elsa Stern, the little round pediatrician with curly gray hair, gave Lily a conspiratorial wink and kept swimming laps.

She would remember it all. Everything about that day would haunt her.

Lily Sampson was on her way to the new YMCA on Julian's Way that morning, to catalogue pottery from the Clarke collection in the little museum being built in the Observation Tower.

She had stayed at the YMCA four years ago when it first opened in 1934 and reveled in its splendor, in its graceful proportions, in its arches and tiled decoration, its tennis courts and gardens, and the grand Moorish lobby paved with Spanish tiles. It had a restaurant, an auditorium where Toscanini played, and a swimming pool—the only one in Jerusalem. Tourists came to ooh and ah and told her this was the most beautiful YMCA in the world. They would climb the Observation Tower for a view of the city and look through telescopes into windows of apartments on Mamilla Street and Jaffa Road.

Lily went there to swim three times a week when she was in Jerusalem, walking from the American School through the quiet lanes of the Musrarra quarter, or cutting through the Old City.

At five minutes to nine, her hair still damp against her ears, her eyes stinging from chlorine, Lily climbed the six flights to the little museum.

Sheets of glass and wooden shelving for cases were stacked against the wall in the corner of a large, bare room that held only an old table, two wooden chairs, pottery wrapped in newspapers and stowed on the floor in old grocery cartons, and a wall clock that said four minutes before nine.

Eastbourne had said he would be here around nine o'clock. Lily suspected that if Eastbourne agreed to help her today, he had reasons of his own. She was grateful that he recommended her for this job, grateful for the small windfall from cataloguing pottery during the short break in excavations at Tel al-Kharub.

Lily stepped onto the balcony that opened off the museum, holding her breath at the sight of Jerusalem, creamy gold in the morning brightness. The great gilded cupola of the Dome of the Rock glinted in the sun. The Old City—its stone walls adorned with towers and battlements, steeples and minarets—loomed behind the King David Hotel.

She could see the grim-faced young Arabs she had passed this morning at Jaffa Gate, the crowd now grown to two hundred or more. The tops of their heads bobbed like so many black-and-white checkered beach balls.

Smoke twisted from small fires in the Valley of Hinnom. Lily looked through the telescope toward Government House on the crest of the Hill of Evil Council. She could just make out the Union Jack, flopping limply from its tower.

On the street, a dapper American tourist in a Panama hat and seersucker suit came out of the King David across the way.

The ladies left the YMCA one by one—Mrs. Klein, still frowning, her hair pulled back tightly in a bun, marched down the street. Dr. Stern walked toward the corner.

Lily heard Eastbourne enter the museum. "Let's get to work." He looked at his watch. "I don't have much time."

Full of his usual charm this morning, she thought. "I was watching for you. I didn't see you in the street."

"I had breakfast downstairs."

"You actually ate here?"

"I was hungry for some good English cooking and a real breakfast."

Of course you were, Lily thought. Good British housewives get up early every morning to cool the toast and put lumps in the porridge.

"You don't have a cook at the British School?"

"He's an Arab. This morning I had ham and eggs."

Lily noticed the newspaper under his arm and twisted her head to read the headlines.

Eastbourne folded it into a small packet and put it in his pocket. "I haven't finished with the paper." He looked out at the street and checked his watch again.

On the wall clock, it was exactly 9:00 a.m.

An explosion somewhere in west Jerusalem rocked the air.

After a tick of silence, a shout of "Allah Akbar" erupted in a full-throated roar from the crowd gathered at Jaffa Gate.

Lily rushed to the balcony, Eastbourne close behind. A mob spewed out of the Old City, propelled by the rhythmic chant, onto Mamilla, around the King David Hotel, spreading in a torrent toward west Jerusalem. Five or six men carrying rifles ran down Julian's Way. They encircled a truck, rocking it back and forth until it turned over.

At first the impassioned madness and destruction seemed strangely distant to Lily, choreographed and rehearsed, like a slow-moving pageant. She watched three men rush from the gas station at the turn of the road with full jerry cans, spilling gasoline on the street as they ran.

Waving fists, brandishing rifles, kefiyas flying in the wind, the horde swarmed into the warren of back streets with old Jewish shops and houses, down Jaffa Road toward Zion Circus. A blare of sirens, scattered shouts and screams carried from the direction of west Jerusalem on wind heavy with smoke.

Lily heard the crash of shattering glass. Looking toward Mamilla she saw a man with a jerry can splash gasoline through a shop window. A rumble of flames erupted and danced in the currents of heat from the rush of the blaze.

"It's that bloody Grand Mufti, al-Husseini," Eastbourne's nostrils dilated with anger and he wiped his hand across his mouth. "You can't trust him. He's orchestrating this from Syria, with the backing of Hitler and his crowd."

The tourist from the King David, his back arched in a posture of fear, stood in the middle of the street now, tilted this way and that by rioters who swirled around him as if he were a lamppost.

Eastbourne watched from the doorway, looking toward the tourist in the Panama hat, and glanced at his watch again.

Mrs Klein advanced on the rabble like a tank, shouting and flailing her arms. The mob surrounded her while she punched and kicked and screamed. They pressed against her, pushing her back onto the road. She floated to her knees, her skirt billowing around her, falling to the asphalt, her hair undone and sticky with blood that began to puddle on the pavement.

Dr. Stern turned back, hurrying toward her friend splayed on the sidewalk. A man careened to face Dr. Stern. He stepped into her path, thrust a fist in her direction as if to greet her. Her eyes widened, her mouth opened. She staggered against him. He pushed her away and slowly, carefully, she plummeted straight down, silent, onto the sidewalk.

Benumbed, Lily reached over the balcony railing as if to help. Trembling, she closed her eyes in horror and Eastbourne pulled her back, back to the notebook on the table, back to the comfort of the past to count clay lamps, juglets, burnished bowls with turned-back rims. She picked up a lamp, the nozzle smudged with ancient soot, and put it down again, drawn back to the balcony with a horrified fascination.

The tourist in the seersucker suit, without his Panama hat, disappeared into the revolving door of the hotel.

"Get inside," Eastbourne said. "This isn't a peep show." He looked at the street. "When this is over, they'll cover the bodies, take them away, and hose down the streets."

What will be left in two thousand years, Lily wondered? Just a thin layer of charcoal, without memory, without skeletons to mark the day, just one more level in the stratigraphy of Jerusalem?

People hung out of the windows of the King David Hotel, one man with field glasses, others leaning against balcony railings, some aghast, some curious. A father led his small daughter inside, shut the door and pulled down the blinds.

The tourist in the seersucker suit was gone.

Dr. Stern lay on her side in the street. Little rivulets of blood seeped from beneath her, flowing downhill and staining the pale blue cloth of her skirt. The little tea bag lady lay on the steps of the YMCA as if asleep in the wrong place.

Mrs. Klein lay in a widening dark pool, her hair, beginning to mat with blood, loose and wild against the asphalt. She looked oddly peaceful, her frown gone, her jaw fallen open in death.

False teeth lay beside her softened cheek. A man stopped, looked at the teeth on the sticky pavement, picked them up, wiped the blood on his sleeve, and put them in his pocket. He pulled a knife from his belt. Brandishing the knife, he ran on toward Mamilla.

"The name Jerusalem means City of Peace, you know," Eastbourne said.

Shuddering, Lily edged back to the table. The haze of smoke from the fires, the blare of fire trucks, the sounds of sirens from ambulances, of sobs, of wounded and mourners, of shutters ringing down with a clatter, penetrated the room. Lily was drawn to the balcony, and back inside to the table, too mesmerized to stop, too terrified to watch, mourning for the ladies who would never again skim across the green water, for Canaanites and Jebusites, for Israelites and Judeans, for Crusaders and Mamelukes who fought in this city with its twisted streets, its strange mystique and power, its heritage of blood and vengeance.

"Go downstairs and get me a packet of Players," Eastbourne said, reaching into his pocket. "Here are fifty mils. Bring me the change."

Lily dropped the money when he held it out. Her fingers numb and shaking, she picked it up slowly. "Sorry. I wasn't looking." She turned toward the door.

In the lobby, the desk clerk looked at her dumbly, his eyes glazed, his face pale. A bushy mustache hid his mouth and quivered when he spoke.

"Rioting in the streets and you ask for cigarettes," he said in a hushed monotone. "Cigarettes? Are you mad?"

"Players," Lily repeated.

"I don't sell them here. In the dining room."

Lily trudged into the dining room. The desk clerk followed and placed himself behind the bar.

"Players," Lily said again and put the money on the counter.

He counted it and pushed back the change. "You cold-blooded English. You have no feelings. Here are your cigarettes."

"I'm American."

"Crazy American. You're all the same."

She climbed the stairs, catching her breath at the landings, looking down empty halls at laundry carts stacked with fresh linens for unmade beds. She felt heat from hidden pipes radiate through the whitewashed walls, heard the elevator knock and clatter as it moved from floor to floor.

On the sixth floor, the museum was silent. The notebook was still open on the table. The clay lamp was where she had put it down.

And Eastbourne was gone.

TWO

⟋

LILY PUT THE CIGARETTES and change on the table and waited for Eastbourne. She wavered back and forth between the table and the balcony, picking up a black juglet and putting it down. "He's a grown man," she said aloud and sat down at the table. "He can take care of himself."

She pulled the pottery registry toward her and turned a page. He's probably down the hall. Maybe downstairs.

She dipped the pen in India ink to write a registration number on the juglet. Maybe he was out strolling down Julian's Way with a gentlemanly swagger, scorning the brouhaha with his usual bravado. Register the juglet. What number? What comes after two hundred forty-seven?

She imagined Eastbourne trying to shout down a clutch of angry rioters, lying on the pavement in their wake, his white Bermuda shorts and knee socks bright with blood.

Is it two hundred fifty?

Oh, God.

She put down the pen and started toward the balcony. The elevator door clanged open and shut. Steps sounded in the hall. For a moment, she was relieved. But it wasn't Eastbourne—the gait was faster and heavier. Lily moved toward the far side of the table as the footfalls came closer, clicking and reverberating on the tiled floor.

The tourist in the seersucker suit, his Panama hat gone, faced Lily from the doorway. He stared at her, his eyes deep-set, a distracting electric blue. He glared at the notebook on the table, the pen, the bowl, the juglet in Lily's hand.

"Can I help you?" she asked.

He hesitated. "Beg your pardon." His voice was deep and resonant. He watched her come around the table and waited, his expression blank, his fists clenched.

"You're looking for Eastbourne? He was here a minute ago," Lily told him.

The eyes of the man in the seersucker suit traced her movements. She went to the balcony, and he followed.

"He might have gone out," she added.

His jaw protruded and the side of his face twitched. The man leaned over the rail. "I don't know anyone named Eastbourne." His eyes continued to search up and down the street.

If not Eastbourne, who was he looking for?

"You lost your hat."

"Beg pardon?" He worked his jaw again. His eyes glinted at her, hard and angry. "Sorry to bother you." He went back through the museum, pausing at the table, eyeing the cardboard boxes on the floor, turning a page of the notebook.

"Something you wanted?" she asked.

"Just curious."

Lily followed him into the hall. The elevator had remained at the sixth floor. She watched the man get in and close the glass door. She waited for the light from the car to descend, then returned to the balcony to scan the street.

Where in hell could Eastbourne have gone on a day like this?

Smoke swirled around the lower floors of the old stone Windmill, almost obscuring the squat rows of Montefiore cottages nestled against it. Looters, their kefiyas flapping and nodding as they ran, dragged a dazed old man into the street and flogged him with a heavy stick in rhythmic blows, like a housewife beating a rug. One gang of men brandishing rifles converged on Barclays' Bank on Mamilla just past the Palace Hotel, another moved toward the new Post Office on Jaffa Road.

In front of the YMCA, only pigeons strutted and pecked on the grimy sidewalk. The dead women, silent and desolate, lay uncovered on the pavement, open to the sky.

Lily shuddered.

She started down the stairs, closing the door behind her. She stopped at a landing to gather sheets from the linen cart. In the lobby, the sheets hidden in her bag, she passed the clerk, still pale behind his bushy mustache. He sat at the desk, holding a sandwich, his fingers shaking.

"Can't go outside," he said, without looking at her. "Too dangerous."

"It's all right," she told him. "I have an errand. I'll be right back."

He came around the desk to stand in front of her and block her way. A crumb hanging from his mustache fluttered with each breath. "You can't go. Door is locked. I summoned police. They arrive soon."

She moved around him toward the women's locker room. He called after her, and she kept going, past the showers and dressing room, out to the tennis courts, and around to the front of the building where the ladies lay, their blood crusted and brown on the street and buzzing with flies.

Stepping carefully, first she covered Dr. Stern. The sheet whipped in the wind and spread over the silent corpse, drifting and sagging like a blanket over a restless sleeper. Then, eyes

averted, she hid Mrs. Klein's bruised face and bloody hair. Next
Lily covered the little tea bag lady as though she were tucking
her in for the night.

Lily's legs began to tremble. Hardly aware of what she was
doing, she started to run toward East Jerusalem, away from the
sounds of screams and sirens that carried toward her from Zion
Circus, away from the smoke that caught at her throat.

Heart pounding, breath burning, she ran—away from Julian's
Way toward Princess Mary, away from the relentless sight of
the ladies on the sidewalk with their staring eyes, to the safety
of home at the American School, to the familiar world beyond
its iron gate, behind its green-shuttered windows.

Stay away from banks and post offices, she remembered.
That's what they hit first.

Not that way.

She zigzagged through the streets, still running, gasping for
breath, toward the Musrarra quarter, her legs moving automatically, her sandals hammering the street.

She hurried past houses with locked gates and empty gardens. Panting, she slowed when she reached Musrarra. Her footsteps echoed along the deserted alley. Gunfire crackled from
somewhere in west Jerusalem. She began to run again. Winded,
she paused at the top of a narrow road, the sound of her pulse
beating in her ears, and ran again.

Across the field on Nablus Road, the high walls of the École
Biblique hid the serene compound, with its tombs and chapels,
its library and hostel, and the ruins of the ancient church of
Saint Stephen. Almost home, she thought. Almost home.

Four young men, dark and thin, with pinched chests and
narrow shoulders, their shirts hanging open and creased with
soot, turned the corner. Street punks, Lily thought. They carried heavy sticks and sauntered toward her, four abreast, a gang
of hoodlums on the prowl, slashing at the air.

"Hello, darling," the shortest called out. He had a knife in his belt.

Lily ran toward the École. Her sandal slipped on a stone. She lost her balance, threw out her arms to steady herself, and kept running.

They were closer now. "Darling, I love you," the short one said. A cigarette was propped behind his ear.

Lily pressed the bell next to the small door in the wall of the École. The explosive ring echoed through the street. The two on the right flourished their sticks and sniggered.

"You know you want me, darling," the one with the cigarette called out.

Lily pressed the bell again.

The one on the right brandished the stick up and down "You waiting for me, darling?" He leered at her while he licked the downy moustache above his upper lip. His nose was running.

The door opened just wide enough for Lily to see dark eyes and the tilted head of the guard. "Library is closed," he said.

"I have an appointment with Pere de Vaux," she told him.

The guard started to close the door. "He's not here. He's at En-Feshka."

The thugs were closing in. Lily jammed her bag into the door to keep it open.

The tallest one had a cracked front tooth and the beginning of a pimple on his chin. He waggled the stick at her and whipped the air with it, close enough for Lily to feel the rush of wind when it passed. She grabbed the end, pulled it toward her, and jabbed it back into his chest. He fell backward against the one with the knife.

Before they could regain their balance, Lily shoved against the door with her shoulder, forced it open, and pushed her way inside, knocking the guard aside. She slammed the door behind her and the lock clicked shut.

The guard gawked at her, then bent down to pick up the pencils and keys that had fallen from her bag. Lily leaned against the wall to catch her breath. Outside, the hoodlums banged against the door, cursing in guttural Arabic.

The guard handed Lily her bag and peeked through a peephole at the street. "You stay," he said and motioned toward a chair in the small guardhouse next to the gate.

He poured coffee into a small cup from a battered *finjan* and brought it to her. "Rest here." His voice was almost drowned by the pounding at the door.

Still gasping for breath, Lily tried to sip the sticky-sweet coffee in the steaming cup. The hot liquid spilled over her fingers and onto her skirt. She stared at her shaking hands, put the cup on the ground, and rubbed at the warm brown stain in her lap, rocking back and forth with the motion of her arm.

The clamor at the door gradually subsided, first curses, then mutters, and finally silence. Lily leaned back in the chair and cradled both hands around the warm cup.

She breathed the aroma of the coffee laced with cardamom, of the pine needles that carpeted the remains of the ancient Byzantine church of Saint Stephen. Vestiges of columns from the atrium stood open to the sky, seeming to grow among the trees. A monk in a light summer robe glided from the chapel toward the library, his sandals crunching on the gravel.

The guard searched through the peephole again, then unlocked the door. He held it ajar and inspected the street.

"Safe," he said. "You go now."

She hurried through the rocky field across from the American School, snaking around stones from ancient walls scattered on the ground, avoiding remains of old excavation trenches now overgrown with weeds.

The dogs in the yard at Sinbad's Taxi on the corner threatened and growled, straining at the ends of their chains. They never got used to her, no matter how often she passed.

They snarled. Lily tried a smile. Behind the closed gate, across Salah-edh-Din Street, was home. Lily read the sign, *American School of Archaeological Research*, attached to the iron fence.

A large American flag fluttered on the railing of the balcony of the room next to hers, like bedding set out to air.

She lifted the hidden latch in the fence, stepped through the gate, and took the path around the building toward the refuge of the garden.

A shrill din of at least fifty people mulled about. They clustered on the sandstone walk, sat on the ledge of the fountain, stood in the rose beds. They talked in high-pitched American voices about hotels, restaurants, the cost of taxis, the riots in the streets outside.

Sir William and Lady Fendley sat in a corner behind posts of the portico, rigid in their chairs. Lady Fendley had once told Lily that they had retired to Jerusalem for the mild climate and because expenses were one-third of what they were in England. "In Jerusalem, the air is like champagne," Lady Fendley had said and told Lily shamefacedly that they chose to live at the American School instead of one of the other archaeological missions for the creature comforts, for ". . . the beds with springs instead of those horrid straw mattresses. We wanted hot water and steam heat in winter."

Lily walked toward Sir William. "Who are all these people?" She gestured in the direction of the Americans thronged in the garden.

Lady Fendley, her back straight, her elbows close to her body, eyed the crowd as if they were rabble. "They're refugees from some sort of madness in the street." She stood up and helped Sir William from his chair.

"Come inside to the Common Room," she said to Lily. "Less noise in there."

Lady Fendley led Sir William, holding him by the arm, guiding his steps. Lily never knew how he was going to behave, or how to speak to him. Some days he was his old self, the genius of Near Eastern archaeology, blunt and brilliant, with a nimble-witted sparkle in his eyes. At other times he was dithering and helpless, losing the thread of conversation, asking foolish questions. Lady Fendley hung over him like a nesting bird, arranging his collar, smoothing his long white beard, pushing hair from his eyes.

Lily paused at the door, adjusting to the incongruous peace of the Common Room, the dimmed stillness, shadows and silence hovering over woven hangings and heavy leather furniture. Only the drawn blinds rattled with gusts of explosions and gunfire. Small and frail in the large black chair, Sir William smiled at Lily.

"What's going on out there?" Lady Fendley asked.

"A riot." The heavy tick of the wall clock was the loudest sound in the room behind the shelter of the closed drapes.

"They've been rioting for the past two years. Never been such a fuss before." Lady Fendley looked offended. "This is the time we take our walk. Why are you shaking like that?"

"It's worse now," Lily said. "People are dead in the streets." She pointed vaguely toward west Jerusalem and saw her arm shaking, her fists tightly clenched. She sat down in the nearest chair, consciously opening her fists, resting her wrists against her thighs to steady her hands.

"They behave like savages," Lady Fendley said. "No one uses restraint nowadays."

Lily tried to picture Lady Fendley somewhere in the misty rain of the English countryside tending a rose garden.

"It will be all right," Sir William said in a quiet voice. "When I got off the boat in Alexandria in '82, smoke filled the air. Sounds of guns and screams were everywhere. Europeans lined the wharves in wagons, their household goods piled in carts behind them, ready to flee to safer refuge."

Lady Fendley brushed some hair behind his ears. "That was a long time ago, my dear, over fifty years. This is a different matter." She patted his arm. "It's the Mufti, you know. He called for this insurrection. Because of the influx of Jews."

"All the same." Sir William looked up at her. "It's about Suez. Makes us look bad."

"We brought it on ourselves, you know," Lady Fendley said to Lily. "Promising Palestine to the Jews and independence to the Arabs. Ned Lawrence's work. I never did like that young man. Not after that dreadful slaughter in Damascus."

"Lawrence of Arabia?" Lily asked.

"Lawrence of Arabia indeed. Prostituted archaeology for politics. His Negev survey in 1914 was just an excuse to stir up the Bedouin."

Sir William smiled at her. "Has a flair for the dramatic." He wagged his finger. "Without young men like him, we can't win the war."

"The war is over." Lady Fendley gave a sigh of impatience. "Enough about Lawrence. Speak no ill of the dead."

"Ned Lawrence is dead?" Sir William clutched the arms of his chair and leaned forward. "Killed in the line of duty?"

"In Cambridge. Three years ago. I told you then."

Sir William closed his eyes and tilted back his head. "They're all dead. Cairo, Khartoum, Damascus."

"That was all a long time ago."

He screwed up his face as if he were caught in a nightmare. "Nothing is the past. It's always with us. Everyone who died left the ghosts of their unborn children." A tear appeared in the corner of his left eye.

Lady Fendley wiped it away with the back of her hand. "It's all right, my dear." She stroked his cheek and smoothed his hair. "It's all right."

Lily looked away self-consciously, at the window, at the clock, at the newspaper on the table behind the sofa.

She heard Sir William's voice again, coming from the depths of the chair. "So you work with Eastbourne and Kate. They were my students, you know. With me in Egypt. Did I tell you they were Fendley's Foals?"

Many times, Lily thought. Each time she saw him he would babble about Kate Hale and Eastbourne and their student days in Egypt. Sir William kept talking, words spilling out of him in a scatter from a repository of disconnected facts, like bits and pieces from a torn encyclopedia. Now and then there were glints of lucidity. He talked about Egypt in 1882, the plunder and burning of Alexandria, his innovations in archaeology, a toothache at Tel al-Hesi.

Lily glanced down at her hands. Her curled fingers still quivered. Sir William Fendley was the greatest genius archaeology had ever produced. That must be remembered, Lily thought, while his voice went on. Fifty years ago he developed the technique of dating pottery that still bears his name. Visiting scholars come to tea at the American School just to see him and pay him homage.

"Kate's brighter than Eastbourne," he was saying. "But she has a harder time because she's a woman. She should be the director of the dig. They were lovers, you know."

Lady Fendley leaned over and wiped the corner of his mouth with a handkerchief. "Now, now," she said, "we mustn't repeat naughty tales."

Lily looked away again, embarrassed, in the direction of the newspaper. From this distance, the picture on the front page looked like the American in the Panama hat who was in front of the King David Hotel.

"That's an old paper, a *Paris Tribune* from last week," said Lady Fendley. "Someone left it."

Lily went around the sofa to pick it up. The man from Julian's Way had the same powerful jaw and deep-set eyes.

"Whose picture is this?" she asked.

"Konrad Henlein. Leader of the Nazi party in Czechoslovakia," Lady Fendley told her. "Where have you been? He's the Pooh-Bah of the crisis in Sudetenland."

"On the tel I never catch up with the news," Lily said. "We only have an old *Liberty* magazine. Last I heard, Hitler took over Austria."

"The *Anschluss* was months ago. You should keep up, my dear," said Lady Fendley. "Henlein is agitating for German autonomy in Bohemia, wants the Nazis to control Czechoslovakia."

Sir William stirred in his chair. "I met him, you know. In Prague. He came to my lecture and interrupted with questions about Indo-Europeans. Aryans, he called them." He smiled and wiped the side of his mouth with the back of his hand. "And his brother Karl." He shook his head and gazed at a spot on the carpet. "Bismarck says that whoever controls Bohemia, controls Europe," he began, and launched into another series of disjointed recollections. He listed every brick and tile in his schoolroom, the grain of wood on every desk. And Lady Fendley answered "Yes, dear . . . I know, my dear . . ." as she stroked his hand.

Lily became drowsy from the drone of his voice and the still air of the room. Sir William paused, looking at her expectantly, and she realized that he had asked a question that she hadn't heard.

"Eastbourne had the paper with him this morning," Lily said into the silence, "but he wouldn't let me look at it."

"Ha!" said Sir William. "He's so stingy he's afraid you'll wear off the print." He shook his head and wagged his finger. "He may have a lonely-hearts notice in the personal column he doesn't want you to see. I could tell you stories—"

"But you won't," Lady Fendley told him, leaning toward him gently, her hand on his arm.

Lily shifted in her chair and gazed at her hands again. "I'm worried about Eastbourne. He disappeared from the YMCA this morning in the midst of the riots."

"You ought to ring the British School," said Lady Fendley. "He may be there."

In the hall alcove, Lily picked up the telephone receiver and waited. She jiggled the hook impatiently, but still no operator came on the line.

"Try again later," said Lady Fendley. "Nothing works in this fool country. Go upstairs and lie down. You look tired."

As Lily left, she could hear Sir William saying, "When I was a boy, before there were telephones, you could send a street urchin with a message for a ha' penny . . ."

*   *   *

Upstairs in her room, Lily stared out the window at the street and the empty field across the way, where *fellahin* from Isawiya usually grazed sheep. She sat at the desk, conscious of the smell of smoke, the distant sounds of chaos in the New City, and fingered the coffee stain on her skirt.

She sat, numb, until the noon call to prayer from the distant mosques in the Old City. The call echoed from the minaret on Nablus road, from a mosque in the Sheik Jarrah quarter, as muezzin after muezzin chanted in unmatched cadence. The gunfire and shouting in west Jerusalem stopped, and one by one the rioters returned from the New City, crossing the field and trudging through the street in their stained clothing, their faces heavy with exhaustion, their backs loaded with carpets, stacks of dishes, a European gas range. A bearded man carried a satin evening gown, still on its hanger. It caught the wind and billowed behind him like a sail. They were going home to wash, to take lunch, to take afternoon siestas, Lily thought. And in west Jerusalem, children will return from school through empty streets to find their homes looted and gutted, their parents dead, lying in the wreckage with their throats slit.

*　*　*

A week ago, someone shot at Eastbourne as he drove down Bethlehem Road. Lily could think of a thousand reasons why someone would take a potshot at him. But as long as she was on the staff of his dig at Tel al-Kharub she could overlook his stinginess, his sour moods, his bouts of petty malice.

Four years ago, Lily's dissertation advisor at the Oriental Institute in Chicago had told her in the tangle-tongued jargon of academia that "mixed groups of men and women are not compatible in a field situation." That was in 1934. Everyone was out of money then except for Rockefeller, who sponsored excavations at Megiddo.

"I'll work with a team of women," she had said.

"I don't think you'll get funding, Miss Sampson. You can work on jewelry. There's some in the storeroom, left over from Breasted's excavations in Egypt. Jewelry, Miss Sampson, jewelry."

Her advisor always called her Miss Sampson. Male graduate students were Chuck and Hank and Flip, and they drank beer together in a saloon on the other side of the Midway.

But ladies didn't. Ladies didn't go south of Sixty Third Street, or sit around in saloons. Ladies didn't dig up ancient skeletons and get dust in their hair. Ladies married field archaeologists, followed their husbands to excavations, slept in their tents, wore rubber gloves to wash pottery, and said, "Yes, dear. Of course, dear. Don't forget your lunch, dear."

Eastbourne wasn't like that. Women were the same as men to him—he was condescending to everyone.

*   *   *

At three o'clock, Lily went around the corner to the British School on Azarah Street to see if Eastbourne was there. Tony Something-or-other, who was working on Crusader Churches, answered the door.

"He was here earlier today, but he's gone back to Kharub," Tony told her.

She had already started home when he called after her. "He said to tell you to get down to the dig as soon as you can."

THREE

At Tel al-Kharub, Lily awoke every morning still tired, to shake out her shoes for scorpions and dress in the dark. The tent flap, snapping in the wind, barked like rifle shots and woke her from another fitful sleep. Since the riots two weeks earlier, her dreams had been haunted by frenzied pigeons hovering over the lifeless face of Dr. Stern, the slack-jawed stare of Mrs. Klein, hollow-voiced inside a mask of tragedy, intoning the words of Antigone ". . . unwept, unsepulchered, a welcome store for birds to feast upon . . ."

Soon it would be first light and time to be on the tel, to clamber up the slope, avoiding scattered clumps of thorny weeds, skitter around fallen ashlars and tread on the broad stone walls that rimmed the remnants of ancient pavements.

I must be crazy to live in a tent with a cracked mirror on a peg, with clothes strung on a rope across my cot, with only a bucket of water and a sponge for a shower, she thought. There was a *hamsin* in the making. It was hot; it was windy; dirt blew in her face; her skin itched; her tent veered ominously. And to-morrow, more blasts of dusty hot wind would feel like an oven and smell of turkeys from the kibbutz over the hill.

It was her third season at Tel al-Kharub, and every year, she cursed the weariness of mornings like this. But during dark Chicago winters at the Oriental Institute, she missed the clean heat and the blue sky, the romance of tension and curiosity, the release of mindless physical labor. Then she longed to be here, to see the sunset from the tel reflected in the dappled gold of the distant sea, to watch cars and wagons moving in the dusk along the self-same road that had been the ancient King's Highway.

She yearned for the excitement of mysterious streets, the pleasurable shock of the exotic. She hungered for the whispers of the past that swirled in the remains of ancient houses and echoed in broken and discarded jugs—messages from long-buried cobblestones and old footsteps in the dust, shadows of laughter eddying in cooking pots and jars filled with the dried remnants of pomegranates.

But today she was so tired that she envied the Bedouin, in spite of their waterless days and tents that smelled like goats. She watched them in the field below the tel, sitting around a campfire in the shelter of a rock, drinking their morning coffee. Jamal had left the kitchen and sat with them, nodding and talking, cradling a small coffee cup in his hands.

They were probably gossiping about Eastbourne again, how stingy he was, how mean and unfeeling, how poorly he paid them. Yesterday a wheelbarrow ran over the toes of one of the workmen, who screamed, pointing to his bleeding foot. Eastbourne told him to shut up. When Lily ran to help, he waved her back to the pottery shed.

"They always complain," Eastbourne had said. "They do anything to get out of work."

She tried to right the tent, pulling the rope taut and hitting the tent peg with a rock. Eastbourne swaggered toward her with his sandy-haired, horse-faced British elegance, his shining boots and white linen breeches, carrying plans and sections, ready for the day.

"What do you think you are doing?" Always immaculate, even the dust was afraid to settle on him. "We have workmen for that," he said. He spread the plans on the ground, positioning rocks on the corners to hold them down in the wind. He marked where they would dig that day and told her what they would find.

Lily listened and nodded and said I know, I see, I understand. When he finished, she asked for a ride up to Jerusalem for the opening of the Rockefeller Museum the next day.

Old John D. Rockefeller had been an endless font, funding the University of Chicago, the excavations at Megiddo, her fellowship, and now the museum. Praise John, from whom oil blessings flowed. She met him once in the Oriental Institute at the fellowship awards. They had cleared a path for the old man's wheelchair and he congratulated her, his eyes rheumy, his nose pointed with age.

"It's called the *Palestine* Museum," Eastbourne said. He rolled up the map and stood over her. "You were invited?"

The wind furled the tent flap over the rope again, and he watched her struggle with it.

"There's a bus stop not two miles up the road," he said, and walked away to get his tea.

She pounded the tent peg until the rock broke. The flake scars on the stone and the small pieces of flint-shatter looked like a Paleolithic hammerstone and debitage, and she was tempted to put it on the shelf in the dig house to fool Eastbourne. Not likely. He would say it was unprovenienced and throw it away.

He was a nitpicker on the tel, and ran the camp with military discipline, but his digs had the cleanest squares, the straightest balks, the most meticulous plans and records in all of Palestine.

Eastbourne had an instinct for archaeology. Two seasons ago he found *ostraka*—messages of fear scratched with burnt sticks on broken pieces of pottery—mingled with arrowheads and missiles, buried beneath a pile of burnt bricks in the guardroom of the city gate. The scrawls called out unanswered cries for help: "May Yahweh cause my lord to bear the tidings of peace this very day. . . . Nedebiah has fled to the mountains . . . Let my lord send help . . . We are watching for the signal fires of Lachish . . . We can no longer see Azekah."

And last year, on the side of the tel, down toward the wadi, Eastbourne had merely brushed a stand of wild mustard back and forth with his shoe before he called the surveyor. They put in a trench and uncovered a mass grave.

Lily had looked down at a disordered sea of bones, and Eastbourne pointed out the organically darkened soil, the blood-shadowed remnants of humans, and reminded her of the Assyrian stele in the British Museum with an inscription commemorating the conquest of the site. He described scenes on the column— defenders crawling through the debris of battle; the walls above them breached and in flames, the refugees fleeing the city. These are their bodies, he told her. She was fortunate, he said. Few people had the chance to excavate skeletal material.

She learned to work with bones, to identify the rounded surface of a patella, differentiate cervical from thoracic vertebrae, to separate earth matrix gently from bones and place each one in a box on a cushion of tissue paper. The first time she lifted a femur, she was surprised by its heft, and for a moment a shock of intimacy and the phantom life that had once surged through the leg made her skin prickle. That season, she recovered remains of over 1,500 men, women, and children.

A week ago, Lily had found the ancient skeleton of a young woman in the remains of the storeroom near the gate—the bones of the feet charred, arms across the chest embracing a spectral memory. Near the sternum some baby teeth were all that was left of an infant. Lily imagined how the woman had run, trapped and cowering into the storeroom, flames catching at her long gown. She had fallen, clutching the infant, and was buried for over 2,500 years under a tumble of burnt and calcined mud brick.

In the ruins of a house along the casemate wall at the back of the site, Lily had found part of an arm, hacked off by a heavy blade, next to the remains of an oven. Lily envisioned the victim, alone in the courtyard where women once had spun and woven and dyed coarse woolen cloth. Others already had fled the deserted town, leaving the soup still on the table. The lone woman stood before the attackers, trying to shield her face with her forearm before the blow came.

This week, Lily was working on the steep eastern slope of the tel where Iron Age tombs were hewn into the weathering limestone bedrock. Yesterday she had seen a glint of blue through the dust, and brushing carefully, exposed a glass amphoriskos, dark as lapis lazuli—a perfect little pear-shaped vial with a long neck and delicate handles.

It fit into the palm of her hand. She brushed at it gently, moved into the light and turned it. As a child, she held one like this. She had taken it from the shelf in her father's study, stood at the window, and rubbed her finger along the smooth surface, shaded and glowing in the sun. Her father had come into the room and taken it from her hand. "We mustn't break it," he had said. "It's from long ago. Such things were rare and coveted, and belonged to princes."

That was before the day that she had opened the dark wooden door and saw the terrible sight in the closet under the stairs.

*   *   *

Lily slid through the entrance to the Iron Age tomb, through the small opening that had been cut into the hillside. Inside the sepulcher, a tangle of bones and pottery lay on the floor and on stone benches hewn into the walls of the man-made cave.

What would she look like in three thousand years, she wondered? Would someone dig her up and say, "Ah yes, there's Lily. I recognize her from the shape of her eye sockets and her nasal aperture. I'd know her anywhere."

She spent the morning carefully freeing one bone after another from the compacted mass with dental picks and sculptor's spatulas, with camel's hair brushes and pouf bulbs that emitted soft puffs of air when she squeezed them to blow away the dust. The anthropologist in London told her she was the first to recover the delicate nasal bones of the face, and she dug carefully, proud of her expertise.

Lily knew she had to finish the tomb quickly, before the Bedouin looted it. Jewelry, figurines, whole pots from tombs were the handiest source of revenue they could wrest from the dry, impoverished Palestine soil.

Especially since Eastbourne refused to pay them enough to guard the site.

* * *

By noon, the heat of the sun penetrated inside the tomb. White limestone powder from the walls of the cave dusted her arms and clothing. She brought the morning's finds up to the pottery shed—the bones wrapped, labeled and boxed; the pots in tagged buckets. From this height, she could see the coastal plain shimmering in the heat. Eastbourne was below in the Bedouin camp, waving his arms and shouting at the foreman. Jamal had turned away and had started up to the tel.

She saw Kate, with her wide-brimmed hat and her gardener's gloves, clambering to the pottery shed. Kate had been working on the ramp the Assyrians had built when they laid siege to the city. Lily thought of what Sir William said about Kate and Eastbourne and tried to imagine a pimple-faced Kate and a callow Eastbourne as lovers in each other's arms.

Jamal came up the hill from the Bedouin camp. His dark eyes always followed her, like those on a recruiting poster. "You are very beautiful," he whispered as he passed through the pottery shed on his way to the kitchen. It was barely audible, and Lily wasn't sure what she had heard.

She looked into the spotted mirror above the sink. Her face and the scarf on her head were blanketed with limestone dust, little rivulets of sweat ran down her cheeks, and her lashes and eyebrows were covered with white powder. Only her eyes, gleaming bright blue in the mask of dirt, were visible. She laughed. "I look like a clown."

Jamal had already disappeared into the kitchen. Kate, flush-faced and sweating, carried a bucket into the pottery shed, the tag, attached to the handle with a string, swinging back and forth as she walked. Her boots were covered with dust, her white linen breeches were wrinkled and soiled, and she wore an expression of jubilant satisfaction.

"Look, look," she said, "part of a bronze helmet from the last defenders of the city. From the ramp, stuck into the city wall. It was covered with ash, hard as a rock, and buried in mud brick. Digging through that mess wasn't easy." Kate hugged the bucket with one arm and ran a finger along the crest of the helmet.

For a instant, Lily felt the chill of the moment when a blow had sent the broken helmet tumbling into the fallen wall, now only a green fragment of corroded metal, gnawed by time.

*　*　*

Lily awoke from the afternoon siesta to the clatter of the cooks preparing tea in the kitchen. She had been asleep in the shade of the pottery shed, exhausted from the heat, dozing in a rickety beach chair with torn canvas that Jamal's Samaritan helper, Abu Musa, presented with a flourish after lunch. Wind had scattered a fine dust over everything—store jars, boxes of figurines, cooking pots, even the carton that held the small blue glass amphoriskos.

She blew the dust off the outside of the box, opened it, and took out the amphoriskos. She held it up to the light, ran her fingers along the edge, and placed it gently back into the container. She could feel her father's hand softly on her shoulder and the ghost of his kiss waft against her cheek. He didn't mean to leave you, the amphoriskos told her. He sends you this as a message of love.

She lovingly replaced boxes that had blown off the shelf and assured the long-gone owners of the artifacts that they would be remembered. She shielded the boxes with a tarp, weighting it down against the wind with a heavy rock.

A jar handle, with the impression of a fingerprint where the clay had been pressed into the body of the vessel, had fallen. Lily picked it up. She fit her own finger into the depression, and felt as if she spoke to a potter across 2500 years.

Abu Musa, with his silent steps and subservient manner, startled her when he came into the pottery shed. "Jamal wants to see you in the kitchen." He gave her his brown, gap-toothed grin. "He has something important to tell you."

In the kitchen, there was dust on the teacups and saucepans, and even a fine film on the dishwater where Jamal rinsed the tea things.

"Don't ride to Jerusalem with Eastbourne tomorrow." His voice was low and secretive. "And don't let him see you leave here."

FOUR

ONLY A MUD-SPATTERED LORRY was parked on the gravel behind the dining shed. Both cars—the camp station wagon that Eastbourne used and Kate's sun-streaked Austin—were gone. Kate and Eastbourne would not be at tea again. Lily imagined their assignation in some dusty pensione on the outskirts of Ashkelon, where they sweated and groaned in the afternoon heat on a straw mattress with creaking springs. She smiled at the ludicrous picture and continued toward the dining shed.

Avi, the boy from the kibbutz on the other side of the hill, sat at a table, his red hair and freckled face shining in the dappled shade. She could dimly make out snatches of an argument between him and Jamal.

When she came into sight, they stopped. Avi smiled and jumped up to greet her. Jamal, arms crossed, legs straddling the threshold, still glowered from the kitchen door.

"I was waiting for you," Avi said. He picked up a crate from the bench beside him and planted it on top of the table. "I brought grapefruit."

Jamal leaned against the doorjamb, his arms still crossed over his chest. "We don't need them. We're closing camp."

Avi turned to Lily. "You're leaving?"

"Just for the weekend." Lily sat down at the table near the crate. "For the opening of the Rockefeller."

"Okay, then." Avi got up and reached for an empty basket from the pottery rack. "You can take fruit with you."

"Too much to carry on the bus," Jamal said.

"You're taking a bus to Jerusalem?" Avi asked.

Jamal unfolded his arms. "How else?"

"Pretty blonde ladies aren't safe riding by themselves through Hebron," Avi said. "These are bad times. They shoot at buses." Avi sat down next to her. "I have the lorry here. I'll drive you to Qiryat Gat to find a taxi."

"Too expensive," Lily said.

"A shared taxi. A *sherut*. Costs the same as a bus." He waited while she thought about it. "There's a *hamsin*." He picked up a grapefruit and began to peel it. "You want to sit in a smelly bus with broken springs?" He offered her a section of the grapefruit, and said she could leave now instead of tomorrow morning.

"I have work to do," Lily said. "Clean up my notes, draw plans and sections."

"You can do that in Jerusalem."

Jamal leaned forward. "Go with him." He spoke with the same hushed voice that he had used in the kitchen.

Lily hesitated, looking from one to the other. Then she picked up the dusty field notebook from the table, told Avi to wait, and went back to her tent.

When she returned, Jamal, still frowning in the kitchen doorway, was eating a grapefruit section by section, as though it were an orange.

Avi left the crate on the table. "*Shalom, shalom*," he said, and carried Lily's bag to the lorry parked behind the dining tent.

They rode along a dirt road lined with orange groves. Avi asked Lily about Eastbourne. He asked why Kate and Eastbourne were not at tea; he asked who Eastbourne's friends were; he asked where Eastbourne went in Jerusalem.

"Why do you want to know?"

"There's going to be a war. Hitler is mobilizing on the Czech border. Archaeologists sometimes dig for more than antiquities."

He talked about Lawrence of Arabia and his archaeological survey of the Negev in 1914, just before the war; of Palmer, who did a survey of the Sinai in the last century and made friends with the Bedouin when the British were building the Suez canal. "Palmer was killed as a spy," Avi said, "by his Bedouin friends."

"How do you know all this?"

Avi shrugged and lifted his hands from the wheel in a questioning gesture. "Common knowledge. Even the director of the American School works for the intelligence agency. That's why he's doing the Trans-Jordan survey."

Lanes of eucalyptus from Australia, planted for shade and windbreaks in the orange groves, lined the route. The Fertile Crescent, Lily thought. Where agriculture was invented. Where the oranges came from China, the peaches from Persia, and the prickly pears growing on the side of the road came from Arizona.

"Are you a native of Palestine?" she asked.

"I was born here. I'm a sabra. But I'm no bloody native."

"I didn't mean it that way."

"I hate the British. Wherever they go, they make trouble."

"They're only trying to keep peace."

"Before the British came, Arabs and Jews were friends. They're our cousins, you know. We fought together against the Turks in the war."

"Cousins?"

Avi laughed. "The children of Ishmael, Abraham's other son."

Dust blew into the lorry. Lily covered her hair with a scarf and closed the window.

"The Brits took up the white man's burden," Avi said. "They pit one side against another and then say. 'These people are incapable of ruling.' Divide and conquer. That's their policy."

"The partition plan . . ."

"Is a bunch of bull. Partition won't work. It's doomed to failure."

"Don't be so cynical. Something has to work."

"Who wouldn't be cynical?" He downshifted and carefully drove around a pothole in the dirt road. "There's a saying in the Talmud: If I am not for myself, who shall be?"

"Sounds like an excuse to be selfish."

"It's political. Written when the Romans controlled Palestine. Things are not much different now. The rest of the text goes: And who am I?" The motor whined as they started up a small hill. "Everything is in the Talmud. There's another maxim: The fish say there is too much land. It all depends on your point of view, doesn't it?"

"And what do Arabs say?"

"With my brother against my cousin. With my cousin against the world."

They drove through foothills covered with stone terraces planted with figs and grapes, the slopes criss-crossed by goat paths.

"It's nice of you to drive me," Lily said.

"An excuse to be with you." Avi blushed. "Besides, it's not safe now. Not since the Grand Mufti began to conspire with Hitler to get the British out of Palestine."

The lorry groaned up a steep incline. "Things are worse since the general strike started two years ago. Violence escalated. Brits lost control of the mandate, can't keep the peace. The Hebron Massacre in '29 was bad enough. I was just a little kid, but I remember it." He shook his head and stared straight ahead. He stepped on the gas, and the motor stammered and stalled. "But this time . . . Jews are always the victims, never the victors. I'm getting sick of it."

He downshifted and let out the clutch. "There's just so much you can take. There's not a Jew in Palestine who hasn't had a friend or relative killed by the Mufti's men."

"I was in Jerusalem two weeks ago during the riots," Lily said.

"Then you know." He looked over at her. "We're beginning to organize to fight back."

"Stockade and tower settlements like the new kibbutzim?"

"What good is a water tower with a searchlight and a barbed wire fence without arms? I'm thinking of joining the *Irgun*."

"*Irgun?*"

"Organized about a year ago. Now the Mufti's mob won't kill us and get away with it."

"Doesn't the Jewish Defense Force stop the attacks?"

"The *Haggana*? They hem and haw, and use 'admirable restraint' according to the British. The *Irgun* retaliates with reprisals." Avi pushed his foot down on the accelerator until the lorry retched and sputtered. "In this part of the world," he said, "no one forgives, no one forgets."

His words hung in the air.

"You know what I think?" he said after a while. "I think the Mufti is angry because Abdullah is Emir of Trans-Jordan instead of him. Now he gets revenge with these bloody raids on settlements and bombs in markets. Riots in Jerusalem and Hebron."

They rode in silence until the truck hit a rock in the road and they bounced in their seats, landing with a jolt on the springs and bounding up again, their heads almost hitting the roof of the cab. Both of them laughed.

"Sometimes I dream that we are married and have three children," Avi said.

"How old are you, Avi?"

"Nineteen."

"I'm six years older than you. When you're thirty, I'll be almost forty."

"Thirty-six to be exact. Anyway, I won't reach thirty."

"Don't be so dramatic."

They drove between distant hills on one side, the sea on the other, through orange groves and melon patches, along the dusty road to Qiryat Gat. Orange groves fluttered in Lily's side-vision and she closed her eyes, thinking of the day a few weeks after her tenth birthday and the long drive to the cemetery with the heavy scent of orange blossoms in the April air. She had sat numb in a limousine following a hearse, listening to her mother sob behind a drapery of black veils. She clutched the blue vial that her father had given her on her birthday. He had held it out to her after she blew out the candles on her cake, turning it so that the dark cobalt reflected the light from the chandelier like a jewel. "This is for you," he had said. "A gift from the past." It was the last thing he gave her. Two weeks later, she had opened the door under the stairs.

And now, to have found another amphoriskos. She knew from the moment that she saw the deep blue shimmer in the dust. She knew as she brushed away the dirt and saw it emerge a few centimeters at a time. She knew when she finally freed it with a careful stroke of the dental pick. Her father had sent it.

The amphoriskos. It was registered in the site catalogue all right, but she didn't remember writing it up in her field notes. She had fastened a slip of paper with its description and measurements to the notebook with a paper clip. I'll fix it in Jerusalem, she thought, and pulled the bag up from the floor.

"Oh damn," she said.

"What?" Avi said.

"I forgot my field notebook. Left it in the tent."

"You want to go back?"

"It's okay. I'll take care of it Monday."

"You work too hard anyway. You deserve a few days rest."

"You work hard, too."

"But I don't have to sleep in a tent. On a cot."

"Neither do I. In Jerusalem at the American School I have a real bed. And a bathtub."

* * *

"I'm not sure we can find a *sherut*," Avi said. "It's a matter of luck. You might need a bus after all."

"You and Jamal…"

"Jamal is in love with you."

"Don't be silly. He's a cook."

"And I'm a tractor driver."

"That's different. You're an American."

"Only my passport. I told you, I was born here, on a kibbutz in Palestine. Don't be so class conscious. You've been working with the Brits too long."

"Defending your cousin?"

Avi smiled and nodded. "With my cousin against the world," he said.

A taxi chugged along in front of them. It pulled to the side of the road to let them pass.

Avi skidded the lorry around it and stopped. "A *sherut*. You're in luck."

"The way you drive, I would have been safer on a bus through Hebron," Lily said.

Avi got out of the lorry. "Come on," he said to Lily and called out to the driver of the *sherut*. "*Yerushalayim*? You going to Jerusalem?"

Lily reached for her bag and followed.

The driver didn't answer and turned away.

"Beni?" Avi leaned his arm on the window frame of the cab. "That you, Beni?"

Beni motioned his head in the direction of the back seat. A pretty, pregnant girl, who seemed broader than she was tall, sat between two men in khaki shorts and white shirts open at the collar. The girl began to giggle. Beni spoke to Avi in Hebrew, his voice hardly audible. Lily could make out only a few words.

"You know what's happening," Beni said. "I'm taking Ora . . ."

The man behind the driver's seat interrupted Beni. "We're taking her to the doctor." He spoke in English. "It's an emergency."

Avi leaned further into the taxi to speak to him. "Rafi, this is Lily. I told you about her."

Rafi looked toward Lily, pushed back a strand of dark hair that had fallen onto his forehead, then glared at Avi. "You know better than that. There's no room."

Lily noticed Rafi's foot resting on a folded jump seat. "There's plenty of room," she said. "It's a seven-passenger car." None of this made sense. "And I don't have any communicable diseases."

"For God's sake, Rafi," Avi said, exasperated.

Ora put one hand over her mouth, the other on her stomach, and tittered again.

"It'll be all right, Rafi," Avi said. "I can't leave Lily here in the middle of the road." Rafi scowled at him. "For me, Rafi."

Beni, the driver, pointed to the seat next to him. "She can sit here. In front."

Rafi frowned, shrugged, and pushed back his hair again. "Get in," he said to Lily.

"The best seat," Avi said, leading her around to the other side of the car. "Right next to the driver," and he opened the door for her.

He put her bag in the trunk, slammed the lid and stood in the road waving as they drove away. "Have a safe journey. I'll visit you," he called after them.

FIVE

LILY SAT IN THE FRONT seat of the *sherut*, the wind blowing against her face as the driver gripped the steering wheel, his hands slippery with sweat. From time to time, she glanced at the back seat in the rear-view mirror. The pregnant girl laughed about her ill-fitting dress, about the size and shape of her stomach. They talked about going to Patt's on the Street of the Prophets for special pastries, about yesterday's ambush on the road near Tulkarm, about the bombs in Haifa market.

The man on the left was called Gadi. Rafi, the good-looking one, the one who spoke English, leaned forward to tell the driver, "Don't go so fast. The police will stop us." He had green eyes.

Beni shook his head and clicked his tongue against his teeth to show he disagreed. "Any slower and we'll be an easy target."

They rode in silence for a time, Gadi reading a newspaper; Ora, eyes closed, leaning back in the seat. Lily stole a glance in the rear-view mirror and saw Rafi staring at her. She watched him, watched the flashes of sunlight filtering through passing trees play on his face, his eyes greener in the bright light, his hair dark and shining.

He winked into the mirror. She turned away, embarrassed, and looked out the window. Haughty camels, loaded with sheepskins, trekked across the horizon from a village beyond a hill.

"It's as peaceful as a poster for Travels through the Holy Land," Lily said.

"An illusion. Children used to hike through this countryside by themselves with water and sandwiches in their rucksacks." Rafi said. "They can't anymore. Too dangerous."

They drove around a truck groaning up the hill and stacked with water bottles.

"How long have you known Avi?" Rafi asked the mirror after a while.

"I'm digging at a site near his kibbutz, that's all."

"He talks about you a lot."

Beni swerved to avoid a bundle in the road, and Lily heard the faint ring of metal on metal.

"What was in the road?" asked Gadi, looking up from the paper.

"Just garbage," Beni answered. "Melon rinds, probably. Want to go back to look?"

Ora laughed unexpectedly. "It could have been a bomb."

They bounced over a pothole and this time it was clear that the metallic clang came from inside Ora's dress. Lily turned around to look at the girl's stomach. Bulging and knobby, it shifted with each bump in the road.

They drove past rocky hills scarred with goat tracks, the taxi droning, still climbing toward Jerusalem. A turbaned Arab on a mule jolted along the edge of a distant path.

Beni careened around the next crack in the road in an elaborate slalom, throwing the occupants of the back seat together against the window, first to one side, then the other. Lily glanced in the rear view mirror again and saw the distinctive outline of a gun jutting from the bulge around Ora's middle.

Rafi patted it back in place. "Pull yourself together." She giggled once again. "And for God's sake, stop that laughing."

"I cannot help it. Always, I laugh when I'm nervous."

Lily turned around to watch Ora adjust the bundle around her waist. "That's all I need," Lily said. "To be arrested for smuggling arms."

No one answered from the back seat.

"Either you're hiding weapons under your dress or you're pregnant with a strangely shaped robot."

"You insisted on going with us," Rafi told her.

"Not to get arrested."

They passed a truck loaded with crates of purple grapes spilling through the slats, exuding the smell of ripe fruit.

Melons grew on tangled vines in the fields. An Arab woman in an embroidered dress sat under a green silk parasol next to a pile of ripe melons for sale. Lily glanced in the mirror again. Rafi was still watching her.

"It reminds me of a story," Rafi said. "Jacob and his son were traveling from Minsk to Pinsk. . . ."

"In Palestine, everything reminds someone of a story," Lily said. "And they all take place on that crowded road from Minsk to Pinsk."

"Jacob didn't have enough money for two tickets," Rafi continued, as though she hadn't spoken. "So he told his son to hide in a sack under the seat when the conductor came to take the fares.

"When he asked Jacob what was in the sack under the seat, Jacob told him, 'Just some glass that my poor sick mother is sending to my daughter's wedding.' The conductor had heard it all before, and he kicked the lumpy sack. The sack jumped and Jacob's son said . . ."

Rafi paused here for emphasis. They drove over another bump and another clank came from Ora.

"Tinkle. Tinkle." Rafi said and leaned back, holding out his hands, palms up like an offering.

"It doesn't make it any better," Lily said. "Last month they sentenced a Druze woman to ten years in Acre prison for smuggling arms."

"Maybe next time you should ask if anyone is breaking the law before you get into a taxi." Rafi rolled down the window next to him and closed his eyes as the wind ruffled his hair back onto his forehead. "Anyway, they don't arrest pretty blonde American ladies."

"Or pregnant women, I suppose." Lily wound up the window next to her against the gusts of wind that blew dust into the taxi. "I could always tell the police that you forced me into the car at gun point."

They were coming into the hill country now. They passed terraces planted with grapevines and olive trees, passed Arab men at bus stops who were squatting on the side of the road, smoking.

"I knew it." Rafi leaned forward.

"We thought you were a friend of Avi's so you'd be all right. Now I'm not so sure."

"I'm fine. But I don't know about you."

He sat back again with a grunt.

They drove through villages where boys rode alongside them on rusted bicycles and men in white *kefiyas* sat at small tables drinking coffee and playing shesh-besh. Women with white veils covering their heads and spilling down their backs, the hems of their black embroidered dresses scraping the rutted mud, struggled with bundles of vegetables.

And 400 yards up the road, two British constables were flagging down cars.

Beni slowed the taxi, maneuvering it onto the shoulder. "Roadblock ahead." He gestured toward the army lorry and the striped black-and-yellow barriers that blocked the highway.

"Don't stop here," Rafi told him. "It looks suspicious."

A taxi with Arab farmers had pulled up to the checkpoint. The police gestured for them to leave the car, and they stood on the side of the road, one holding a chicken by its legs. The bird cackled and fluttered while a constable searched the trunk and under the seat.

Ora laughed again. "If they make me leave the car, I give birth right here on the side of the road."

Beni drove up behind the Arab taxi and stopped. The *sherut* idled noisily, swaying from side to side while Ora gripped her stomach.

"Don't worry," Lily said. "They'll let us through. They always wave me through roadblocks."

"Why?" Rafi asked. "You have a special pass?"

"I wondered myself. Last week on the Ashkelon road near Negba, when they waved me through, I pulled up and asked." She looked pointedly at Rafi. "They told me they don't stop blondes."

"Can you make it work again? "

"As long as Ora doesn't clang."

They waited, motor idling, and watched the *fellahin* pile back into their taxi, the chicken flapping and losing feathers in a struggle to escape.

"How do you know you can trust me?" Lily asked.

"I don't. I trust Avi."

The taxi in front of them pulled away and Beni drove slowly up to the roadblock and brought the car to a careful stop.

Lily rolled down the window and smiled at the soldier. "What seems to be the trouble, officer?"

"Just checking for weapons. You have any guns?"

"Why? Do we need them?" she asked, still smiling.

He laughed. "I hope not, luv. I'd hate to have anything happen to someone who looks like you."

"We're archaeologists. On our way to Jerusalem for the reception at the new museum tomorrow." Lily heard mumbling in the back seat. In the rear view mirror she saw Ora clutching her stomach and holding a handkerchief over her mouth. Rafi had one arm over her shoulders, the other tight across her belly. "You all right, dear?" he asked Ora.

The constable leaned into the car, his hand on the window, peering into the back of the taxi.

"We're graduate students from the University of Chicago," Rafi told the policeman. He nodded toward Ora. "This is my wife. I'm taking her to the doctor in Jerusalem. Hope we make it in time."

The soldier hesitated. Lily laid her hand on his arm. "Are you married, Constable?" she said. "Pregnant women are so touchy. The least little thing upsets them."

He looked at her and smiled. "My sister in Colchester has five children. Whenever she gets in a family way, I give her a wide berth. No pun intended."

"Colchester," Lily said. "A lovely town, full of history, with Roman walls and castles. Where Queen Boadicea led the revolt of the Britons against Roman rule."

The constable nodded. "When I was a lad, I would find bits and pieces of Roman pottery in the lanes after a rain and dream I was a Roman soldier. I've always been partial to archaeology."

Lily glanced at the back seat again. Rafi and Ora were still clutched in an embrace. Lined up behind the *sherut*, she saw a lorry piled with bundles of hay, and beyond that, an old Arab in a white *kefiya* sitting in a cart filled with melons. Behind him were two taxis and a bus.

"Heavens," said Lily. "There's a queue behind us. We're holding up traffic. I'd better let you get back to your duties."

"Oh—yes." The constable stepped back from the sherut. "Yes, of course. Nice to meet you. Have a safe trip." And he waved them through.

Ora waited until the checkpoint was out of sight before she began laughing. "Sorry," she said. Her shoulders shook; her stomach rattled and banged. "*Kol hakavod*. Well done, Lily."

"She had no choice," Rafi said.

Ora laughed again. "The constable will tell all his mates tonight about his friend the archaeologist."

"And he'll remember us," said Rafi.

After a while, Rafi said to the mirror, "Come to Patt's sometime and try the special pastries."

* * *

Lily left the *sherut* on Jaffa Road in Jerusalem. She passed shops burned in the riots, their floors blanketed with blackened remains of counter tops and fallen beams. The acrid stench of stale fire from the charred debris filled her with unexpected panic. In two thousand years, Eastbourne had said, only a layer of charcoal, wall-stubs, foundations, sandwiched between other strata, would remain.

She ran across the street in the face of the traffic near the corner of the Old City, toward the White Sisters and Notre Dame.

She cut through a courtyard where a nun struggled with freshly washed sheets that billowed in the wind. A gust lifted the wings of her coif and whipped the sheets, with their fresh smell of soap and sunshine, around Lily's head.

Laughing, the nun untangled her. "*Bonjour*," she said, still laughing.

"*Bonjour*," Lily answered.

"*Va bien*? You are all right?"

They both laughed, together. "*Va bien. Merci,*" Lily said.

Still smiling, she crossed the field where villagers in white *kefiyas* and long cloaks, *abayas* they called them, came into town from Nebi Samwil and Beit Safafa, Beit Hanina and Deir Yasin, with vegetables to sell, with watermelons and figs, and oranges from Jericho. A Bedouin woman held out a bundle of spices, of thyme and capers. Blue and green tattoos, the colors of paradise, decorated the rims of her eyes and mouth and guarded the entrance to her soul. Women from Lifta in dark embroidered dresses squatted on the street next to baskets of beans, of okra, with piles of apricots—holding them up for display, calling to passersby.

Lily hated walking through this section. No matter how she behaved, no matter what she wore, it was like running a gauntlet. Men would step in the way to brush against her; women gestured and shouted at her with guttural cries that sounded like curses.

Lily threaded her way between rickety wooden buses with peeling paint and shattered windows; scribes sat with old typewriters perched on card tables, writing letters and completing forms for clients. Vendors with goatskins of water and shiny bottles harnessed to their backs pushed through the throng, the bottles filled with colored syrup and sticky with flies. The street was slippery with discarded and half-rotted fruits and vegetables, crowded with people milling and pushing, and heavy with the smell of sheep.

She broke through the crowd onto the quiet street where sheep grazed in the field near the high walls of the École Biblique, and rounded the corner. She crossed the road to the gate of the American School, lifted the latch, scurried up the walk and climbed the steps into the calm of the entry hall next to the library.

* * *

Lily heard the bell for dinner and started down the stairs, bathed
and rested. A tall man with straight shoulders, a tanned face,
and a prominent jaw stood at the bottom of the steps. His hand
clutched the newel; he looked up as if he were waiting for someone. Lily recognized him as the man in the Panama hat whom
she had seen the day of the riots in front of the King David.

"It's you," she said, and continued down the stairs. "Secretary's gone for the day."

"I came here especially to speak with you, Miss Sampson."

"You know my name?"

"May I see you a moment?"

"What's wrong?"

"I'm Henderson. Colonel Keith Henderson. From the consulate."

"What happened?"

"Can we go outside?" he asked. "Not the garden. Too many
people."

Lily led the way down the steps to the tennis court. Only Sir
William and Lady Fendley were in the garden. Lily looked back
over her shoulder to see if Henderson followed. He took long,
loping steps, his hands in his trouser pockets.

"You been keeping up with the news?" he asked.

Where was this leading? "I've been on the tel for the last six
weeks. When I come to town I sleep and bathe and see old friends."

"There's going to be a war," he said. "Hitler is mobilizing to
enter Czechoslovakia. Over the Sudetenland."

That was the second time that day that someone talked about
war. Avi had said the same thing in the lorry. "What does that
have to do with me?"

"You heard about the bomb at Jaffa Gate last month. It killed
four people. Thirty-eight more and one hundred and fifty

wounded in the riots that followed. You were here then, in Jerusalem. I saw you." He watched her, waiting for her to speak. "Last week, forty-five people were killed by a Jewish bomb in the *souk* at Haifa." His voice was taut. "You know the situation in Jerusalem. The British are proposing partition." He paused. "Arabs and Jews are both against it."

"I'm not interested in politics," Lily said. "As a scholar, I can't take sides."

"The Grand Mufti—al-Husseini—is allied with Hitler."

"I have to go to dinner," she said, starting back toward the garden.

"Would you like to have your own site?" He asked so quietly that she wasn't sure she heard him.

She turned around and looked at him. "I couldn't get a permit." Her voice was almost a whisper. "And the funding..."

Something was wrong with this conversation. She didn't know him. She had no idea why he was talking to her, and now he was making some kind of incomprehensible offer.

"You have a good reputation as an archaeologist."

"What is this all about?" she asked.

"With the right recommendations, the Smithsonian would look favorably on a grant proposal from you."

Lily felt a momentary thrill of excitement and danger.

"Archaeologists can go anywhere," said Henderson. "I thought you might like to do a little archaeological survey before you select a site."

There was something vaguely disturbing and unethical about this, and she shook her head.

"You have nothing to fear," Henderson reassured her. Almost as an afterthought, he added, "They never hurt women." He waited again for her reaction.

Who are "they"?

"Think about it," he said. "I'll call you in a few days."

SIX

Lily pirouetted in front of the mirror at the top of the stairs, composing a smile, turning this way and that, watching the fringe of her shawl slither. Her eyes reflected the blue silk, bright against her tan; her hair shone pale and sun-streaked.

Sir William came out of his room on the arm of his wife. "You shouldn't preen like that. It's bad for your character." His eyes were bright and amused and he was laughing, anticipating attention and admiration at the museum reception. Lady Fendley smiled and brushed a stray hair from his forehead.

"We called a taxi," he said. "Care to join us?"

Lady Fendley hesitated and glanced at Sir William. Her smile stiffened. "She's not ready."

As welcome as an ant at a picnic. The curtains at the window next to the mirror wafted clear summer scents from the garden toward Lily. "Too beautiful a day to be inside a musty taxi," Lily said. "I'd rather walk."

"Remember, my dear," said Lady Fendley, "you take your life in your hands near Herod's Gate." Now she seemed offended. What's wrong with her today? "You have a habit of roaming the streets during riots."

Only one riot. "I'll be all right."

"Everyone has guns these days. Someone took a shot at Eastbourne's car a few weeks ago near Solomon's Pools." Lady Fendley brushed a speck from Sir William's collar. "No one is safe in this Godforsaken country."

Not even Englishmen with public school educations, Lily thought.

* * *

Lily wore high heels for the first time in months. They pinched her toes. She limped along to the museum, feeling broken bits of sidewalk and pebbles through the thin soles. And next winter, she thought, after the rain begins, it will all be knee-deep in mud.

The new museum sat grandly on raw ground, planted across from the northwest corner of the Old City, just past Herod's Gate. Smooth blocks of creamy gold Jerusalem stone glared in the sun. Ladies in broad summer hats and flowered dresses, men in dark jackets and white trousers crowded the steps before the high open doors of an octagonal tower. Bastardized Moorish like the YMCA, Lily thought, the British vision of East meets West.

Inside, a cacophony of shrill voices echoed in the stone halls. A dense press of people talked in groups, men nodding, smiling, women waving gloved hands, all looking around, waiting to be noticed. Lily pushed her way through the crowd, searching for a familiar face—Eastbourne, Sir William, Lady Fendley. She saw the entire staff of the excavations at Hazor, the senior staff from Jericho and Samaria, even the new High Commissioner from Government House.

It was too crowded to see anything in the cases. In the exhibit hall, men in striped school ties ate canapés in front of stone carvings from Hisham's Palace in Jericho. People lounged against vitrines stacked with ancient jugs and jars.

"Hello, hello," Lily said to no one in particular.

"My God, it's a sea of pots," she heard a woman's voice call out, "and every one of them has a name." The woman wore a hat with an ostrich feather shaped like a question mark that trembled with each word.

"Have you seen Eastbourne?" Lily asked someone who looked familiar. Before she could get a reply, she was driven back toward an exhibit case by a new surge of people.

Rickety in her high-heeled shoes, she stumbled against a physical anthropologist from the hospital. "So sorry," she said.

The press of the crowd was suffocating. Lily forced her way toward the open air of the courtyard, repeating "Beg your pardon, excuse me," in a rhythmic murmur.

Outside, a fountain, dancing and dappling, caught the rosy evening sun. Guests jammed into the shade of a loggia, leaned against stele carved with ancient inscriptions, elaborate sarcophagi and empty stone ossuaries with peaked tops and rosette decorations. In the first century, the ossuaries had held the bones of the dead.

She found a gin and tonic at the bar, already poured and waiting for someone. No ice; they never have ice.

Sir William held court for a brace of admirers in the comparative quiet of the loggia, nodding graciously and offering his cycle of recollections. Lady Fendley stood a little behind, smiling as she watched his animated face. Words came in and out of his head all day long, Lily thought. Some stayed, some slithered away like water. And if they stayed, he repeated them over and over for the comfort of their sound.

"The germ of the idea came from my friend Francis Galton," Sir William was telling a young man, who listened dutifully and nodded deferentially. "Darwin's cousin, you know. He did a study on family resemblances. I just transferred the idea to pottery."

"There you are, my dear." Lady Fendley said to Lily, and continued to scan the crowd. "Arrived safely, I see. I don't see Kate. Isn't she coming?"

"Stayed in camp again. She's anti-social."

"Just shy," Lady Fendley said.

What was wrong with Kate, hiding behind her square shape and face like a cartoon in *Punch*? Someday, when he's in the right frame of mind, I'll ask Sir William about her. He knows about everyone.

"Pity," Lady Fendley said. "It would be to her advantage to show here."

"She never goes anywhere. Except some mysterious place in Ashkelon. Sometimes she stays the night."

"Probably because of the curfew," Lady Fendley said.

"She goes there every day. Eastbourne here yet?"

"Haven't seen him."

Sir William was telling an admirer in a mustard-colored jacket, "I landed in Alexandria during the uprising of '82."

"Must have been an exciting time," said Mustard Jacket. He had a Cambridge accent.

"Much like what's happening here. In those days, the Sultan of Turkey paid the rebels. Today it's Hitler. We put a stop to it then. Arrested the leader, put him on trial."

"Those were the glory days of the empire," Mustard Jacket said. He looked off into the distance, and his eyes misted over.

"We had to protect Suez. Lifeline of the empire."

Across the courtyard, leaning against a column, the woman with the feathered hat was talking to a short, balding man, her feather wavering like punctuation.

"Is that Margaret Sotheby?" Lily asked.

"That?" Lady Fendley followed her gaze.

"The one with the feather."

"Oh that. Yes. Elliot Blessington's wife. She's a novelist."

"I think I met her once," Lily said.

"Writes about one murder after another. I think she's deranged." Lady Fendley leaned forward and lowered her voice. "Her first husband was a philanderer." She came closer to Lily, almost whispering. "She's terribly extravagant. Last year, she spent a hundred pounds for a desk she kept in the tent at Eliot's excavation. Writes in the dig house while he excavates." Lady Fendley leaned closer still. "Won't let Eliot out of her sight. Older than he is, you know," she said into Lily's ear.

"I never heard about the desk. Who's she talking to?"

"Haven't the slightest. I never saw him before. Looks American."

"She's coming this way," Lily said.

Lady Fendley straightened up, but continued in a low voice. "They just finished at a site in Turkey. On their way to Mesopotamia, I think. We'll ask."

Margaret Sotheby approached and nodded at Lady Fendley. "Cordelia." The feather danced. Dame Margaret took both of Lily's hands in hers. "Lily darling," she said. "It's been ages since I saw you."

We hardly know each other. Why the effusive greeting?

Dame Margaret dipped her feather. She exuded a pleasant scent of vanilla. "You're working with Geoff Eastbourne now at Tel al-Kharub," she said while she continued looking around the room. "I don't see him here today."

"I haven't—"

"You didn't you drive up with him?" Dame Margaret held onto Lily's hand while her eyes searched the crowd. The short man she had been talking to earlier signaled her from the other side of the loggia. "Will you excuse me?" Dame Margaret said and left, her feather fluttering in the wind. The short man followed her.

"What was that about?" Lily asked, watching them disappear into a side room.

Lady Fendley glared after Dame Margaret. "Rudeness. That's what it was about."

A British major pushed past, almost knocking against a stone column. He made a circuit of the courtyard, glanced around the loggia, tapped his hand on a Roman sarcophagus, and went back into the building.

The hum of conversation from inside the museum stopped. Lily heard the cadence of a garbled announcement. A sound like a collective sigh reached the courtyard. Then silence.

The major returned, followed by the pale, distraught director of the British School. The director took a position in front of the fountain, cleared his throat, tapped on a glass with a spoon, and turned to speak to the major, who nodded.

"Ladies and gentlemen, if I may have your attention . . ." His voice broke. Perspiration stood on his upper lip and ran along his temples. He whispered to the major again. This time the major shook his head and shrugged.

"I have the unfortunate duty to announce that Geoffrey Eastbourne . . ." He reached into his pocket for a handkerchief and wiped his face. "Geoffrey Eastbourne was killed this morning on the Beit Jibrin track near Hebron."

He wiped his face again. The handkerchief fell to the stone pavement of the courtyard. For a moment, Lily wasn't sure what she heard. She felt the blood drain from her cheeks. The courtyard hushed. People stood in clusters, shaking their heads, murmuring in low voices.

All around her, she heard snatches of conversation ". . . died in the line of duty . . . a terrible waste . . . a brilliant archaeologist . . ."

Recollections of the moment when she found her father in the dark closet under the stairs surged through her again—the specter of desolation, the loneliness that came with news of sudden death.

She watched the water play in the courtyard fountain, burbling and flashing in the dusk, and stared at the sarcophagus next to her. A plate with a half-eaten canapé was balanced on the rim.

She remembered Eastbourne pacing along the shadowy stub of an ancient wall; swaggering along a balk, his eyes squinting at the faint outline of stratigraphy emerging on the side of the square; kneeling down on one knee, tracing the outline of the wall on the site map.

Sir William's voice broke into her reverie. "What happened?"

"It's Eastbourne," Lady Fendley said, reaching for his hand. "I'll tell you about it later. We must leave now."

Lily stopped the major before he left. "How did it happen?" she asked. "A traffic accident? Did he skid? Was he speeding? Was he hit by another car?"

"No accident," the major said. "He was shot." He walked away.

People began to leave. Dame Margaret emerged from the side room and looked at the thinning crowd and grave faces.

"What happened?" she asked. Lily told her about Eastbourne.

Only her feather trembled. "I'm not a bit surprised," she said. Lily had no idea why. Dame Margaret leaned forward as if to explain. "We have to talk. Stop at the American Colony on your way home. I'll buy you a chocolate gateau."

She moved into the scattering crowd, her face expressionless, her feather erect.

SEVEN

LILY PUSHED HER WAY through the crowded street across from the Old City wall, thinking of Eastbourne's death. Killed in a flicker on a dusty road in a strange land. He had missed the Great War with its poets and heroic good-byes, its nightmares and festering trenches. Now he died on a desert track, a meaningless death in a nameless by-lane.

Across from Herod's Gate, she turned up Salah-edh-Din Street. An accident? A case of mistaken identity? An angry workman? It made no sense. "The Arabs are my friends," Eastbourne had always said. "There's no danger here for me."

Jamal had warned her. Jamal knew something was going to happen.

Distracted, Lily passed the American School, passed the Tombs of the Kings. She stepped around the bends and cracks in the narrow sidewalks, her feet aching, her toes pinching.

Dame Margaret knew something. I'll find out when I talk to her, Lily thought. She turned into the narrow lane that led into the entrance of the American Colony Hotel, passed the whitewashed walls of the anteroom decorated with tiles, passed the lobby, the air permeated with deep-scented tuberoses in vases of Hebron glass, brilliant as jewels on the glistening copper tables.

In the courtyard the polite murmur of voices and quiet sounds of china and silverware moving gently on linen tablecloths were punctuated by the peaceful splash of the fountain in the center.

Dame Margaret waited at a table in the corner, beyond two tall palms that wavered above the flagstone pavement, beyond the blooming roses, near the bright masses of red and orange and purple bougainvillea tumbling against the stone walls. Dame Margaret had already shed her hat.

Lily took the chair across from her. "You wanted to see me?"

Dame Margaret didn't look up. She rearranged the spoon and fork in front of her. Lily expected her to express some sort of half-hearted condolence, to say something like, "Sorry about Eastbourne."

Instead, Dame Margaret asked, "Why were you working with Geoffrey?"

Is that what she wanted to know?

"He was willing to put me on the staff."

"Why not Megiddo? That's a Chicago dig."

Lily was startled. She knows more about me than I thought, knows I'm from the University of Chicago. "They don't mix the sexes on American excavations, say it's bad for morale."

"Nonsense. Sex has nothing to do with gender. Wooley and Lawrence always dug together, and the British Empire survived."

"The Turkish Empire didn't," Lily said. So the stories about them were true?

An enormous brass key lay on the table in front of Dame Margaret. She moved it aside. "You're thinking of Ned Lawrence's friend, that little Saudi sheik? It had nothing to do with archaeology."

"He became king of Iraq."

"Political obligation, that's all. Ned had to make promises."

"Balfour made promises too," Lily said.

Dame Margaret shrugged. "All's fair in love and war. Without promises, Turks would still control the area. I ordered tea for you."

"Thank you."

"You could have worked with Hetty Goldman at Tarsus." Dame Margaret straightened her fork again, ran her finger along the handle of the spoon. "Kathleen Kenyon and John Crowfoot worked together at Samaria without any trouble. We've come a long way since the twenties. You have Fendley to thank for that. As long as students put up with his field conditions, he took them on. Cordelia ran the camp and mothered them all, men and women alike."

"I have to thank him for more than that. He's responsible for my being on Eastbourne's staff. I came to Palestine on my own, used my fellowship money. When they turned me away at Megiddo, Sir William found me moping in the library at the American School and called Eastbourne."

We should be talking about Eastbourne, Lily thought, should be lamenting his untimely death. "Eastbourne's murder is a terrible shock to me," Lily said.

They sat in silence, Dame Margaret glancing from table to table around the courtyard. Lily waited.

"What did you mean when you said you weren't surprised?" Lily finally said.

"At what?"

"That Eastbourne was killed," Lily said.

"Nothing. Nothing at all. He may have made enemies. The workmen or other archaeologists may have resented him. He was not a pleasant man."

"Unpleasant enough to be killed?"

"He was secretive and bad tempered."

"He had good points too, you know," Lily said, surprised that she felt forced to defend him.

"*De mortuus nil nisi bonum*? Speak only good of the dead? No, my dear. Quite the contrary. The dead are beyond hurting. It's the living who deserve kindness."

Dame Margaret picked up the key and put it down again in front of her. "I have that room over there." She pointed to double doors heavy with paint that led from the courtyard. "They tell me it was Lawrence's room. When he died, he was working on a survey of Crusader castles."

Most of the castles were in the north—on either side of the Palestine border, like Monfort in the upper Galilee and Nimrod in the Golan. Some were along the coast, Caesarea, Atlit; or in the Judean hills, like the ones at Latrun and Ramle.

"You're smiling," Dame Margaret said. "What's so funny?"

"I was picturing Lawrence, getting into that role. Lumbering around the countryside in costume, clattering in medieval armor, mapping a castle keep."

"Ned was an unhappy man," Dame Margaret said. "Maybe a little insane. But he was no buffoon." She paused and fingered the key again. "He worked with Eliot and me at Ur." She looked away at the fountain, watching the water splay and whisper as if it held some secret, and then looked back to Lily. "How did Eastbourne get on with Kate?"

"All right, I suppose." Lily said. "Well, I'm not sure."

Dame Margaret shook out her napkin and laid it in her lap. "Tea is here." She moved the brass key to the side and sat silently while the waiter arranged plates and cups. He poured with an elaborate show of arcs and dips. She waited until he left before she spoke again. "When did you last see her?"

"Kate? Yesterday, when we came in from the field for lunch. I left the tel early. Why do you ask?"

"No reason. There was a time when they had a problem, that's all. I know her well. We worked with her once. You didn't see him leave or know who drove up with him?"

"No. I took off too early for that."

"You'll be going back after the funeral? Will you continue digging?"

"It all depends on Beacon Pharmaceutical. They sponsored the dig."

"By the way, is anything missing from the excavation?"

The question seemed offhand, almost an afterthought. So this is what she's after, Lily thought. "Not that I know of. Why do you ask?"

"No reason. With the situation in Palestine now, the British police are helpless. You might need the protection of your own consulate."

"You think things will get worse?"

"Who knows? For the past two years, with this awful general strike, there's been nothing but violence—a thousand people killed in the last two months alone." Dame Margaret seemed more impassioned than Lily expected. "The whole thing is orchestrated by the Grand Mufti, you know. Inspired by the Nazi forte—to magnify small fears and disagreements. They tease at wounds until they fester, nurture hatred until it erupts."

"Divide and conquer?" asked Lily.

Dame Margaret took a sip of her tea and put the cup down carefully. "The British are the bastion of civilization in the Near East."

"I didn't mean it that way."

Dame Margaret narrowed her eyes. "You were in Jerusalem with him that day." Another casual statement that seemed to come out of nowhere.

"What day was that?"

"July tenth."

"The day of the riot? We were working on pottery at the YMCA."

Dame Margaret paused, wiped the spoon with her napkin, and put it down again. "Both of you disappeared that day from the YMCA."

What is she trying to say? Is she accusing me of something?

"See anyone else?" Dame Margaret asked.

"Just . . ." Lily hesitated. What was Dame Margaret after?

"Just what?"

"Just a tourist," Lily said. "Sir William thinks the whole thing, the riots, the general strike, is a plot to sabotage Suez and destroy the empire."

"He may not be far off. Where do you think the poor *fellah* gets guns and ammunition? We know the Mufti gets his money from Hitler." She picked up the brass key and held it in her hand, idly polishing it with the napkin. "You know Henderson, the new American military attaché?"

"I met him yesterday."

"He's just arrived." Dame Margaret seemed surprised. "His predecessor was killed in an accident near the Kastel on the road up to Jerusalem."

"I know that curve. It's dangerous. The road is narrow there and slippery when it's wet."

"Wasn't raining when he skidded off the road."

"Henderson's a nice-looking man," Lily said.

Dame Margaret shrugged. "There's no accounting for tastes." She put the key on the table next to her spoon and picked it up again. "I'm concerned for your safety, my dear. What will you do now?"

"I don't know. I thought I might do a survey. Iron Age fortresses, maybe. And then write up some proposals for my own excavations."

Still holding the key, Dame Margaret stood up. "Will you excuse me? I'm very tired."

She headed toward Lawrence's room. Lily was dismissed.

* * *

The murder made the front page of the *Palestine Post* the next morning, right under the headline "Eleven Separate Incidents within Seventy-Two Hours." Lily read it at breakfast.

BRITISH ARCHAEOLOGIST MURDERED NEAR HEBRON

Geoffrey Gorton Eastbourne, distinguished British archaeologist and director of the Beacon Research Foundation excavations at Tel al-Kharub, was killed Saturday morning on the Beit Jibrin track northwest of Hebron. Eastbourne was shot in the back and sustained a crushing blow to his head.

Eyewitnesses, including his driver and a member of the excavation staff who witnessed the shooting, say that armed bandits stopped their car two kilometers from the main highway and ordered Eastbourne out of the car. The driver was told to continue on to Hebron. Two shots were heard as they drove away.

The car was intercepted as Eastbourne was on his way to the opening of the new Palestine Archaeological Museum.

According to a spokesman from the British Archaeological School, "Eastbourne demonstrated his usual rash courage and conscientious attention to his professional responsibilities" by insisting that work on the tel be completed before leaving camp. The director of the British School said that Eastbourne had no known enemies but had often been warned against traveling unarmed in the present political climate.

The body was brought to Jerusalem by ambulance late Saturday. Funeral services are scheduled for 2:30 p.m. today at the Protestant Cemetery on Mt. Zion.

* * *

When Lily finished breakfast, she brought the newspaper inside to the telephone table in the alcove next to the Common Room and put it on top of the stack of old papers. She remembered the morning of the riots, when Eastbourne had folded the paper and put it in his pocket, and searched through the stack for July 10, wondering what he had been hiding, and where he had gone that day.

She scanned the headlines from twenty days ago. Air raids in Canton; Spanish insurgents thirty miles from Valencia; Haifa curfew in force after yesterday's bomb; Nazis demand self-determination for Sudeten Germans; arrival of the Italian steamship *Marco Polo* in Haifa port; record New York-Paris flight by Howard Hughes; Aspro tablets cure hay fever, nervous exhaustion, neuralgia, colds, malaria, asthma, sleeplessness.

Nothing there.

She remembered Sir William's joke about a lonely heart's notice in the personal columns. Flats for rent; English-speaking secretary wanted; shipment from the Marco Polo to arrive at the King David this morning; new dresses at Rosenthal's Clothing Emporium.

Nothing there.

Lady Fendley came into the Common Room and Lily handed her the morning paper. "The funeral is at 2:30."

"It's so sad," said Lady Fendley, sighing. "Geoffrey was a fine young man, really. He did it all on his own, you know.

With scholarships and hard work. His father was just a clerk in a haberdashery."

"You really liked him."

Lady Fendley nodded. "It wasn't just that. He had responsibilities that would have distracted another man who wasn't that dedicated. People laughed at him for being stingy. But the truth is, he was just squeaking by financially. He was sympathetic and helpful to all his workmen, seeing to their health and comfort. And he was good with children." Lady Fendley looked down at the paper and then at Lily. "Village children adored him."

"*De mortuus nil nisi bonum?*" asked Lily.

"Of course."

EIGHT

THE HIGH COMMISSIONER himself delivered the eulogy. Lily, drowsy from the sun, listened to his voice drifting in and out with the breeze that floated through the tall cypress and gently shifted their branches back and forth.

Snatches of his words reached her. "Brutally shot down in mid-career . . . outstanding discoveries . . . a scientist and a leader of men . . . inestimable loss."

The whole British community was there—the Anglican Bishop who read the service; the Chief Justice; Dominicans from the École Biblique, dressed in their light linen summer robes; the Attorney General; the Special Commissioner; members of the British School; bearded scholars from the Hebrew University. They crowded around the open grave and coffin draped with the Union Jack. Perspiration beaded on upper lips and ran down temples.

Jamal was there, watching from the verge of the path. Kate, buttoned into an ill-fitting black dress, her face puffed and blotched with tears, lingered on the edge of the crowd. A child sat near her in the shade of a tree.

Sir William stood in front, erect and resolute, looking toward the tawny desert hills and the Dead Sea, the water clear

and blue as the sky and rimmed with white patches of salt crys-
tals floating like miniature icebergs. Lady Fendley held his arm.
Dame Margaret stood next to them, wearing the hat with the
astonished feather.

"Gave his life for this land . . ." the High Commissioner was
saying. Bees and butterflies hovered among wreaths that sepa-
rated the funeral from tombstones that grew like broken teeth
out of the dry weeds. Fresh graves, decked with faded flowers,
were scattered here and there under soft and irregular ground.

Dame Margaret approached Lily. The breeze straightened
her feather into a point, trembling a moment at apogee and
then subsiding.

Lily heard whispers behind her, ". . . that's not what I heard.
I heard he was killed by some dissatisfied workmen."

Before Lily could turn around to see who was talking, Dame
Margaret reached her. The pleasant scent of vanilla mingled
with the pungent odor of cypress and the fragrance from lavender growing on the side of the hill.

"We have to talk," Dame Margaret said. "Not tomorrow.
Tomorrow's Tuesday. Let's make it Wednesday, for lunch. At
the American Colony." What is it this time, Lily wondered?
Dame Margaret left without saying goodbye, her feather rising
again, the smell of vanilla wafting in her wake.

Sir William tossed the first shovel of dirt into the grave after
the coffin was lowered. He turned away to take his wife's arm
and they walked down the path to a waiting taxi before Lily
could reach them. Kate had vanished before the group dispersed.
Only Jamal remained.

Lily left the cemetery. Weeds brushed against her sandals,
releasing the pungent aroma of wormwood. She scrambled past
the Church of the Dormition at the crest of the hill, past its
turrets and conical dome. Jamal followed her down the hill to
Zion Gate.

They went through the great double doors, heavy with iron hinges. Jamal strolled by Lily's side, silent and watchful, through the crowded lanes—past donkeys and camels that blocked the way; Jewish men with fur hats and black, belted suits; women with head scarves and shapeless, long-sleeved dresses.

Jamal stayed with her as she maneuvered through the swarming bazaar of the Khan ez Zeit, through the slippery streets, past butcher shops redolent with flyspecked legs of lamb. The ruddy-faced woman behind her, wheezing garlic, had her ample belly caught in the small of Lily's back. A man wearing a *kefiya* and a long, loose *abaya* jostled her. For a moment, the crush was so dense that Lily could barely breath.

Jamal was still with her.

Through the stifling throng snaked priests in long black robes and thin-lipped Protestant missionaries in dark suits leading their pale wives in baggy print dresses with dainty lace collars. Jamal glanced at Lily with his hooded eyes and smiled.

Somewhere near the Via Dolorosa, he disappeared.

*   *   *

Lily arrived at the American school hot and tired. She went to the kitchen and reached into the icebox for the water pitcher. The telephone rang. It was Henderson.

"Can you meet me at Samir's Patisserie inside Damascus Gate in half an hour? Something urgent we must talk about."

"Make it forty-five minutes."

"Forty-five minutes then."

She washed her face and took the glass of water outside into the garden, pressing its cool surface against her cheek and temples. She sat in the quiet of the garden with her feet up, her eyes closed, under the shade of the cedar tree until the lift of the late afternoon breeze revived her. Then she went back to the Old City.

She elbowed her way through Damascus Gate, avoiding beggars with swollen legs lying on the pavement in the shadow of the gate; beggars with pitiful faces and outreached hands; beggars sitting cross-legged on the ground, praying, their copper begging bowls silent reminders; beggars with accusing eyes who babbled and reeked of old urine. Assailed by a swarm of the destitute—by urchins and greedy children snatching at her— she reached into her pocket for a mil, a penny, a dime, anything to ease the guilt, to counteract the curses of their eyes. There but for the grace of God . . .

"Don't give them anything." It was Henderson who came up behind her. "Only encourages them."

He led her to Samir's Patisserie at the corner. "European Pastries," the sign said. "We deliver tarts to your home for your pleasure." The window was banked with sticky cakes and pastries mounded in geometric patterns, like three-dimensional optical illusions. A boy stood near the cakes with a whisk, beating back the flies drawn by the redolence of clarified butter and sugar syrup.

The proprietor smiled, with a sweeping bow. "*Ahlan wa sahlan.*" He waved them to a table. "Welcome in peace."

"*Fiq,*" Henderson answered. "*Minfadlak*, please, just some coffee." He sat down at the table and pointed to the seat across from him.

He waited until she was seated. "Have you thought about the survey of Iron Age fortresses?"

"It depends on whether we continue digging at Tel al-Kharub."

"Without Eastbourne?"

"Kate knows what she's doing."

"You think Beacon Pharmaceutical would sponsor an excavation headed by a woman?"

"The Brits don't mind. Excavations have woman directors, trained on the playing fields of England. Women play field hockey there."

A fly danced along the ceiling, swooped down toward the top of Henderson's head in wide arcs and then back up again, flitting across the room.

"You've heard of the Tegart lines?" he asked.

"I'm not sure."

"Double electrified fences. The Brits are installing them along the northern border," he said. "Two sets of barbed wire, about three meters high, ten meters apart. And roles of barbed wire between."

"To prevent infiltration from Syria and Lebanon by the Mufti's men?"

He nodded. "Personnel, arms, ammo. Tegart wants to build fortified command posts. The best locations were worked out in antiquity. We're looking for defensible hillsides with a good overlook."

"Maybe they weren't the best locations," Lily said. "Assyrians and Babylonians invaded and conquered anyway."

"Depends on the terrain and back-up."

"Locations of Iron Age fortresses were based on the use of fire signals from hilltop to hilltop," Lily said. "Now there are radios."

"The principle's the same."

She leaned closer. "You believe the new forts will keep out the Mufti's men?"

"I don't know. He's daring, resourceful."

"He hid in the Haram-al-Sharif and sneaked away in the night to Beirut disguised as a woman," Lily said. "You call that daring?"

"I call that resourceful." The fly buzzed above his head in narrowing circles. "I met him once."

"What was he like?"

"Disarming personality—a gentle man, smiling, soft-spoken. Light eyes. Pleasant."

"He kills people."

"To defend his home. The Jews are trying to drive Arabs from their own country, murdering their sons, burning their houses. Probably plotting to destroy the Dome of the Rock," he hit the table for emphasis, "as we speak."

"He kills Arabs too."

"Only traitors. Like a surgeon cutting away diseased tissue."

Lily moved back in her chair. "He sounds like Hitler."

"Exactly." The fly lit on the rim of his cup and he brushed it away. "Hitler is giving Germans back their pride. Like the Mufti is doing for Arabs."

"I suppose you met Hitler and found him charming too."

Henderson lifted his cup, and spooned some sugar and water into the saucer. He held the cup in his hand, waiting for the fly to light, then slammed the cup into the saucer, turning it around and around.

"You have to understand Hitler," he said. "He was wounded in the Great War. Trapped in a trench for two weeks with a dead comrade who'd been blown to bits. He was shell-shocked—blind for two months. Recovered his sight, but not his naiveté. He swore vengeance."

"That's no excuse," Lily said.

Henderson lifted the cup, put a paper napkin on the saucer over the splayed fly, and took a sip of coffee. "Something similar happened to me. Horrible. Buried with the dead. Hemmed in for a week. I'll never forget the stench, the bloated stomach, the eyes open to the rain."

"Yes, but you didn't . . ." Her voice trailed off. "Hitler behaves like a madman," Lily said. "Especially toward the Jews."

Henderson shrugged and took another sip of coffee. "He blames them for the war and the defeat. I don't trust them either. Most of them are Communists. They control the press and banking."

"Communist bankers?"

He grasped the coffee cup in his fist. "Between Marx and Rothschild, they control the world."

"You forgot Freud and Jesus."

He tried to smile. "Them too." The knuckles of his hand tightened around the coffee cup.

"Confucius and Buddha probably had Jewish mothers."

He nodded. "I wouldn't be surprised."

"And Mohammed and Chief Sequoia."

"Chief Sequoia?"

"A member of the Lost Ten Tribes. Where were you brought up?"

"Cincinnati."

"It sounds like a whole different world. Keep talking," Lily said. "It's time to put the other foot in your mouth."

Henderson leaned forward. He was looking at her carefully now, ignoring a second fly that danced around his head, his deep-set turquoise eyes glinting. "You are a very attractive woman. The gold of your hair and the blue of your eyes . . ."

"Is a blend of the western skies?"

"Yes. Something like that."

Lily moved her chair back. "I'm the sweetheart of Sigma Chi."

He leaned his arms on the table. Lily stared at the napkin in his saucer, puckered and discolored. "I have to be going." She started to get up.

"By the way." He reached for her arm. "Something is missing from your excavation. You registered it in the catalogue."

Another offhand statement, this time from Henderson.

"What is it?" she asked.

"Nothing much. Just a little blue glass vial."

Her amphoriskos! "What do you mean 'missing'?"

"Not at the site or in the stuff Eastbourne was bringing to the museum," he said.

"How do you know about it?"

He didn't answer. His nostrils flared for a split second and he narrowed his eyes. "I'm not at liberty to say." He glared at her through icy slits. "Let's just say it's a matter of great interest to the State Department."

"What's this about?"

"It's hush-hush." He stood up. "You're too upset to talk now. You just came from Eastbourne's funeral." He tossed two piasters on the table. "We'll talk about this another time. How long will you be in Jerusalem? When do you go back to the excavation?"

"I'm not sure."

"There's a reception at the Austrian consulate tomorrow evening. I have to be there. What say I pick you up tomorrow at six and we have dinner at the King David before the reception. We can talk then."

"Talk about what?"

"The blue glass vial, of course."

NINE

THE NEXT MORNING LILY slept late. She dressed quickly, reached for her saddle shoes, considered disguising the scuffs under a coat of fresh polish, and then thought better of it.

She carried her breakfast into the garden. Avi sat at the table under the pine tree, his legs up on the chair next to him, his face hidden behind the front page of the *Palestine Post*.

"*Boker tov,*" he said. "Good morning."

Lily read off the headlines. "Bomb Outside Hotel in Tel Aviv Wounds 21; Air Raids in Barcelona; Henlein Bloc Victorious in Czech Poll. Not very good as mornings go."

"We're alive." He looked over the edge of the paper. "I was waiting for you. Thought you might like company after the funeral yesterday."

"You came to Jerusalem to console me?"

"I had errands." He closed the paper and looked around the garden, at the roses dropping their petals on the flagstones, stretched his arms and took a deep, satisfied breath. "A beautiful day. Flowers are blooming. The sky is blue. Finish your breakfast and we'll go for a walk."

77

He went back to the paper. "I see they arrested someone and let him go."

"For Eastbourne's murder?"

"Police dogs tracked a scent from the murder scene to a house in Kharass."

He took his legs off the chair and sat up. "'The dog followed a trail for 22 kilometers to Kharass where it went straight to the house of the accused,'" he read aloud, "'stopped at the door and went to the wall of the courtyard, jumped against it and barked. A German Luger loaded with four rounds was found hidden behind a stone in a hole in the wall. The firearm was handed to Sir Charles Tegart, who assisted in the investigation.'"

"They let the man go?"

"He said he was looking after a sick cow when Eastbourne was shot. He claims he never locks the courtyard and anyone could have hidden the gun."

"What was Tegart doing there?"

Avi shrugged. "Eastbourne was an important man."

"How much does a Luger cost?" Lily asked.

"I don't know. Fifty pounds, maybe."

"Where would a poor *fellah* get the money? It would take years to earn that much."

Avi shrugged. "From the Waqf, maybe?"

Lily shook her head. "That's a religious fund. For widows and orphans, maintaining holy places."

"It's a form of religion. The Mufti feels he has a sacred duty to kill anyone who doesn't agree with him. That's what religion is all about."

"Don't be so cynical."

Avi put down the paper and began to chant. "Who killed Geoff Eastbourne? I, said the sparrow, with my little bow and arrow."

"It was a Luger."

"Sorry. Make that: I said the Hun, with my little German gun."

"You're pleased with yourself today."

"Ever walk along the ramparts on top of the city wall?" Avi asked.

"Spying on secrets hidden in the old stones and crooked alleys?" she said. "Let's go."

They spent the morning in the tangle of streets—Feather Lane, Watermelon Alley, Dancing Dervish, Needle's Eye—crowded with camels and donkeys, sheep and goats. They made their way through water vendors and men sitting on the stone pavement with olivewood camels for sale. They listened to nasal love songs of Umm Kousum blaring from shops.

They ran along the catwalk on the top of the city wall, looked down at traffic on Suleiman Street, at tourists studying maps. They peered into courtyards with wash hanging on the line, at spires of churches, at children playing in schoolyards, at the arches of the Church of the Holy Sepulcher.

"I feel like a peeping Tom," Lily said, and stopped to watch tired buses on Suleiman Street gasp up the hill between carts drawn by donkeys or spavined horses.

Avi stood on the parapet facing the Old City. He spread out his arms and declaimed, "If I forget thee, O Jerusalem, may my right hand forget her cunning, let my tongue cleave to the roof of my mouth, if I remember thee not; if I set not Jerusalem above my chief joy."

"And is Jerusalem your chief joy?" Lily asked.

Avi dropped his arms. "I don't know. Sometimes I wonder how many lives must be lost for this pile of stones. Then I remember all the stories of Jerusalem. This is where my forebears wrote the Bible. Over there," he pointed to the Dome of the Rock, "King David bought the threshing floor of Araunah the Jebusite."

He gestured at the narrow lanes of the Old City. "This is where David danced when he brought the ark from Kiryat Yearim. And over there," he pointed toward the cemetery on the Mount of Olives, "are the tombs of my ancestors."

He turned to Lily. "Did you know that if you're not buried in Jerusalem, you must tunnel your way back on your hands and knees? Just think, Eastbourne is already here."

He gazed across the hills. "At the end of days, the Messiah will sacrifice a red heifer and a miraculous bridge will lead from the Mount of Olives to the Temple Mount. Souls of the dead will walk across it for divine judgment." He gestured toward a wadi where small rubbish fires burned. "All the dead will rise from the Valley of Hinnom, right over there." Avi swept his arms from hill to hill like a conductor at a concert. "Franciscans will rise from the Olivet, Eastbourne from Mount Zion. The dead from everywhere will come to Jerusalem."

"There's not enough room."

"It is written." He dropped his arms. "That's the tragedy of Jerusalem. There's always room for the dead." His voice dropped to a hoarse whisper and his tone flattened. "There are no more red heifers. The species is extinct. The Messiah can never come."

The sounds of a quarrel seemed to erupt in the street outside the Old City. Lily looked down at vintage taxis parked in front of Damascus Gate. A flock of sheep blocked traffic. The shepherd leisurely guided them down the center of the street, ignoring the man shouting and shaking his fist from the running board of a Pierce Arrow marooned in the sea of sheep.

"Don't argue with the past," Avi called down in a mournful voice to the red-faced man. "You can't win."

"I had enough of the Old City," Lily said. "Let's go into town. I'll buy you an ice cream."

"Had enough of my sentimental hogwash?" He gave her a nervous smile. "Better yet, let's go to Patt's, and you'll buy me lunch."

They descended from the city wall at Jaffa Gate and started down Bethlehem Road toward the Sultan's pool.

"The Old City looks different," Lily said. "Last year it was full of men in red tarbooshes. It looked like a Shriner's convention. Now they all wear *kefiyas*, like *fellahin* from the villages."

"Statement of political solidarity," Avi said. "Even Arab judges wear *kefiyas* nowadays. Everybody wears costumes." He stopped and looked at her dress and down at her shoes. "I know you're an American because of your funny shoes."

Lily was sorry that she hadn't covered the scuffed toes with shoe polish.

"You know I'm a kibbutznik because I wear sandals and shorts and a *kova tembel*." He pointed to the white hat perched on the top of his head. "My idiot hat."

He grinned and started uphill toward Mamilla Street.

A bearded man from one of the yeshivas, dressed in black from his homburg to his shoes, strutted past them on the narrow sidewalk. Fringes of a prayer garment peeked from beneath his open frock coat. Side curls hung along his curly beard down to his lapels and danced with each step.

The man covered his eyes with his hand in an elaborate gesture and turned his face away.

Avi chuckled. "You see, everywhere silent messages shout at you. He was flirting, letting you know you make him think carnal thoughts."

They had reached Julian's Way and were near the King David Hotel.

A taxi, its motor idling noisily, waited at the corner of Mamilla. Two Arabs sat in the front seat.

A man dressed in a striped vest over baggy pants, his head encased in a bright turban, strolled down the street toward the King David Hotel. He carried a brown paper package tied with string.

"Another costume," Avi said as the man approached. Avi squinted at him. "Isn't that the workman from your site?"

"Abu Musa?"

Abu Musa looked up at the sound of his name and ducked into a shop near the entrance of the hotel.

Avi watched him scurry out of sight. "He looks like an illustration from a David Robert's print."

"Costumes again. He's Samaritan," Lily said. "I wonder what he's doing here." The shop had a gold-lettered sign, Judah Arnon, Antiquities. "I know Judah, the owner of the shop." Lily approached the display window adorned with Roman lamps and coins and peered inside. "Sometimes he works with archaeologists. Dug with us one season at Kharub."

Ancient bowls and jars stood beneath tiny spotlights on lacquered stands. Abu Musa, holding an Iron Age decanter, gestured and argued with a man who stood behind a glass case laden with jewelry.

"That's Judah," Lily said. "Behind the counter. The decanter looks like one from Tel al-Kharub."

Abu Musa waved his free hand insistently while Judah shook his head.

With a final nod of dismissal, Judah turned away from Abu Musa. The Samaritan wrapped the decanter in newspaper, put it back into the brown paper sack and retied the string. He came out of the shop with the package under his arm.

This time, he grinned at Lily. "I go to Ramallah. Wrong bus." He slid his tongue around the gaps in his brown teeth. "Ask in shop to find bus."

The taxi on the corner of Mamilla and Julian's Way pulled away from the curb and started toward them.

"Bus terminal is on Jaffa Road," Avi pointed up the street toward town. "That way."

Abu Musa's glance followed Avi's finger. "You sure that the way?" He flashed his stained teeth in a friendly leer.

Behind Abu Musa, Lily saw the driver of the approaching taxi lean back in the seat while the passenger reached down and brought up a rifle.

The man with the rifle swung it across the steering wheel to aim in the direction of the shop.

Judah looked through the window, waved his hands in warning, opened the door and grabbed Lily's arm. "Inside. Quick."

Abu Musa, alerted, ducked into the hotel entrance.

"Down!" Avi shouted.

An explosion erupted from the cab with a fiery flash. A loud pinging sound reverberated somewhere near the shop window and something flew past Lily.

Lily brushed her hand against her cheek. "What was that?"

The taxi sped away and Lily saw Abu Musa run down the alley that led to Herod's family tomb.

"Rifle shot," Judah said. "Hit the building."

"Don't be silly," Lily said and felt her knees buckle.

"There." Avi pointed to a spot near the door. "Took a chunk out of the stone."

Judah grabbed Lily's arm and propelled her inside. "Worry about that later."

He pulled at the straps that closed the metal shutters. They clattered down. He settled Lily into a chair in the back of the darkened shop. "You all right?" He held out a glass of tea in a silver holder. "Why would someone try to shoot you."

"I don't know." Her hand was shaking as she reached for the tea.

"First Eastbourne. Then you." Avi's high-pitched voice and rapid speech echoed his alarm. "Something to do with Tel al-Kharub?"

"I don't understand." Lily took a sip of the tea. "There's nothing there. No reason I can think of." She dropped a cube of sugar into the glass and stirred the tea. "You were at the site, Judah. Can you think of anything?"

Judah held out his hands and shrugged.

Avi said and leaned forward. "Think. There must be a reason."

Lily took a deep breath, sipped from the glass, shook her head. A marble clock on the shelf behind the counter ticked with a steady rhythm. She stirred the tea again. "What did Abu Musa want?"

"Tried to sell me an Iron Age decanter. Said he found it when he was plowing fields near his village."

"You didn't buy it."

"It wasn't from Samaria. Rim and neck were wrong. More a Judean type. Still . . . You think it's a fake?"

"Or stolen."

"From Kharub?"

"Maybe. I couldn't swear to it."

The clock whirred as if it took in a breath. Soft chimes carefully struck twelve o'clock. Lily finished the tea and handed the glass to Judah.

Avi glanced at the clock. "We have to leave."

Judah set the glass on the counter. "You sure it's safe?"

"I'll be all right," Lily said and stood up.

"I have an appointment. At Patt's," Avi said. "We'll be fine."

* * *

They headed for the New City through narrow alleys redolent with garbage, where armies of cats stalked and perched on the lids of cans, ready to pounce on their prey. Iridescent pigeons pecked at melon seeds and detritus scattered around the edge of oily puddles the same color as the birds.

"Wild life in the city," Avi said. "Years ago the British brought cats here to control the rats. And now look." He skirted a discarded melon rind. "I could never live in a city."

They continued up the hill toward Zion Circus, passing machine shops, skirting grimy pools of grease, passing a Hebrew sign painted on the wall between two doors.

"Holy place. Forbidden to urinate here," Avi read. "You see, even that is forbidden." He smiled at the sign and the faint dark rivulets trickling along the wall below it.

"You know what happened back in the twenties?" he asked. "The Brits built a public toilet near Zion Circus. They were miffed when the Arab mayor refused to commit public urination for the opening ceremony. Told him they do it in France. He said he didn't have to go, he went before he left his house."

"Ever seen a photo in the *Illustrated London Times* of the Lord Mayor of London in full regalia," Lily asked, "using a public latrine in Picadilly Circus?"

"No."

"Neither have I," Lily said, and was surprised that she had almost forgotten the rifle pointed in her direction and the stone chip from the building that had flown past her cheek.

At the sidewalk outside of Patt's, Avi pulled a canvas chair away from one of the small wooden tables. "We can sit out here and watch the world go by. Sooner or later, everyone comes to the Street of the Prophets." He gestured up and down the empty street. "It's like Times Square."

The only other person on the street was a woman who hurried out of the little grocery at the corner, weighted down with full shopping bags balanced from each hand.

A waiter stepped outside, wiping his hands on a towel.

"Cheese sandwich?" Avi asked Lily.

She nodded.

"Two. And orange juice twice," he said to the waiter. He turned to Lily. "You don't want the coffee. It will dissolve your teeth."

The waiter continued wiping his hands on the towel. "The shipment of *rimmonim* you brought this morning from the kibbutz?" he said to Avi. "Some of them were rotten."

Avi pushed away from the table. "The pomegranates? Maybe the whole crop is spoiled. I better go see."

He entered the shop and disappeared through a door in the back of the bakery. Lily waited for a while in the shade of the locust trees, watching occasional passersby. An old man wearing threadbare, faded clothes shuffled along on the other side of the street, hugging buildings, tilting his face to the sun as though he were blind. A ButiGaz truck stacked with cylinders of butane for kitchen stoves rumbled by.

Lily fidgeted in her seat and wondered what was keeping Avi. A boy carrying a soccer ball ran down the street. A pale young woman in a long-sleeved dress pushed a child in a carriage.

Finally, Lily left the table and opened the door of the café to the yeasty aroma of bread and pastries fresh from the ovens, the bitter smell of boiled coffee, the clatter of dishes on small marble tables where people leaned toward each other and murmured in quiet voices. She walked past them to the back of the room where Avi had gone through the door. She turned the knob.

The door was locked.

TEN

LILY KNOCKED. SHE HEARD movement behind the door and knocked again.

Avi's voice, strained and apprehensive called out "Who is it?" He opened the door a crack and looked through the narrow opening still secured by a chain bolt. "Oh, it's you." He hesitated. "Sorry I left. Emergency."

"A shipment of over-ripe pomegranates?" Lily looked past him into the back room, unfurnished except for a sink and towel roller in the corner.

What was so secret about a shipment of pomegranates from a kibbutz? Pomegranates—*rimmonim*. There's another meaning, Lily remembered.

Hand grenades.

Ora stood in the middle of the room, in the same baggy maternity dress, this time loose around the waist.

"Ora gave birth to an unhealthy brace of hand grenades, didn't she?" Lily said.

Avi flushed. "Who told you that?"

Ora twittered.

"You did," Lily said. "Just a little while ago. The waiter said something about a shipment of pomegranates, *rimmonim*—hand grenades in Hebrew. That's what you and Ora brought to Patt's this morning."

Ora giggled, sending the ripples of loose fabric from the dress surging around her middle like the tide.

Rafi, his hands white with flour, emerged into view, coming up from below. He stopped on the stairs.

"Are there flour bins in the basement?" Lily waited for a confirming titter from Ora. "Is that where you hide them?"

Rafi moved to the sink to wipe his hands. "Get her out of here," he said in a low voice.

"She's all right, Rafi. You told me . . ."

"I'll take care of it." Rafi reached for the towel and looked Lily over speculatively. "We'll go for a walk." He started for the door.

Lily heard the lock click behind them as they went back through the café and into the street.

They strolled under the trees, not looking at each other, brushing leaves out of the gutter with their shoes.

"Where are we going?" Lily asked.

"I don't know." He walked slowly, looking down at his feet, his hands in his pockets. "I'm just a tourist here."

"Sure you are."

They turned the corner at Rothschild Hospital and continued on toward Ethiopia Street.

"What are you really doing here?" Lily asked.

"Not much to tell. My name is Ralph Landon. I'm an orthopedic surgeon from Chicago, here for a few months to demonstrate new trauma procedures at Strauss Hospital."

"I'll bet."

"A tourist. Here for a couple of months."

Lily watched him as they sauntered up Ethiopia Street in the quiet of the siesta. "You want the grand tour," she asked, "or the intimate one of back streets that tourists never see?"

"Intimate is always better."

She smiled. He took his hands out of his pockets and smiled back.

"Over there," she waved toward a building on the other side of the road, "is the former home of the American School. Before they built the one in East Jerusalem."

"That where you live? The American School?"

"Where do you live?"

"I rent a bed-sitting room with board and laundry in Katamon, for eight pounds a month."

"You're overpaying. You can get a whole apartment for five pounds a month."

Lily pointed to a house next door to the black-domed Ethiopian Church. A guard in a white uniform stood at the door. "Haile Selassie, the Lion of Judah, Emperor of Abbysinia, descendant of Solomon and the Queen of Sheba, lives right there, in the Abbysinian Palace."

"In parts of Chicago," he said, "the South Side, some people think he's the new Messiah. A new religion, Ras Tafarians. We used to get called to the South Side sometimes to fix up knife wounds when I was a resident at Michael Reese. That's when I found out."

"You really are a doctor, aren't you?"

"I told you."

"You said Ora was your wife."

"I don't always tell the truth."

"You honestly work at Strauss Hospital?"

Rafi nodded and kept walking, slower, his hands in his pockets, brushing his shoe along a pile of leaves on the curb, scattering them into the roadway.

"I like the quiet this time of day," Lily said.

They strolled along the street, the only sounds their own footsteps, the crickets, and leaves stirring in the afternoon breeze.

"But that's not the real reason you're here, to teach trauma techniques," Lily said. "You're smuggling arms."

"Where'd you get that idea?"

Lily shook her head. "I caught you white-handed. Why the alias?"

"Don't know what you're talking about."

"I'd have to take lessons in stupidity to miss what you're doing."

"I don't have an alias. Just simpler to use a Hebrew name. Raphael."

"You said you don't always tell the truth."

"And you believed me?" He stopped walking and faced her. "I'm getting hungry. How about you? There's a new café on Chancellor Road, across from the hospital."

They turned left on Chancellor Road, their footsteps echoing in the silence. In front of the cafe, they sat at a table under an umbrella and waited in the eerie hush of the siesta.

A car was pulled up on the sidewalk in front of an arched doorway; bits of torn gray paper scudded among the leaves on the pavement and eddied in the wind.

A beggar sat cross-legged next to the steps of the Health Center across the road, his eyes closed, an open book across his lap, an engraved copper begging bowl next to his knee.

Rafi went into the café, emerging after a few minutes with two bottles of orange soda. "We have to make do with this. *'Geschlossen zwichen Zwie und Vier fur Schlafstunde.'* Closed between two and four for the siesta."

Lily took a sip of the soda. "What are you doing here really?" she asked.

"I told you. Demonstrating techniques for treating traumas at the hospital."

"Just working at a hospital? Every fourth man in Jerusalem is a doctor," she told him. "Taxi drivers and hod carriers are doctors. They don't need one more doctor in Jerusalem. You're here to smuggle arms."

"What makes you think that?"

"The *sherut* for one thing. And today at Patt's."

"I don't know what you mean."

"Why would a doctor take chances like that?"

Rafi shifted in his chair. He looked down at the table and took a sip from the soda bottle. "That reminds me of a story," he said. "Moishe and Chaim . . ."

"Were on the road from Minsk to Pinsk?"

Rafi shook his head. "No. This time they were on the high seas in a leaky boat. In a storm. The boat was pitching and tossing, pitching and tossing." Rafi rocked back and forth like the tide, his hands and forearms rising and falling. "Moishe cried, 'Help! Help! The ship is sinking! The ship is sinking!' And Chaim answered, 'So why are you worried? Is it your ship?'"

Lily sat quietly for a moment, not smiling, her arms crossed over her chest.

"You were supposed to laugh," Rafi said.

"Why were they in a leaky boat?"

"It was the only one they had."

She leaned forward and touched his arm. "You have to be careful. Penalties are getting more severe. They sentence people to death for smuggling arms now."

"I am careful. Besides, they always seem to commute the sentence."

He took another swallow of soda, tapped his foot and looked toward the beggar asleep at the steps of the Health Center. "What would you like to do now? We could go tea dancing at Café Europa. Or to the Edison and watch a movie. Walter Huston is enlarging the British Empire in *Rhodes of Africa* this week. We can spit shells from sunflower seeds onto the floor the whole afternoon. Or we could go to a salon—a genuine salon—at an artist's house."

"I have to meet someone for dinner at six o'clock."

"The salon it is," he said and tilted the soda bottle to finish it. "We'll drop in and leave after an hour, like important people."

"I've never been to a salon. What do people do?"

"Sit around in a circle and take turns talking about themselves."

"Does anyone reveal a guilty secret?"

He shook his head. "They come to flex their egos. They say, 'I won this prize; I invented that; I wrote that.' It's edifying."

"Sounds boring."

"It is. High society in Jerusalem. For visiting dignitaries like us." He stood up. "Leave the bottle on the table."

"Where is the salon?"

"A little way from here. Kalman House. He's an opthamologist. Runs an eye clinic out of his house. She's an artist and has her studio there. They hold open house every Thursday afternoon."

"How do you know them?"

"From the hospital." Rafi looked at his watch. "If we walk slowly, we won't arrive too early."

They strolled in the direction of Zion Circus. In a small alley with steps that led down a steep incline, the sensuous smell of roasting nuts drifted toward them from a shop built into the stairway.

"Someday I'll buy you a bag of pistachios," Rafi said.

"I'd rather have rubies."

Dissonant sounds of muezzins' calls for prayer wafted toward them from loudspeakers on a multitude of minarets near the Old City.

"It's three-thirty," Lily said. "Siesta's over."

"That's how you tell time?"

"Muslims are called to prayer five times a day—when they wake up just before first light, in mid-morning, at noon before the mid-day meal, at the end of the siesta, at sun-down, and before they go to sleep. Like a factory whistle. Tells you the time, even though you don't work in the mill."

People appeared in the streets; shopkeepers unlocked their doors. Ancient cars gasped along the road; motorbikes squealed between sputtering trucks and careened around horse-drawn wagons.

A man in a black felt fedora brushed against Lily, knocking his briefcase against her leg as he hurried past.

From somewhere near the Old City, hoarse shouts drifted toward them, faint and indistinguishable at first, then growing in intensity, punctuated with cries and shrieks. Lily stopped and grabbed Rafi's hand. Not another riot, another bomb, another lifeless face like Dr. Stern's. Rafi pressed her hand for a moment, then put his arm around her waist.

Around them, traffic slowed, people stood silent with harried faces animated by fear. Lily waited, anticipating horror, waited for the sound of gunfire, the jolt of an explosion, the howl of sirens through the streets.

ELEVEN

THE HAIRDRESSER, READY to open his shop, left the shutters half-closed; the greengrocer, carrying a box of apricots, halted on the sidewalk. Traffic on the road barely moved. A man on a motor bike lingered at the corner, one foot on the ground, the bike canted against his leg, his head tilted toward the Old City. All waited, listening in mute fellowship for echoes from the Old City.

The man in the black fedora knelt on the sidewalk, opened his briefcase and took out a gun that glinted blue-black in the sun. He thrust it into his belt, catching it in the fringes of a prayer-vest that dangled beneath his shirt. A tall man behind him peered over the rim of his sunglasses and backed away. A woman glanced at the gun, smiled at her friend and raised an eyebrow.

Noises from the Old City abated. Fear dissipated; shoulders that had been hunched relaxed. People still waited until the street filled with familiar sounds—mothers calling to children, taxis honking, buses coughing their way through the streets—and then turned away from each other. They walked around the man in the fedora, their eyes straight ahead.

Rafi let out a long breath. "Well, that certainly got my adrenals flowing."

Lily noticed that her fingers were still shaking. "The man in the fedora . . ."

"He wasn't Hagganah," Rafi said.

"How do you know?"

Rafi put his hands in his pockets. "What were you going to say about the man in the fedora?"

"He could be arrested for carrying arms," Lily said after a while.

Rafi kept walking, kicking at imaginary pebbles with the toes of his shoes. "Not if he's a supernumerary." He didn't look up.

"Supernumeraries carry spears. At the opera."

"British police recruit locals, Arabs and Jews, as reserves." He took his hands out of his pockets. "Call them supernumeraries."

"What kind of gun was it?"

"A Luger."

"The Brits issue German weapons?"

"Probably his own."

"Are they expensive?" Lily asked.

"Forty, fifty dollars." Rafi reached for her arm. "You want one?"

"Where would a *fellah* get the money?"

"A *fellah*? What makes you ask that?"

"It said in the paper that the police tracked Eastbourne's attackers to an Arab village and found a Luger hidden in a wall."

"Maybe he stole it?" Rafi shrugged. "Got it from the Mufti?"

"I think it's odd, that's all. They didn't arrest the man, or question him, just let him go when he said he didn't put it there. . . ." Her voice trailed off.

They strolled in silence, Rafi's fingers still lightly on her elbow. She could feel the warmth from his body, and was surprised at how comfortable she was with it.

After awhile, he pointed down the road to a house where green shutters stood open on the upstairs balconies and white curtains fluttered softly in the afternoon breeze. "Kalman's is over there, the big house with the awnings, near the corner."

Rafi rang the bell. The sound echoed inside the house, and penetrated through the tall arched windows. Footsteps clattered on a stone floor.

A small, bald man with glasses and a gray mustache opened the door. "*Baruch haba*. Come in. Come in." He swept his arm in a welcoming gesture. "What was the commotion in the Old City?"

"Who knows," Rafi said.

The man shook his head. "It's getting so bad, I can't even count sheep to go to sleep. In the middle of counting, someone shoots them."

Rafi's hand still rested on Lily's elbow as they entered the hallway. The man looked from Lily to Rafi and winked. "This is the first time you brought a friend."

Rafi winked back. "Lily Sampson," Rafi nodded at Lily. "Albert Kalman."

Kalman led them into a room with whitewashed walls and a high domed ceiling. Four blue settees were arranged around a polished brass table exactly in the center of a Persian rug. Bookcases ran the full height of two walls, the books punctuated with blown glass pitchers and vases—blue, deep red, green. Lily stopped in front of a wall hung with framed woodcuts and drawings of street scenes in Jerusalem, old Turkish houses, bearded Hassidim in the religious quarter of Mea Shearim, women shopping for vegetables among the stalls at Machneh Yehudah.

A woman came into the room, her sandals slapping on the marble floor, her loose skirt swaying with each step. "You like them?" she asked of the drawings. Her thick gray hair was pulled into a coil at the back of her neck, her cheekbones shone in the light, and her eyebrows, heavy and dark, underscored the intensity of her large brown eyes.

"Very nice," Lily said. "They look like a Jerusalem version of Kathe Kollwitz."

"Really? They look like Anna Kalmans to me."

Albert Kalman came up to them, smiling. "Here you are, Anna. You met Rafi's friend Lily?"

"Anna? I didn't mean . . ."

"Of course you didn't. Actually, I'm flattered," the artist said, and tilted her head to look at Lily. "It's time Rafi brought someone here." She took Lily's arm. "Come out to the garden. You need a bit of sunshine." She called over her shoulder to Albert, "Two more spritzers," and turned back to Lily. "Our holy water. Wine from the Galilee and soda water from Jerusalem."

Steps led down to a garden shaded by Aleppo pines, filled with the sweet scent of Victorian Box and blooming roses. A dark man stood on the edge of the terrace, looking out over the garden.

"This is Rafi's friend Lily," Anna said. She turned to Lily. "Yaacov is in Jerusalem to learn trauma techniques from Rafi. He's a doctor at Hanita."

"Hanita?"

"The new Hagganah settlement near the Lebanese border," he said. "Built the watchtower and stockade last March."

"I read about those settlements in the *Palestine Post,*" Lily said. "They're built like Iron Age forts, inside a double wall of wood filled with rubble."

"Exactly. We have to protect ourselves. Armed bands from across the border are killing Jewish farmers, attacking buses and trucks on the highway."

"And they had a time building it," Anna said.

Yaacov beamed at her. "It was quite a day. Got there before dawn. We thought we'd finish before nightfall, present the Brits and Arab villagers with a *fait accompli.* But..." he shrugged.

"What happened?"

"We had to leave the vehicles behind. Hill was too steep; there was no road. We hacked out a trail to carry equipment and supplies up the hill by hand. And the wind! Couldn't even put up tents. It took longer than we planned—hadn't finished by dark. They attacked at midnight."

"You lived to tell the tale," Anna said.

"Drove them off, thanks to Orde Wingate."

"The British army captain?"

Yaacov smiled. "He trained us. Carries a Bible with him. He says he's working for the victory of God and the Jews."

"You see, God works in mysterious ways." Albert Kalman said. "He gave us Rafi and Orde Wingate. And Yaacov, still a student who learns from everyone. He learns from Rafi, who learned to treat wounds in Chicago, the Sodom and Gomorrah of America where gangsters roam the streets."

"And what did you learn from Orde Wingate?" Lily asked.

"I learned how to move in the darkness, how to whisper orders, how to shoot, how to hide, how to anticipate an attack," Yaacov said. "In the Hagganah, I swore by candlelight, with a Bible and a revolver on the table before me. When I was a boy, growing up in Peqi'in, I never dreamt that all but one family would flee from our village."

"Peqi'in?"

"Mountain village in the Galilee. A Jewish community since the days of the Temple," Yaacov said. "Everyone else is just a newcomer."

Anna sat in one of the garden chairs and pulled another closer, gesturing for Lily to sit. "So you've come to visit Rafi while he works in Jerusalem?" She leaned toward Lily with a conspiratorial smile. "Tell me all about it."

"Actually," Lily said, "we met in a *sherut*."

"And since then you've become friends?"

Albert came toward them carrying a tray, with Rafi close behind. Rafi brought a small tiled table from the other side of the terrace, then carried two more chairs to where Anna and Lily sat.

"You're a tourist, then?" Yaacov asked.

Lily took a sip of her drink before she answered. "I'm an archaeologist."

"Ah, the archaeologists," Albert said. "They flit here in the spring like flocks of migratory birds. They peck at the ground all summer long and fly away in the fall. Only three industries in Jerusalem. Hospitals, British, and archaeology."

"I work at Tel al-Kharub."

Anna passed a plate of orange slices. "Unpleasant, that unfortunate incident with the director. My condolences. Things are completely out of hand." Anna shook her head.

Lily placed her glass back on the table. "What do the Arabs want?"

"Arabs?" Yaacov answered immediately. "To stop Jewish immigration, prohibit sale of land to the Jews."

Albert reached for an orange slice. "In the end, the British may have to give in. They have to put a stop to this brouhaha before the war with Germany. And then, who knows?"

"And the Jews?" Lily asked. "What do they want?"

Albert's sigh was deep and thoughtful. "Just a little corner of the world where we can live ordinary lives in peace."

"Why are the British so interested in Palestine?" Lily asked. "It isn't exactly the land of milk and petroleum."

"The gateway to Suez," Albert said.

"It's the poor farmer I feel sorry for," Yaacov said. "The *fellah*. He's caught in the middle. If he obeys the law, he's a target for the Mufti's men. If he doesn't, the British throw him in jail."

"Not to mention armed brigands who infiltrate from Syria and Lebanon to steal crops and animals," Anna added.

Yaacov nodded. "The *fellah* can't sell his land for fear of reprisals."

"It's not all bad," Albert said. "The Arab strike of the last two years is the best thing to happen to the *Yishuv*. First they closed the port at Jaffa, so we built one in Tel Aviv. Then they closed their shops. Been a stimulus for our economic development."

"Maybe if it hurts their pocketbooks enough they'll mutiny," Anna said. "The Mufti's men murder any Arab who has commercial dealings with Jews. Nobody stops them."

Albert leaned over his wife, shaking his head. "It won't help. German and Italian propaganda fan the flames."

Lily picked up her glass and held it in her hand.

"More spritzer?" Anna asked.

"Not really. It's making me a little sleepy. I haven't had lunch."

"Oh, dear," Anna said, and picked up a bowl from the tray to move it closer to Lily. "Here. Have a peanut."

Albert looked at his watch. "Time for the BBC. Maybe today we'll be able to hear some news."

He led the way inside. A glistening mahogany cabinet with dials for a short wave receiver stood in the corner. Albert squatted in front of the radio, twisting knobs until they heard a faint crackling. "This is BBC calling with news of the world. Today in China, the Japanese bombed . . ." The voice faded in and out.

"Where did they say?" Anna asked. "Nanking? Peking?"

Kalman put a finger to his lips. He sat in the chair next to the radio, listening, frowning in concentration, his eyes focused on the tip of his sandal.

". . . On the streets of Barcelona . . ." the voice said before it faded again. "In Czechoslovakia . . . Konrad Henlein . . . the Sudetendeutsche Party . . . eight-point program. . . ."

Intermittent high-pitched screeches and the dead noise of static drowned out the words. They all leaned forward, watching the loudspeaker like lip readers.

"Ah. The Italian air war," Albert said. "They're strafing the broadcast frequencies."

Anna looked at her watch. "Try the BBC Arabic broadcast. They increased the signal."

Kalman turned the dial until they heard a few words in Arabic. This time Morse code signals and the voice of a soprano singing *Un Bel Di* cut off the sound.

"I've always enjoyed Puccini," Anna said, and glanced at the wall clock.

Albert turned off the radio. "Hopeless." He stood up and began to pace, his hands behind his back. "The only thing that's certain is that to the victor belong the ruins."

"Not that the British are all that impartial," Anna said. "Lloyd George says that Hitler is the greatest German of the century."

"He's a bastard," Rafi said. "All Nazis are bastards."

"Thank God all bastards are not Nazis." Albert sat down and looked toward Lily. "We must be more careful of our language in the presence of the young lady." He inclined his head in her direction. "Did we insult you?"

Lily shook her head. "Not me. Just bastards."

"So tell me," Albert said to Lily. "Will you remain in Jerusalem?"

"I go back to the University of Chicago when the digging season is over to work on my dissertation."

"Just as well. No room at the Hebrew University. Since the *Anschluss*, the university is full, gymnasiums are overflowing, and every hospital is overstocked with physicians. Soon doctors will pay hospitals to practice instead of vice versa," Albert said. "Every one is an exile. Strangers here, strangers there, strangers everywhere, filled with longing for the past, the familiar smells of their childhood."

"The influx of immigrants from Europe is crowding every-one out," Anna said. "That's what makes the Arabs angry."

"Arabs are no better," Yaacov said. "They immigrate here from neighboring countries at the Mufti's instigation. Most of the immigrants of the last fifty years have been Arabs. Last century there were about 25,000 Jews in Jerusalem and only 14,000 Arabs. Now the proportions are reversed."

Anna looked at the wall clock again. "It's almost five o'clock, and almost no one is here. I'm beginning to worry. Something must have happened in the Old City," she said to her husband.

"Wait another fifteen minutes," he told her. "If no one comes, then you can begin to worry."

Chimes from the wall clock interrupted their conversation. Anna looked at her watch, threaded her fingers together and looked at her watch again.

"It's getting late," Lily said. "I have to go."

"Stay a little longer," Dr. Kalman said. "We hardly got to know you."

"Besides," added his wife, "we don't know what's happening in the streets."

"I have an appointment," Lily said. "At the King David for dinner. I still have to change."

"Rafi won't mind if you're a little late," Anna told her. "Will you, Rafi?"

"She's not going with me."

Lily was already in the hall when the doorbell rang. Anna opened the door to a short round woman with reddish hair and sharp features and a small dark man. Both began speaking at once in an excited mix of German, English and Hebrew.

"The *ganze* city is a *balagan*, everything is topsy-turvy," the woman said. "We saw it. The whole thing. From Jaffa road."

"Sorry we're late. We were held up at check points."

Anna leaned forward to kiss the air behind the woman's ear. "*Ma kara*, Tsipi? What happened?"

"*Alles* is *beseder*. It's all right," Tsipi said. "This time the police were ready."

"It started at Al Aqsa mosque," the man said. "The Arabs were whipped up by a sermon after someone passed around fake photos of Jews attacking the Dome of the Rock."

"Poured out of the mosque like madmen," Tsipi said. "We saw them at Damascus gate, shouting and waving their fists, running up the hill."

"Police surrounded them before they got to New Gate," the man broke in.

"The police blocked the roads into the New City and the gates of the Old City." She stopped to catch her breath. "The crowd threw stones and bottles and the police charged with batons."

"Anybody hurt?" Rafi asked.

The woman turned to her companion. "*Welche Nummer, Pauli? Ulai*," she began in Hebrew, "Maybe?" she switched back to German. "*Sechs? Sieben*?"

"Six Arabs, five policemen," Pauli said. "Light injuries, nothing serious."

"This time," Anna said.

Albert shook his head. "The Mufti hangs over Jerusalem like the angel of death."

They stood at the crowded doorway, Tsipi's hand on Pauli's arm.

Lily looked at her watch. "I have to leave. Thank you both for a lovely afternoon."

Albert walked down the steps with them. "Don't take the bus," he said. "Walk. Between snipers and ambushes and gelignite bombs, buses are too dangerous." He took Lily's hand. "It was good to meet you. Come back soon."

"*Shalom*," Rafi said.

"*Shalom, shalom ve ein shalom*," Albert said. "'Peace, peace, there is no peace.' They said that in the ancient days in Jerusalem. Little has changed." He pointed to metal disks hammered into the asphalt to mark the crosswalk. "You see how bad things are," he said and smiled at them. "They have to nail down the streets so that no one will steal them."

TWELVE

IT WAS A QUARTER TO six by the time Lily returned to the American School. Hardly enough time to dress for a gala evening at the King David. A note from Lady Fendley, tacked on the message board under the stairs, said that Kate had called and wanted Lily to come down to Tel al-Kharub to help close the camp. I'll call her in the morning, Lily thought, and ran up to her room to wash and put on the blue dress and high-heeled shoes she had worn at the museum reception. On the way to the mirror at the end of the hall, she glanced out the back window and saw Henderson waiting in the garden.

"Be right down," she called to him, ran the comb through her hair, tossed the fringed scarf over her shoulders and hurried down the stairs.

* * *

"Wrong side," Henderson said when Lily opened the door of the sleek green car. "Right-hand drive."

"What kind of car is it?" Lily asked, looking over the polished chrome trim and leather seats.

"Jaguar. Like it?"

"Nothing is in the right place."

"Depends on your point of view."

Henderson turned the key and the car purred to life. The powerful motor vibrated gently. "Motor mounts need adjustment," he said.

The Old City gleamed in the evening sun as they turned down St. Paul's Road.

"Beautiful, isn't it?" Lily said.

Henderson eyed the array of gauges that decorated the burled wood dashboard. "Not a bad car," he said, "but expensive to keep up."

They turned down Julian's Way, toward the King David Hotel.

The domed bell tower of the YMCA stood against the soft glow of the evening sky, serene with its graceful proportions, its tiles and vaulted arches. The morning of the riots still quivered in Lily's memory—the face of Dr. Stern, lax and pale in death on the sidewalk—her first glimpse of Henderson, buffeted by the mob in front of the King David.

Henderson drove past the grand entrance of the hotel, where the doorman, in a turban and galabia, unloaded cars and taxis under the porte-cochere. He turned onto the side road on Abu Sikhra Street. They pulled up in front of the ancient tomb with the rolling stone where Herod had buried his murdered relatives.

"We'll park here," Henderson said. "I may have to leave early."

Inside the rotating glass doors of the entrance, tall Sudanese waiters wearing white pantaloons and red tarbooshes glided along the marble floors of the majestic lobby.

"Looks like the British Colonial Office conquered the Ancient Near East too," Henderson said, eyeing the ornate lobby with its Assyrian décor, the dining room's ancient Phoenician theme. "They think they own the world."

They waited for a table in a lounge that was ornamented with Hittite motifs. A *thé dansant* trio played the *Tango de la Rose*. Lily watched couples twirl, stiff-backed, on the tiny dance floor.

"What would you like to drink?" Henderson asked signalling a waiter. "Two Scotch and Coca-Colas." He ordered without waiting for her answer, pulled out a chair at a small table and sat down.

"Is that what they drink in Cincinnati?" Lily asked.

"What?"

"Cincinnati. Your hometown."

"Oh, yes. Of course."

Lily picked a pretzel from the dish on the table.

"About the blue glass vial," Henderson said.

"Amphoriskos."

"Yes. Of course. Amphoriskos. You have any idea where it is?"

"It was on a shelf in the pottery shed when I left the camp. The day before the museum opening."

"You haven't seen it since?"

Lily shook her head. "What makes you think it's missing?"

"Tell me something about it," Henderson said.

"Dates to about 800 BC, made of sand-core glass. More opaque than the blown or molded variety."

"How's that?"

"Before glass-blowing was invented, a core of sand used as a mold was coated with viscous glass, and the sand was removed when it cooled."

"What's it look like?"

"Dark, opaque blue. Small, about three inches high and one and a half inches around. Pear-shaped, with a long neck and handles from the shoulder to the neck. It was wound with yellow glass threads combed into an ornamental pattern."

The waiter appeared behind Henderson, arched the tray downward with a flourish and poured their drinks.

Lily took a sip. "Interesting taste."

"Never had Coca-Cola before? It's the great American drink."

Of course I've had Coca-Cola. Not with scotch. Lily tried it again. She rolled the sticky sweetness on her tongue. There was an aftertaste of peat. "It tastes like cotton candy made of mildew," she said.

"The glass vial—amphoriskos," Henderson said. "Is it worth a great deal of money?"

"You mean, would someone steal it? I suppose a collector might pay as much as a thousand dollars for it in a New York gallery." Lily picked up another pretzel and broke it in two. "I don't know what people pay for these things. I don't approve of the antiquities trade. Artifacts mean more in an archaeological context than in a vitrine in a New York apartment."

A pageboy, his uniform jacket buttoned up to his neck, a little cap slanted on his forehead, came toward them. "Mr. Henderson, sir. There's someone to see you at the concierge desk."

Henderson said, "Excuse me a moment," and left the table.

Lily could see him, nodding and gesturing, intent in conversation with someone who remained out of her line of vision. She watched couples on the dance floor, pomaded and bejeweled. She picked up another pretzel and tried the drink again. She decided she didn't like it.

The music was smooth and soothing. "Let's Face the Music and Dance." She took another sip of the drink. It was still too sweet.

After a few minutes, Henderson returned and asked for the bill.

"What is it?" Lily asked.

"They were looking for someone named Karl."

"What did they want?"

"How should I know?"

"Well, maybe . . ."

"There must be two hundred Karls in Jerusalem. I'm not one of them. Finish your drink. We have to stop by the Polish consulate."

*   *   *

At the consulate, Henderson deposited Lily next to a buffet piled with plates of herring and sausage, little fish balls on tooth-picks, platters of bread and mounds of butter. A large bowl of shaved ice embedded with small silver cups of vodka stood in the center of the table. Henderson disappeared into a side room.

A tall gray-haired man with a trim goatee unexpectedly grasped Lily's hand and bent over, kissing the air above her fingers.

"Charming," he said. "Now you try our Polish vodka. Bet-ter than the Russian." He plucked a silver cup out of the mound of ice as if it were a grape and handed it to her, skewered a piece of herring on a toothpick and pressed it to her mouth.

Lily had swallowed three cups of iced vodka, two little sau-sages, and a piece of herring by the time Henderson returned and told her that they had to stop at another reception, this time at the Austrian consulate.

"Don't worry," he said. "Their buffet is good. Champagne, pastries, and of coursc," and now he smiled, "*schlagsahne.*"

"*Schlagsahne?*"

"Whipped cream. A Viennese specialty."

*   *   *

They rode south on Julian's Way, past the railroad station and into the German Colony, with its Bavarian houses and window boxes bright with geraniums. They parked in front of a large house.

"Here we are," Henderson said.

Lily was startled to see a Nazi flag flapping on the flagpole over the doorway. When she hesitated before getting out of the car, Henderson said, "Austria is part of Greater Germany now. Since the *Anschluss*."

A red carpet, anchored with polished brass rods, covered the marble steps in the entry. In the whitewashed foyer, a large black eagle hung against the wall.

In the inside rooms, Arab waiters in starched white jackets stood behind tables lavishly laid with pastries and wine. Small groups of people—some men in uniforms encrusted with medals, others in tailcoats and high wing collars, and ladies in long dresses—leaned toward each other, talking earnestly. The lilt of a Strauss waltz emanated from an adjacent room. Here and there, the sound of laughter punctuated the quiet murmur of conversation.

Lily noticed an Arab in a dark suit near a table in the corner. He stood apart, and his dark eyes moved from one group to another.

It was Jamal.

Henderson followed her gaze. "You know him?"

"Who?"

"The Arab. You know him?"

"I didn't notice," Lily said. "What Arab?"

Henderson watched her for a moment. "I'll be back soon. Someone I have to see." He disappeared into another room.

THIRTEEN

LILY MOVED TO THE TABLE. "A glass of wine, please," she said to Jamal. "Didn't expect to see you here."

Jamal asked a waiter for two glasses of wine and handed one to Lily.

"You don't work here?" she asked.

"I'm working right now. Attending physician at the reception."

"Physician?"

"Graduated the American School in Beirut," Jamal told her. "That's where I met Eastbourne."

"You worked at Kharub as a cook."

He took a sip of wine. "To earn extra money. Hospitals don't pay enough to live on. There are more doctors in Jerusalem than patients."

"I didn't know Arabs drank wine."

"I'm not a Moslem."

"There's a lot I don't know about you. I didn't know you were a doctor."

Jamal reached for a plate and contemplated the pastries on the table, looking over eclairs, cream puffs shaped like diminutive swans, little tarts, mocha and chocolate tortes. "I'm on staff at the Austrian Hospice," he said. He heaped pastries on the plate and handed it to Lily. "They do wonderful sweets here. Try a cream puff and some *Sacher torte*. Viennese specialty."

Lily put down the wineglass. "You were on the Beit Jibrin road with Eastbourne when he was killed, weren't you?" she asked. She tasted the *Sacher torte*.

"They reported it all in the newspaper," Jamal told her. "Gunmen ordered him out of the car and told us to drive on. Then we heard the shots. Nothing I could do."

"You didn't go back to see if you could help?" The *Sacher torte* was delicious.

"Driver wouldn't turn around."

Lily took another forkful of torte, luxuriating in the rich chocolate, rubbing her tongue against the roof of her mouth. After a while, she said, "Did Eastbourne have the amphoriskos with him when he was shot?"

"The one you found in the tomb? He might have done. Could have been bringing it up to the museum."

She tried the cream puff. "Henderson told me it's missing."

Jamal glanced toward the door to the other room. "Henderson? That his name? The man you came with?"

"You know him?"

"Henderson? No."

"It wasn't found in the car or on Eastbourne's body." Lily took another bite of *Sacher torte*.

"Might have dropped on the road," Jamal said.

"Could you take me there? To the exact spot?"

Jamal shrugged. "Police have been all over the area."

"I want to look for glass shards."

"Is it so important?"

Lily nodded. "When can we go?"

"I have to arrange for someone to cover for me at the hospital."

*   *   *

Henderson came back into the room, shaking his head and holding out his hands in apology.

"Have to go," Jamal said. "See you."

Henderson looked after him. "You do know him."

Why was he so interested? "We just met."

"There's champagne in the other room," Henderson said. "And an orchestra playing waltzes. Come on. I'll teach you the Viennese waltz."

He took Lily's arm and led her through the door. Dancing couples careened in patterned circles, around and around the floor in time to a Strauss waltz—*Blue Danube? Voices of Spring?*—circling the ballroom in wide arcs.

"A toast," he said, handing her a champagne flute and clicking his glass against hers.

"To what?"

Henderson flourished the glass, swirling it in a little circle. "To our friendship. To the blue glass vial. Drink up and we'll dance."

She felt queasy for a moment—but it passed. "I've never danced a Viennese waltz before," she said. When she ducked her head in apology, the room moved—just a small motion—but it passed.

"It's easy," he said, looking down at her with his handsome face. "Just follow me. *One,* two, three, *one,* two, three, *one,* two, three," and they whirled in time to the music, arching and swaying and twirling around the room.

One, two, three. *One,* two, three. *One,* two, three.

He smiled at her, the light from the chandeliers bouncing off his teeth and eyes, the colors of the room twinkling and flashing past his head. Turning and swirling, tilting at the waist— *one*, two, three; *one*, two, three.

Behind him, streaking light and blurring shapes kept moving, kept moving, two three; *one*, two, three. Red tracks flickered behind his ears, his forehead was growing and his eyebrows were getting longer—two, three; *one*, two, three; *one*, two three.

Those horrible cocktails. Two, three; *one*, two, three. Scotch and Coca-Cola.

One, two, three; *one*, two, three.

She was getting dizzier. The Polish reception with herring and sausage and little glasses of iced vodka. "Butter the bread thick, then a bite of herring. It lines the stomach and you can drink all night." They gave her one cold glass and then another. "Specially for the American lady."

One two three. Her head felt as if she had drunk Novocain. *One* two three—one—two—three. Her legs were heavy; her mouth was taut and dry.

It was the sausage. You never know what they put in sausage. One two three, one two three, one two three. And the vintage wine. Who knows one wine from another—red wine, white wine, with a nose, without—two three, one two three. And all that pastry. Whipped cream. On everything. Two three, one two three, one two three.

She saw his interminable smile, reeling and gyrating, with the chandelier twirling carelessly on the top of his head, and the room spinning out of control. One—two—three. One. Two. Three. One two three.

"I'm going to be sick." When she stopped, the walls were still heaving and moving. There was no way out. No doors, no windows, just the tilted floor and pulsating walls, waving toward her and receding, one two three, one two three, in and out, two three.

Jamal grabbed her arm and pulled her outside to the terrace, where the cool air was as sharp as an ax. She groped for the railing and leaned over, facing bushes garnished with thorns and little pink roses with open mouths. She bent over, her jaw slack, her stomach cramping, gagging and retching on the roses— two three, one two three. Go away. Leave me alone, two three. One two three. Hold my head.

Behind her, the ballroom was still spinning, the whipped cream still billowing, and the Viennese were still dancing and laughing in the woods, two three.

One two three, *one* two three.

FOURTEEN

AT BREAKFAST, SIR WILLIAM nattered on. "I met him," he was saying to Lily, "Konrad Henlein and his brother Karl."

Her eggs were swimming in grease; her toast was cold and wilted. The sun was too bright; she had a headache; she was sick to her stomach. And now, he was babbling about the Sudetenland crisis. And Konrad Henlein.

"It's the same as my pottery styles," he droned. "Just small changes—in rim shape, curvature of the shoulder—"

Lily tried another sip of coffee

Sir William prattled on. "Galton worked with family resemblances. I knew Sir Francis. Darwin's cousin, you know,"

Lily tried the toast.

"… Just small changes," he was saying, "just a line of the lip, the tip of the nose. Police use it for composite portraits."

Lady Fendley said, "Finish your breakfast, William darling, before it gets cold," and tucked a napkin under his chin.

"Please. Don't interrupt, my dear," Sir William told his wife. "This is important."

He turned back to Lily. "Where was I?" He paused a moment, pressing his hand against his forehead.

Would he never stop, Lily thought? I have to call the police about the amphoriskos. When does Kate want me to come down?

"I remember," Sir William raised his index finger heavenward. "I was telling you about Konrad Henlein and your young man."

"I have a touch of stomach flu," Lily said. "I have to make a telephone call," and left the table.

At the phone under the hall stairs, she tried Kate's number, letting it ring until the operator came back on the line and said there was no answer.

"Connect me with the police post in Jerusalem, please," Lily said. "I don't know the number." When a voice finally answered, she said, "I would like to speak to the officer in charge of Eastbourne's murder investigation."

"Is this an emergency?"

"No," Lily said. "I worked with Eastbourne, and I wanted . . ."

"Sorry," the voice said. "We have no new information."

"I have something—"

"We are making every effort to find his killers, madam."

"But I want—"

"Thank you for your interest, madam. As soon as we finish investigations, information will be released to the public. Goodbye, madam." The line went dead.

Nothing was going right this morning. She felt dizzy, and her head hurt to the tip of her nose.

Must be a migraine, she thought. Or a sinus attack.

The only thing to do, Lily decided, was relax in the shade and close her eyes until it was all over. She went out to the garden.

Avi was waiting near the fountain. He said, "I hear you were out dancing last night," and he raised his arms to hold an imaginary partner and began to waltz over the flagstones.

"Five foot nine; eyes that shine; and he comes from Palestine
. . ." he sang, pirouetting around the fountain and turning past
the table.

"Oh shut up."

"A bit testy this morning? Don't look to me for sympathy."

He danced around the edge of the terrace, twirling around
the roses, almost losing his balance. "You could have spent the
evening with me at the Orion, cheering for Jeanette Macdonald
as she sang through the San Francisco quake, reformed Clark
Gable and defeated the forces of evil, all in less than two hours.
You could have done that.

"Instead," he said, still circling, "you chose to carouse with
the descendants of the Knights Templar and the minions of Mad
Adolf from Berchtesgaden."

"They were Austrians."

"So is Adolph." Avi stopped dancing and dropped his arms.
"Some of my best friends are Austrians," he said, "but they
don't behave like that."

"The amphoriskos is missing," Lily said.

"Yes?"

"Eastbourne had it with him. He was taking it to the
Rockefeller."

"Yes?"

"Henderson told me."

"Is that his name?"

"I tried to tell the police just now on the phone. Something's
wrong there."

"If you ask me, Henderson's what's wrong there."

"I didn't ask you. The police wouldn't listen. They hung up
on me."

"Not to worry," Avi said. "I'll speak to Auntie Major. She'll
get you in touch with the police."

"Auntie Major?"

"Her real name is Greta Landau. She's having an affair with a British major. She says he'll do anything for her. He brings her gifts. Things in short supply, like lipstick and perfume."

"What does she give him?"

"Oranges?" Avi shrugged. "She says he's her fiancé."

"Are you going back to the kibbutz today?"

"I could."

"I have to go down to Kharub. Kate's going to close the camp."

"When do you want to go?"

"Not 'til the afternoon. I'm having lunch with Dame Margaret."

"Don't look so unhappy. Dame Margaret's not so bad. She writes about bloodless murders, she wears funny hats, and she smells like a cookie."

Lily was staring at the table. "Things are worse than I thought," she said. "I see little black spots before my eyes. And they're moving."

"Those are ants," Avi told her.

Lily pressed her fingers against the bridge of her nose. "I don't feel well."

"Serves you right, *habibi*."

Lily said, "I'm going to take a nap," and lay back on a lounge chair with her eyes closed.

She heard Avi tiptoe away and return. He brought a soft, lightweight covering that smelled of mothballs, draped it over her, then tiptoed away again.

Lily fell asleep and dreamed she was whirling in a storm-tossed dinghy, getting seasick as the boat eddied round and round. And the ship was sinking.

When she awakened, it was almost one o'clock. Her insides were churning, her head was aching, and she felt worse than before.

* * *

Dame Margaret waited at a table in the American Colony, crowned with a hat that looked like a miniature garden. If Lily felt better, she might have smiled.

"You look dreadful," Dame Margaret said.

"I feel dreadful."

"Eat something. They do a nice omelet here."

"Nothing fried," Lily said and made a face.

"Some steak tartar?"

Lily pictured the meat, buzzing with flies, hanging in the bazaar of the Old City. "I'm a vegetarian."

Dame Margaret called the waiter. "Bring her a tomato juice with a raw egg."

Lily groaned. "Oh, God."

"As bad as all that? What did they serve at the King David? Or was it the Austrian Consulate?"

"Everybody knows where I went last night?"

"You got a bit tiddley. And with a tall, good-looking man." Dame Margaret's tulips shook in admonition until they rattled. "You left with one man and came home with another. There are no secrets in a small town. Rumors are the only entertainment."

"I don't remember going home."

Dame Margaret leaned forward. The whiff of vanilla stung Lily's eyes and stirred her stomach.

"You think Henderson is good-looking?" Lily asked. "You didn't before."

"I still don't." Dame Margaret sat back in her chair and her tulips swayed in the breeze. "I've been meaning to ask you. Is anything missing from the site inventory?"

"An amphoriskos. You think it has anything to do with Eastbourne's murder?"

Dame Margaret shook her garden. "Who knows? Anything else missing?"

"I don't know. I'm going back to Kharub this afternoon to help pack up."

"They're closing the camp?"

Lily nodded. Her brain tossed around inside and ricocheted against her skull. She was sorry she moved her head.

"Too bad," Dame Margaret said. "Kate is competent. She should have a chance."

The waiter brought the tomato juice and put it in front of Lily. She looked at it with distaste.

"Drink up," Dame Margaret said. "You'll feel better."

Lily took a sip. "Oh, God," she said, "excuse me," and ran from the table.

* * *

They reached Kharub in the late afternoon. Avi swung the lorry onto the rutted field where the excavation's wagon was parked. "How do you feel?" he asked.

"Better, thanks," she answered with a dramatic whine. "But far from well." She placed the back of hand against her forehead and sank back in the seat. "The doctor says I never will be strong."

"Poor *habibi*. That'll teach you."

The camp was deserted. Kate's car was nowhere in sight, and some of the tents had already been taken down.

Avi parked next to the wagon. "Where's Kate?"

"I think she has a house in Ashkelon. Maybe she's there."

"You want to wait here? Go to Kate's? Drive over to the kibbutz?"

"I'm not sure where Kate lives. Anyway, I have work to do," Lily said. "And I want to look for the amphoriskos. In the wagon, maybe. Or the shelf in the pottery shed."

"I'll help." Avi opened the camp wagon, felt under the seats and looked in the glove compartment. "What does it look like?"

"A dark blue vial, decorated with wiggly yellow lines."

He pulled out the back seat. "It isn't here."

"It's in a box, a small cardboard box, maybe three and a half inches long."

"When did you last see it?"

"In the pottery shed. I labeled the box and covered the shelf with a tarp. That was before I left for Jerusalem. Let's look there."

The tarp was gone. Avi looked at cardboard cartons neatly ranged on the shelves. "What are all these numbers?" he asked.

"Kh is the site name, Kharub; 38 is the year; 3 would be the area of the site; T 104 would be the number of the tomb; g, for glass; 3321 is the catalogue number."

"You put these numbers on everything you find?"

Lily nodded. "I put a tag on an artifact and enter it in my field notes. The registrar adds it to the field catalogue and also makes out a card for the other registry over there." She pointed to a speckled file box on the shelf.

"Like double entry bookkeeping."

"Triple entry," she said, "I haven't written it up in my field notes yet." She felt ashamed of her carelessness. "If the amphoriskos is lost, it's my fault."

"Naughty, naughty," Avi said and flipped open the field catalogue on the table.

Lily looked over his shoulder to check the registration number of the amphoriskos. "It's in the registry, but not on the shelf."

"You want to look in all these boxes?"

She shook her head. "Maybe later. First I have to finish my field notes."

"I'll look in the boxes while you work on that."

"It can't hurt." She turned toward her tent to get her field notes. "Don't mix anything up. Watch how you repack the artifacts. Handle them carefully. I'll be right back."

The notebook was still on her cot, lying on top of the sleeping bag. She slapped the dust off the loose-leaf binder and brought it back to the pottery shed.

Avi waved a small box at her." "I found it. I found it."

"Where?"

"It fell behind this pile of cartons." He shook the box.

"Careful with that."

He placed the box on the table and lifted the lid. "It's heavier than I thought it would be."

Inside was a rectangular stainless steel object. Lily placed the notebook on the table and took it from the box.

"It's a cigarette lighter," she said and turned it over in her hand.

The back was inscribed with the word MINOX inside a lozenge with the letters VEF breaking the line at the top. Underneath, it said Riga, and at the bottom the legend "Made in Latvia."

"Latvia? Where did Eastbourne get a cigarette lighter made in Latvia? And what's it doing in this box?"

"It's a camera," Avi said.

"It's too small to be a camera."

"Rafi has one, uses it to copy documents." He reached for the camera. "Let me show you."

He let Lily's notebook fall open and pulled at both ends of the camera. It opened with a click. There was a tiny eyepiece that seemed to be a viewfinder and a lens. He held the camera over the page with the viewfinder to his eye and clicked it shut.

"That's how it works," he said and put it back into the box.

Lily looked over at the open notebook. "Something's wrong," she said and sat down. "These aren't my field notes."

Lily turned page after page filled with Eastbourne's cramped handwriting. She picked up the book and shook it. A map and plans fell out of the back pocket.

FIFTEEN

"IT BELONGS TO EASTBOURNE. Some kind of journal." Lily flipped
the pages of the notebook. "He left it for me. Why?"

Avi reached over her shoulder and pointed to an entry. *"July
10. KH at the King David, 9:30 a.m.* I thought so. He met someone."

"That morning in Jerusalem—the day of the riots. I couldn't
find him all day. Maybe he kept the appointment."

"A scandal." Avi licked his lips and rubbed his hands together. "KH. You think it was Kate Hale?"

"It's not a joke," Lily said. "Anyway, it could be anyone."

"Who then? Kareem Husseini? Some bimbo with a name
like Karla Habibi? Or your own Keith Henderson?"

Lily thumbed through the binder. "He's not my Keith
Henderson."

"No. That one belongs to the world." Avi sat down next to
her, moved the notebook toward him and turned the pages one
by one.

"Don't do that," Lily said. "It makes me feel guilty. Like
we've opened someone else's mail."

"If he left it for you, you owe it to him to read it." Avi read an entry and turned another page. He tapped the journal. "Here's the amphoriskos," he said. "*July 30*—the day he was murdered."

"Let me see."

He ran his finger along the page. "Right here. *Pack amphoriskos*." He read the next entry. "*July 31. KH at King David, 9:30 a.m.* What did I tell you? Another tryst."

Avi began to hum. "Who killed Geoff Eastbourne? I, said his lover, and I did it undercover."

"Stop it," Lily said and took the journal away from him.

They were interrupted by the noise of Kate's Austin. It sounded like a sewing machine that needed oiling as it struggled up the road toward the camp. The dull blue paint of the Austin was streaked and dappled from the sea air.

Lily closed the notebook and slipped it into her bag.

Kate set the brake with an audible ratchet. The motor churned while she squeaked the car open. She got out and pushed against the door with both hands to close it. She had lost weight. There was a fragility about her that Lily hadn't noticed before.

Kate's face was more blotched than ever, her eyes swollen from crying. "I've been trying to reach you," she told Lily. "Beacon Pharmaceutical wants to close the camp."

"I'm sorry," Lily said.

Kate took a ring binder from the shelf near the kitchen door and handed it to Lily. "You forgot your field notebook." It seemed like an accusation.

Lily flushed. "I've been looking for it everywhere."

With a heavyhearted sigh, Kate sat down at the table. "We have to finish the site report." She looked toward the boxes on the shelves behind Lily. "You can do the section on the cemetery. That is, if you want to."

"I meant to work on my field notes last weekend in Jerusalem. But . . ." Lily wondered whether Kate was listening.

It didn't seem to matter. Kate's arms drooped at her sides, her dress hung loosely from her shoulders and had a stain in front, and her face looked like a wound. Her eyes were filling with tears. She doesn't understand what I'm saying, Lily thought.

Lily kept talking, trying to diffuse the dejection that radiated from Kate with an incessant patter. Lily told Kate that the amphoriskos was missing, told Kate about her frustration when she tried to get in touch with the police. Kate listened with a dazed, uncomprehending look.

"I'm awfully sorry," Lily said. "Awfully sorry."

Kate reached for the handkerchief balled up in her sleeve. "Geoffrey was taking the amphoriskos up to Jerusalem for the opening of the Rockefeller. Ask the museum registrar."

She heard what I said after all, Lily realized.

Kate wiped her nose. "All the tomb finds have to be photographed for the site report." She continued to sniffle and looked down at her hands, twisting the corners of the handkerchief into a damp point. "Why don't you pack up the cemetery stuff, work on it in Jerusalem?"

Kate shouldn't be alone, Lily thought, and reached out to touch her arm. "You look tired. You need help here."

"No, no. I have to keep busy. It's the only way." Kate looked at her watch. "I have to get back now."

She rose slowly, faltered to the car, started the motor, and clattered down the road toward Ashkelon.

"Four o'clock." Lily watched Kate drive away. "She always leaves around this time."

Avi stood up. "Let's follow her." The car turned the corner toward the Ashkelon Road. "Find out where she goes."

"Probably goes home. Every day at four o'clock. You think it has anything to do with the entries in the journal? KH."

Avi started toward the lorry.

"Wait a few minutes," Lily said. "So she doesn't know we're following."

They took the Ashkelon road, past orange groves and stands of eucalyptus. The asphalt was white with the sun, and tiny mirages glimmered and disappeared as they bounced over the dips and gullies. The trees thinned out near the dune area, and they could make out Kate's car, shimmering in the heat, about a quarter of a mile ahead. The road went past half-buried brick walls from Byzantine houses punctuated with the bright flowers of wild oleander; past stubs of ancient columns, festooned with tangled branches and thickets of bramble. As they approached the sea, drifts of sand scarred with tracks from bus tires coated the roadway. Spikes of wormwood and dune grass anchored small sand hillocks on the abandoned sidewalks. Here and there, gray, leafless branches of white broom jutted from the cracked macadam.

A lone grocery, its door bracketed with stacks of soda bottles and a small refrigerator, was on the left. A row of small stone houses with flat roofs stood facing the sea. Past the houses, an incongruous Bauhaus structure with a faded sign that said Club Casino overlooked the beach. A single date palm with a leeward bend, hunched and distorted by the wind, grew near the corner of the building.

Kate's car was parked next to a tumble of bougainvillea at the side of the last house. A bright blue door was half-hidden by swags of jasmine that drooped from a matted trellis.

Lily got out of the lorry and started toward the house. "Mind if I go in?"

"Go ahead. I'll walk on the beach."

Lily rang the bell and heard a rush of footsteps. A sandy-haired boy, about six years old—the boy Lily had seen at Eastbourne's funeral—pulled open the door. He had the same imperturbable blue eyes as Eastbourne.

"Geoff. Don't open the door without knowing who's there," a guttural voice called from behind him, and a plump Arab woman in a striped Gaza dress came puffing up to the door after him. "I can help you?"

"I came to see Kate Hale," Lily said.

Kate appeared behind them. "It's all right, Faridah. She's a friend." Kate put her hand on the boy's shoulder. "This is my son, Geoff." Kate smoothed the child's hair and kissed his forehead. "Now you know." She stared at Lily, as if waiting for a comment.

The boy reached to shake Lily's proffered hand. "How do you do?"

"We're having tea." Kate's fingers continued to stroke little Geoff's hair. "Care to join us?"

"Just came to see if you're all right. I can't stay." Lily gestured toward the lorry. "Someone's waiting."

Kate led her into a light-filled room. Deep red Bukharian rugs were scattered over the floor, the marble tiles beneath so loose that they rasped and echoed with a hollow sound as they wavered beneath Lily's feet.

A table in front of a window overlooking the sea was set for tea and covered with a starched, embroidered tablecloth.

Geoff smiled up at Lily. "We have strawberry jam today," he said. "Would you like some?"

"You and Faridah have your tea," Kate told him. "Miss Sampson and I have to talk."

She gestured toward two small armchairs in the corner that stood on either side of a table inlaid with mother of pearl. A glass door behind it led to an atrium with a dusty table and chairs and forsaken bracts of bougainvillea that swirled in the corners like broken paper lanterns. A cluttered desk nearby was surrounded by a typewriter table and bookshelves made of planks and glass bricks. Piles of books were stacked on the desk and spilled haphazardly over a heavy plush chair.

Kate sat down, looked at her hands, limp in her lap, and ran her fingers along the folds of her skirt. "Were you surprised when you met Geoff?" she asked Lily.

"It wasn't what I expected."

"He'll be going back home this fall. To public school."

"You and Eastbourne never married?"

"We couldn't. We were both graduate students. It would have been the end of our careers." Kate looked over at Geoff and smiled. "Lady Fendley took care of everything. She's been a brick. Geoff adores her. He's called her Auntie Cordelia ever since he could talk."

This was a new aspect of Lady Fendley, Lily thought. The doting aunt. "She arranged the public school too?"

Kate nodded. "She told them little Geoff was her dead sister's child. Things are pretty tight financially. But Geoffrey came up with the money. He always does."

"Is that why you went up to Jerusalem to meet Eastbourne?"

Kate shook her head. "I never met him in Jerusalem. Just here. In private. Besides, I wouldn't leave Geoff for a whole day."

"Then who did he meet?"

"I don't think he met anyone. He may have done consulting work for some collectors. We needed the money."

Kate sighed. A picture of Eastbourne and a bowl of apples were on the table next to her. Her nose was still red from crying. She picked up the photograph and cradled it, stroking it with her finger, tracing Eastbourne's forehead and cheek. A tear formed on the rim of her eye and ran down along side her nose, trembling on the edge of her nostril before it dropped to her blouse.

She put the picture back on the table and lifted an apple from the bowl. "He brought these from Lebanon," she said. "They don't grow here. Not enough frost." She ran her finger along the surface of the apple, around a dark spot on its skin. "He was like the apples, you know. A beautiful blossom in its youth and shining in its maturity, with a few surface flaws here and there. But the taste is crisp and sweet. And at the core are seeds for a thousand orchards."

This was the first true moment of mourning that Lily had witnessed through all the speeches and eulogies of the past week. "You really miss him," she said.

"Of course I do. Who wouldn't?" Kate put the apple on top of the table next to the picture. "There was trouble at the site toward the end, you know."

"Oh?"

"Things were turning up missing. Small things. Geoffrey's extra pair of linen breeches, some frying pans from the kitchen, a black juglet, a horse-and-rider figurine." Kate pressed her hands to her face as if they could staunch the tears. "At first he thought it was the Bedouin. It turned out to be Abu Musa. Geoffrey told him to clear out."

"When was that?"

"That last morning."

"You think he stole the amphoriskos?"

"He could have done."

"And waited at the Beit Jibrin track?"

"He was angry enough." Kate's shoulders shook. She took a deep breath and looked out the window toward Avi's lorry. "You can drive the station wagon up to Jerusalem," she said after a while. "I don't need it here. I don't want to see it day after day." She shuddered. "Let me fetch the keys."

She disappeared into the bowels of the house. "You have to bring back the wagon eventually," she said when she came back into the room. "It belongs to Beacon's Pharmaceutical. We have to return it after the camp is closed."

Outside, Avi was waiting in the lorry. "Well?" he said.

"Well what? I have the keys to the station wagon," Lily said. "I can use it until we close camp. I'll bring some of the material up to Jerusalem, work on it there."

"You know what I mean."

"Eastbourne didn't meet Kate in Jerusalem. I'm afraid it was that bimbo with a name like Karla Habibi."

"Bimbo is right. With a name like that, she'd go out with anyone."

On the way back, Lily told him about little Geoff and Lady Fendley, and about Eastbourne's accusations against Abu Musa.

She mused about it until they reached the camp.

"I'll help you load the boxes," Avi said on the way to the pottery shed.

"I must talk to the police." Lily picked up a box to carry to the station wagon. "About Abu Musa."

Avi reached for a carton and stacked it against the back seat of the station wagon. "I'll get hold of Auntie Major," he told her. "She'll arrange it."

                              *   *   *

Lily maneuvered the station wagon along the track to Qiryat Gat, distracted by a whirlwind of thoughts about what Kate had said, about Abu Musa, about the amphoriskos. July tenth, July tenth, echoed with the hum of the tires bumping over the ruts in the road. If not Kate, then who did Eastbourne meet that morning?

On the road, she passed the place where Avi had stopped the *sherut* with Rafi in the back seat. Lily smiled and wondered where he was, what he was doing at that moment.

At the American School, she parked the wagon near the tennis courts and brought the boxes into the back hall, one by one. She hoisted one of the boxes, balancing it against her hip, and unlocked the library door, ready to carry the box down to the pottery laboratory in the basement.

A man stood at Lily's carrel, pawing through books and notes scattered over the desk and onto the floor. Lily recognized him as Eliot Blessington, Dame Margaret's husband. He looked startled when Lily opened the door.

He grabbed for a book.

"Ah, here it is," he said and held it up for her to see. "I was looking for the site report from Tel Beit Mirsim. It was checked out to you. I need to borrow it."

"I don't have the site report from Beit Mirsim at my desk."

He made an elaborate show of reading a title on the spine of the book. "Sorry. My mistake." He put down the volume, left the chaos on her desk and started for the door.

"I hope you're feeling better," he called over his shoulder. "Margaret still wants to talk to you. She'll ring you tomorrow." He closed the door behind him.

"You left a mess," Lily said and heard the front door slam. "I know ancient curses for people like you."

While she rearranged the books in the carrel and picked the papers off the floor, the rhythmic repetition, July tenth, July tenth, continued in her head. The day of the riots. Something happened that day, Lily thought, something that involved Eastbourne.

She went out into the hall to look for the pile of old newspapers. They were still there, on the shelf on the bottom of the telephone table. She hunted through the stack for the newspaper. When she found it, she folded it up, just the way Eastbourne had done, and put it in her pocket.

SIXTEEN

RAFI WAS WAITING in the foyer when Lily came down the stairs the next morning. She felt her face flush.

"Had breakfast yet?" he asked. "We can go into town. My treat."

"We could eat here." The idea of making breakfast for him appealed to her. "Save you money."

"Can't." He shook his head. "I'm on call. I told them I'd be at that little place near the hospital."

"I'm not sure I have time," Lily said. "I'm waiting for Avi to call. I have to get hold of the police. Abu Musa may have killed Eastbourne to steal an amphoriskos—a blue glass vial—from Kharub."

"Who's Abu Musa?"

"One of the workmen at the site."

"Was the amphoriskos valuable?"

"Eastbourne was taking it to Jerusalem for the museum opening."

"Maybe you should let it alone." Rafi's hands were in his pockets. "Let the police handle it. It's a British matter. Eastbourne was a British subject."

"I can't do that. I have to find the amphoriskos. Besides, the police aren't handling it."

"They may have their reasons."

"As far as I can see, it's because they lost control of the Mandate," Lily said. "The terrorists have taken over."

"All the more reason. The same people that went after Eastbourne might go after you."

"They already have. Someone took a pot shot at me a few days ago."

He took his hands out of his pockets and reached out to her.

"They missed," she said.

"Those are famous last words. Maybe the amphoriskos is still at the site. You looked through everything?"

"Its not there. But I found a camera in the box where it was supposed to be."

"A camera?"

When he touched her arm, she noticed his fingers were red and sore. "What happened to your hands?"

"It's nothing." He shoved them back in his pocket. "It's just a rash. I got it in the darkroom."

"You don't use gloves and tongs?"

"I use a special developer for fine grain film. The fumes are pretty strong and there may have been a pinhole in the gloves."

"You need that developer for the film you use in that little camera you have?"

His eyes widened in surprise. "What little camera?"

"The one you use to copy journal articles."

"Who told you I used a camera to copy journal articles?" His voice was edgy.

"Avi told me."

"Avi?" He kept his hands in his pockets.

"Yes. He said you had a little camera like Eastbourne's."

"Eastbourne had a little camera to copy articles?"

"I told you. We found it in the box that was supposed to have the amphoriskos."

"Any film in it? I might be able to develop it in the lab."

"I don't know. I didn't open it."

"I suppose you should go to the police." He looked past her at the wall and seemed to be thinking. "But they won't talk to you without an appointment."

"How can I get one?"

"I'll see what I can do," Rafi said. "I'll get back to you." He turned and hurried out the door.

* * *

Lily had almost finished breakfast when the telephone rang. It was Rafi.

"Avi said you wanted Auntie Major to arrange an appointment with her officer," he said.

"Yes?" Lily was surprised at the glow of excitement she felt at the sound of his voice.

"We made one for ten o'clock, Monday morning," he told her.

"Auntie Major will meet us at Patt's at 9:30 and take us to the police post in the Russian compound."

"Can't it be sooner?"

"I wish it were. But today's Friday—Moslem Sabbath. The Brits close offices for everybody's holidays—Moslem, Christian, Jewish, Chinese New Year. And any day that has an 'r' in it."

"I want to talk to the police as soon as possible."

"I'd like to see you before then." There was silence at the other end. When Rafi spoke again, his voice was muffled. "You sure the amphoriskos was stolen? Maybe it's in the Rockefeller."

Lily could hear Rafi chewing. "What are you eating?"

"Breakfast. How did you know it was missing in the first place?"

"Someone told me."

"Who?"

"I'm not free to say."

"Oh, come on."

This time, Lily heard Rafi sip and swallow. "Coffee?"

"Juice."

Another moment of silence, and Rafi said, "You rilly thimk Abby Musim milled—?" He swallowed, and repeated it. "Abu Musa killed Eastbourne for a glass vial?" Another pause, another bite. "You mink Abumus dukit?"

"You got crumbs in my ear," Lily said.

"Mo do bell."

"*Bon appetit,*" Lily said and hung up.

She sat next to the telephone for a while. Better check the museum first, she thought, before I go to the police. She picked up the receiver again and jiggled the hook to get the operator.

Lily finally got the registrar of the Rockefeller on the line and asked if the amphoriskos was in the museum. "Eastbourne was bringing it up to the museum for the opening," Lily told her.

"We don't have it on exhibit in any cases on the floor."

"It would have come in too late for that. Maybe the police brought it. During the murder investigation."

"Murder?"

"Eastbourne was killed on the way to the opening."

"I know that."

"Do you have the amphoriskos?"

Lily heard the rustle of papers. "I have to check the accession record," the registrar said.

"It's not the sort of thing you could forget."

"You have no idea. It's a madhouse here. We weren't ready by the opening. Haven't caught up since. Nothing in the cases is labeled. We're behind in our records."

"Will you look it up?" Lily asked.

"I'm awfully busy. It may be misplaced. Other things are missing too. It'll turn up."

"It's important." Lily said.

"I'll get back to you."

So much for that, Lily thought. She tried the American consulate next and asked for Henderson. He had gone to Haifa for the weekend, the clerk said, and wouldn't be back until Monday.

She went into the library, sat down at her desk and took Eastbourne's journal off the shelf above her carrel. If Eastbourne had left the journal where he knew she would find it, there must be a message for her in it, something that he wanted her to know.

Lily opened it to July 9, the day before the riots. "KH arrives," it said. The same KH that Eastbourne was scheduled to meet in Jerusalem the next day?

The telephone rang again, just as she started up the stairs to get the July tenth newspaper. The museum registrar, Lily thought, and hurried to answer it.

This time, it was Dame Margaret. "We never did get to talk," Dame Margaret said. "How about lunch tomorrow? One o'clock at the American Colony," and rang off before Lily could answer.

Command performance, Lily thought, another session of casually worded questions. Maybe Dame Margaret knows something about the amphoriskos.

Back in the library, Lily spread the newspaper on the empty desk next to her carrel. She looked at the personal column again, at ads for secretaries and furnished flats. What had she overlooked? What had Eastbourne hidden from her? What really brought him to the YMCA at Julian's Way that morning?

The sentence jumped out at her. How could she have missed it? *The shipment from Marco Polo will arrive at King David this morning*. Marco Polo? A code name?

Something nagged at her memory. She almost had it, when the telephone rang again. Maybe the museum registrar this time, Lily thought.

It was Henderson.

"You got my message?" Lily asked.

"What message?"

"They told me you were in Haifa."

"No, I'm right here in Jerusalem, getting my car fixed. In this damned country, nobody knows what they're doing."

"I wanted to talk to you. About Abu Musa."

"Who?"

"One of the laborers at Kharub. I think he stole the amphoriskos. And killed Eastbourne."

"Do you, now? Meet me here at the garage and tell me all about it. Nissin's, next to the radio station on Queen Melisande Street."

Lily hesitated. "I'll be there in twenty minutes," Lily said. Henderson may know who Marco Polo is.

Lily went back to the library to stash the journal and newspaper upstairs in her room before she left. As she folded the newspaper, a line from the shipping news caught her eye.

The Italian steamship Marco Polo arrived in Haifa port yesterday afternoon. KH had arrived in Haifa on the *Marco Polo* and met Eastbourne at the King David the next day.

She put the paper and journal under her arm and started up the stairs. Lily remembered that morning, remembered looking from the balcony toward the King David just as the riots began, and remembered Henderson in his Panama hat, buffeted by the crowd.

She shoved Eastbourne's journal into the top drawer of her desk, stashed the newspaper on top, and locked her door.

Henderson was the shipment on the *Marco Polo.*

SEVENTEEN

HENDERSON WAITED IN FRONT of the garage, standing near a clutter of engine parts between cars that were pulled up onto the narrow sidewalk.

"Let's get out of here," he said as soon as she came into sight. He glowered at the gutted cars with their engines disgorged on the ground. "They look like torn intestines. And they smell of axle grease and old oil."

He started up a steep alley in the direction of Zion Circus. "Who is this Abu Musa?"

"A laborer at Kharub."

"One of the Bedouin?"

"A Samaritan."

Henderson shrugged. "Anyway, an Arab."

"They claim to be the lost ten tribes. Some scholars say they are the descendants of the Macedonian soldiers Alexander settled in the ancient city of Samaria-Sebast."

Henderson stopped and turned toward her. "Can you find him, get hold of the vial?"

Abu Musa should be easy to trace, she thought. Only about two hundred Samaritans are left, some in a little village near

Nablus at the foot of Mount Gerizim, some still in Sebastiye. She regretted telling Henderson about him. "Abu Musa disappeared after he left Kharub," Lily answered.

Henderson began walking again. "I hate this place," he said. "They can't do anything right here. They'll probably wreck my car."

"Why did you take it there?"

"It's the whole damned city. The whole damned country. Can't do anything right."

He was moving faster now, and Lily had to hurry to keep up with him. "Why don't you wait until you get home to fix it?" She was almost out of breath.

"Bring it back to Cleveland?" he asked.

"Cincinnati," Lily said.

"Right," Henderson said, increasing his pace, forcing Lily to trot after him. "No choice. If the motor mounts give way, I could turn a corner, the car would go one way, the engine another."

He strode into the narrow lanes that led through Nachlat Sheva. "For all I know, they'll bollix the job." He stopped and looked around him. "Where the hell are we?"

They were in the alley smelling of urine that she and Avi had walked through on Tuesday, where pigeons strutted through puddles of oily residue, where cats prowled for their dinner, where the sign said, "Holy place. Forbidden to urinate here."

Henderson stepped on the cobbles carefully as if he were wading in excrement. "Cats and pigeons, pigeons and cats," he said. "The whole damned city is nothing but pigeons and cats. And fleas."

"It's a beautiful city," Lily said, "with unexpected charm. For instance, that sign on the wall behind you—"

"I don't give a damn what the sign says."

A cat rubbed against Henderson's leg and he kicked it away with the toe of his shoe. It slinked toward him—its back poised for pouncing, its tail straight up—and scratched at his trouser leg.

"The sign says—" Lily began.

Henderson and the cat glared at each other. The cat bristled and hissed, its sharp teeth bared.

"I hate it here," Henderson said.

"It says 'Holy place—'"

He reached down and picked up the cat by the tail. The cat squalled and spit, struggling at the end of Henderson's arm.

Henderson mumbled, "Look at that. Look at that," gesturing with his free arm up and down the alley while he swung the cat by the tail.

Its head hit the wall with a hollow thump, leaving a trickle of blood behind.

"Filthy, dirty scum of the earth." He whirled the cat against the stones again, once, twice, as if he were handling a tennis racket.

"Oh my God," Lily said.

He smashed it against the wall again and dropped it on the ground.

Henderson leaned against the wall, next to the sign. His hand shook; he gasped with spent emotion.

"Holy place—" Lily repeated automatically. The narrow alley began to tilt and waver. Cobbles shivered beneath her feet. Walls quivered and closed in on her. Not enough room to swing a cat. Isn't that what they said?

Lily's skin went cold. She backed away from the trickles of blood; away from the cat, one eye smashed and closed, its neck awry, its teeth still bared; away from Henderson, leaning against the bloodstained wall.

She ran through the alley toward Jaffa Road, hardly seeing where she was going, doors and stone walls of houses blurring as she hurried past.

EIGHTEEN

LILY FLED THE DARK ALLEY, the smell of kerosene and dank stones. She ran toward Zion Circus, where she knew the sun was shining, where crowds of orderly people carried shopping bags and waited at crosswalks for the lights to change.

"Lily," a voice called after her, and she kept running.

"Lily," it repeated, and she felt a hand on her shoulder, slowing her flight. Ready to cry out, she turned around.

It was Rafi.

"What happened?" He put both hands on her shoulders. "You're pale as a ghost."

"The cat," Lily said, panting and pointing toward the alley.

"Sure it's not a tiger?"

She was still pointing. "No, no. It's him. He—" She still pictured the cat, discarded on the ground. She shuddered.

"Someone is chasing you with a cat?"

Lily shook her head, still out of breath.

His hands kneaded her shoulders and he spoke in a low, measured tone. "Take a deep breath."

He smelled of soap and bay rum. His fingers, warm and pacifying, rubbed the muscles of her neck and spread across her back, moving gently against the tension. She leaned into him, resting her head against his shoulder.

"That's better," he said and steered her toward Ben Yehuda Street, his arm around her waist, and sat her at a table in the shade of an umbrella in front of Café Atara.

Rafi put his hand on her arm. "Brandy," he said to the waiter and turned back to Lily.

"Before lunch?" she asked.

He stroked her arm, like a mother calming a baby. "You look like you're in shock."

The waiter put a bottle of the local brandy and a shot glass on the table. Drops of water glistened on the exterior and ran down the outer surface. Rafi filled the glass to the brim. Lily sniffed, held her nose, leaned down and sipped. "It tastes awful." She pulled back her lips in distaste.

"Brandy always burns on the way down."

Lily sat back in the chair. "It's dissolving my teeth."

"You want to tell me what happened?" Rafi's hand was still on her arm.

"Not really." She reached for the brandy glass, lifted it, and put it down again. "I'm awfully thirsty. Don't they have water here?"

Rafi signaled the waiter for a bottle of Vichy. She drained one glass, then another. She stopped once for breath, gasping, then drank again.

"What were you running from?" he asked after a while.

She turned the bottle around and around, leaving a track on the table. "He killed a cat. Casually, while he was talking." She reached for a napkin and wiped at the wet circle. "Back there." She nodded her head in the direction of the alley. "He grabbed it by the tail and slammed its head against the wall."

"You saw the man?"

"No expression on his face. And his eyes," Lily shuddered. "His eyes were blank. As if he were dazed. He just kept swinging the cat."

"Dangerous man. Keep your distance if you see him again." Rafi leaned toward her. "Take another sip of brandy." He glanced at the glass she was clutching. "Your hand is still trembling."

"You're trying to get me drunk."

"I could ply you with a cheese sandwich instead."

"Orange juice."

He called the waiter and watched her pour the rest of the water from the bottle, watched her reach for her sunglasses. "You shouldn't wear dark glasses," he said. "Your eyes are too beautiful to hide."

Lily felt her face flush. "The sun is too bright."

Rafi eyed her pensively. "Better?"

She nodded, put down the glass and smiled back.

He turned her palm up and traced her heart line. "It says here," he said, "that love has a deep meaning for you. Are you in love?"

She shook her head; her skin tightened as he ran his finger along her palm.

His hand was still on her arm when the waiter brought lunch. "Are you and Avi close friends?" Rafi asked.

"He visits the tel sometimes."

"He likes you, you know."

"He's a nice boy."

"Boy?"

"He brings me oranges. Sometimes he drives me if I need a ride."

"That's all? Does that leave a clear field for me?"

Lily felt a tick of satisfaction and looked away. Couples around her sat at the tables in front of Café Atara, murmured

in soft voices, bent toward each other, their eyes locked. Rafi
was still brushing his fingers along her arm. Without thinking,
she placed her hand on top of his.

Rafi picked up the sandwich with his free hand. "What were
you telling me about this morning?" he asked and bit into the
roll.

"You always talk with your mouth full? *Bon appetit.*"

He swallowed. "That reminds me of a story."

"About a storm at sea in a leaky boat?"

"This time, Sammy Goldberg was traveling to Europe for
the first time, first class on the *Queen Mary*. The first night, he
went to dinner all spiffed up in his tuxedo and found out he
shared a table with an elegant Frenchman. Just as Sammy sat
down, the Frenchman bowed and said, '*Bon appetit.*' So Sammy
bowed back and said, '*Goldberg.*'"

"Very funny," Lily said.

"Wait. I'm not finished. The next night and the night after, it
was the same thing. The Frenchman would say, '*Bon appetit*'
and Sammy would answer, '*Goldberg.*' Then Sammy found out
what *bon appetit* meant, that it wasn't the Frenchman's name.
So on the fourth night, Sammy came to dinner early. This time
he was ready. When the Frenchman arrived, Sammy bowed with
a flourish and said, '*Bon appetit.*' So the Frenchman answered,
'*Goldberg.*'"

"That's it?" Lily said.

"That's it." Rafi took another bite of the sandwich.

"*Bon appetit,*" Lily said again.

"Goldberg." Rafi reached for a napkin. "You said something about Abu Musa this morning? The Samaritan who
worked at the tel? And a blue glass vial."

"I went to Kharub yesterday. Kate told me that Abu Musa
was fired for stealing."

"That's why you think Abu Musa killed Eastbourne for a blue glass vial?"

"For revenge."

"Anything's possible."

"Abu Musa comes from a little village near Nablus—Sebastiye," Lily said. "I have to go up there to talk to him."

"Don't go alone. If he killed Eastbourne, he might do the same to you."

* * *

Lily went as far as the hospital with Rafi. He paused at the steps, bent to kiss her lightly on the cheek, cupped her chin in his hand and kissed her again, this time on her lips.

People smiled at her as she floated home along the Street of the Prophets. Summer breezes bent leaves to shade her all the way to the American School. The sky was a brighter blue today. Even Sinbad's dogs sniffed gently at the fence when she passed. And a pleasant whiff of vanilla that reminded her of Dame Margaret lingered at her carrel in the library.

* * *

She sat in her room, reluctant to begin working. Too much had happened today to spend time with dusty potsherds and pour over drawings of tombs and the placement of skeletons. She reached for Eastbourne's journal instead, then turned on the radio, moving the dial back and forth until she found an English program with a studio orchestra that played gentle music.

Plans and sections of rectangular buildings were in a pocket in the back of the notebook. They were not Iron Age forts, nor Roman *castella*. Plans of modern buildings. What had Kate said—

something about Eastbourne doing consulting in Jerusalem for extra cash? Consulting? About what? Lily felt a chill of misgiving.

She unfolded the largest sheet in the pocket. It was a topographic map of Northern Palestine—the scale, 1 to 100,000. Sites were marked along the northern and eastern borders. He's been doing some kind of survey, she thought, maybe the one that Henderson had proposed.

She spread the map on the table and traced what she knew of ancient roads and trade routes, trying to make sense of the settlement pattern. The ancient Kingdom of Israel? The Roman period? Crusader castles? Nothing fit except the present. These were the borders of the Mandate.

* * *

A tone sounded three times on the radio to announce the hour, paused, repeated, and then a bland voice announced, "This is the news from the Palestine Broadcasting Service."

The British voice intoned, "In local news, two more bombs were exploded in Tel Aviv. The wounded were taken to Government Hospital. The Jaffa-Tel Aviv death toll for the last two days is now five.

"Emergency Regulations curfews have been imposed between the hours of 7 p.m. and 5 a.m. in the municipalities of Haifa, Jerusalem, Tel Aviv-Jaffa border, and Nablus; the villages of Jenin, Taiyiba, and Umm al Fahm; and all roads and tracks between municipalities, settlements and villages.

"Shots were fired at a bus between Affuleh and Mesha settlement. The attackers fled before police arrived at the scene. Shots were fired from ambush at a taxi traveling along the Haifa-Nazareth road. Troops quickly arrived at the scene and engaged an armed band, inflicting one casualty and capturing three of the bandits.

"German rifles were found in a taxi near Rehovoth. The Arab driver and his passengers were arrested.

"Security in the south is deteriorating. . . ." Lily turned off the radio.

* * *

Lily didn't notice the peal of the telephone until the third or fourth ring. Breathless, she ran into the hall to answer it.

It was Rafi. Lily smiled at the sound of his voice and ran her fingers up and down the telephone as he spoke.

"You're in luck, little tiger," he said. "We have an excuse to go to Abu Musa's village. I have a Samaritan patient who invited me to a wedding there on Tuesday."

"We can drive up. I have the station wagon from Kharub."

"Good. I knew there was a reason that I asked you to go with me."

* * *

That night, Lily couldn't sleep. She stroked her arm where Rafi had touched it, smiled and stretched under the covers.

She listened to the sounds of Salah edh Din Street   an occasional car, the angry dogs tethered in the yard of Samir's Taxi, the clop of donkeys and the strain of cartwheels rolling up the hill toward the American Colony.

She lay awake for hours, hearing the incessant tick of the clock on the bedside table, the dogs barking and growling at shadows in the dark night, footfalls echoing in the empty street outside her window, the clatter of an empty can scudding along the sidewalk as the steps faded.

Eastbourne's murder, the maps and plans in his journal, Kate's tear-ridden face, blood-haunted visions, rumbled through her head. When she closed her eyes, she saw the bloodied cat, its neck askew, lying on the cobbles. Sometimes it looked like Mrs. Klein, with her toothless stare, crumpled on the asphalt in front of the YMCA the day of the riots.

Toward dawn, after the muezzin called the first prayer of the day, Lily fell asleep and dreamed of Eastbourne lying bullet-ridden and bloody in a trench at Tel al-Kharub. In her dream, Kate was keening as his body turned to sand, while Lily brushed away the particles with a camelhair brush and a dental pick. The skeleton of a cat with a crushed skull and a broken tail lay next to him, its sharp teeth, like fangs, buried in Eastbourne's bony hand.

* * *

At lunch, Lily's eyes were gritty from lack of sleep; her neck ached with fatigue. Nothing that Dame Margaret said made sense.

Lily rested her chin on her hand and closed her eyes. "I couldn't sleep at all last night."

Dame Margaret leaned forward, exuding her usual scent of vanilla. She was saying something about the Grand Mufti-Nazi connection.

"By the way," Lily said. "You haven't heard any rumors about the missing amphoriskos, have you?"

Dame Margaret ignored her question. "The danger is real."

"We can't locate it. There's a possibility that one of the workmen stole it.

"You're not listening to me."

"Sorry. I'm tired," Lily told her. "I haven't slept well lately. First the riots, then Eastbourne's murder. And now this missing amphoriskos. I don't know what's going on, or why it's all happening."

"But you do know. You even know who KH is, and what Eastbourne was doing in Jerusalem."

Dame Margaret had been at Lily's desk after all and had looked in the journal.

Lily shook her head. "I haven't the slightest."

The big yellow rose balanced on the brim of Dame Margaret's hat began to quiver. "The Arabs have a saying—He who knows not and knows not he knows not is a fool. Shun him." Lily felt dizzy. Dame Margaret went on relentlessly. "He who knows not and knows he knows not is a child. Teach him. He who knows and knows he knows—"

"Is too darn nosy?" Take that, Dame Margaret.

"There's your problem right there." Her rose waggled like a reprimand. "The rest of it goes—He who knows and knows not he knows is asleep. Waken him."

"I'm too tired to waken. Too tired to think about it."

"Not too tired," Dame Margaret said. "Too frightened."

"Frightened?"

"You escape into the past. You probe old archives of disaster layer upon layer, but your ruins are memorials for bloodless deaths. That's why you're an archaeologist."

"You disapprove of archaeologists?"

"Of course not, I adore them. When you marry an archaeologist, the older you get, the more he loves you." Dame Margaret smiled at her. Lily had heard the quip before.

"I really should go home and lie down," Lily said.

"You refuse to face facts. Americans are so naive. Why don't you look at things head on? This is no time for optimism."

Lily formed her lips to answer but said nothing.

"There's going to be a war. All over Europe, people know. What's happening here and in Spain and China is only the prologue." Dame Margaret's rose was trembling now. "Before it's over, the world will be bleak and changed forever."

"You're afraid."

Dame Margaret reached across the table. "Of course I am. The Great War was just the beginning. The horrors are yet to come."

Lily blinked at her.

"You can't keep your eyes open," Dame Margaret said. "Go home and take a nap."

NINETEEN

LILY SPENT THE MORNING in the basement of the library, taking artifacts out of boxes one by one, tomb by tomb, marking notes on the brown paper she had spread over the long laboratory tables. She had propped open the basement door and the sun shone in from the garden. Site reports were stacked on a small desk next to the accountant's ledger she used as a register.

She reached for a Cypriote juglet with bands of black painted on the shoulder just as Lady Fendley clattered down the stairs in her sensible shoes.

"Someone to see you." Lady Fendley raised her eyebrows and jiggled her head coquettishly. "A young man."

Henderson? "What does he look like?" Lily put down the juglet.

"Like someone very nice."

Rafi?

"You're blushing to your earlobes," said Lady Fendley.

"Tell him to come down."

Rafi had already started down the stairs. "Had an hour to spare. Thought I'd visit. You busy?"

"Working on the pottery from Kharub."

159

"I'll help." He reached for a small black burnished juglet. "What's this?"

"A perfume juglet. Put it back. I'm working on the artifacts from tomb 104, the one that had the amphoriskos."

He reached into a box labeled tomb 104, grasped two handles with his forefingers and lifted out a large pot. "What's this?"

"Don't pick it up by the handles. It's a store jar."

"Why three handles? And what's this, where the fourth handle should be?" He canted the jar against his hip and pointed.

"Be careful. It's called a pillar handle. It's hollow, a resting-place for a little dipper juglet, like this." She picked up a small-necked, round-bottom juglet to show him. "The jar was used for oil. They dipped it out with the juglet." She made a scooping motion with the juglet in her hand and replaced it on the table. "After it was emptied, they placed it on the pillar handle and the drippings went back into the jar."

"Pretty clever." He balanced the store jar with both hands and brought it to the table. As he carried it, a faint sound, like metal rolling seemed to come from the bottom of the jar. "Something's in here," Rafi said, and turned the jar upside down.

"Don't—"

A tiny aluminum cylinder bounced on the table and rolled onto the floor. Rafi placed the jar on the table and picked up the cylinder.

"What's that?" Lily said.

Rafi turned it over in his hand. "A film cassette."

Lily glanced at it. "It's too small."

"Eight millimeter. A new kind of film, fine grain with high resolving power, used in that camera. . . ." He stopped and looked over at Lily. "You say that this is the tomb the amphoriskos came from?"

"Yes."

He twirled the cassette between his fingers. "It's used in a miniature camera with a special macro-lens for copying documents. Like the one you found, no bigger than a cigarette lighter. Snap it open and shut and the copy's made."

"It's used to copy texts, manuscripts, record shots of small inscriptions, coins?"

Rafi nodded.

"Maybe there's a shot of the amphoriskos. Look inside, see if there's film."

He unscrewed the lid of the cassette and looked inside. "Not this time. Film's gone."

"Usually Eastbourne used a professional photographer. They use mechanical boxes with special lights and platforms," Lily said.

"Cameras like this are easier to conceal." Rafi edged toward her field notebook and flipped a page. "What's this?"

"My field notebook. Gives the exact find spot of every artifact. A three dimensional record. All very scientific."

"Will it cure the common cold?" He continued to turn the pages of the notebook.

"You're losing my place." A gust, carrying the scent of lemon blossoms, blew in through the open door and ruffled another page.

Lily looked out into the garden. "Let's go for a walk." Rosebushes along the gravel path bent and smiled in the breeze and offered their buds to the sun. "It's time for a break."

*   *   *

They strolled along the Street of the Prophets, back toward the hospital, hand in hand, their gaits matching. He asked her about Eastbourne's murder, about the amphoriskos, about Abu Musa, about Kate and little Geoffrey. "I still don't think you should interfere with what the police are doing," Rafi said. "Just let the police take care of it."

"But they're not taking care of it."

"Don't get tangled up in this. It could be more complicated than you think."

"I can't help it. Curiosity, for one thing."

"And another?"

"An instinct for self-preservation, maybe. I owe it to Eastbourne. And myself, I suppose. I promised Kate I'd find out what happened. Anyway, I have to find the amphoriskos."

"That's too many reasons. One would be more convincing. Give it up. I worry about you," he said. "I think I'm in love."

Lily glanced at him, flushed with pleasure and squeezed his hand. The wind had blown the cowlick onto his forehead, and she resisted the urge to push it back. "Is it anyone I know?"

"What a self-satisfied smirk," he said. "I'm not sure you know her. She does strange things. Sticks her nose into affairs that don't concern her. Most of the time, she lives in an imaginary world of long ago, like a child."

Lily slowed her pace. "Are you in love with who she is or who you want her to be?"

"I'm not sure of that either." Rafi let go of her hand.

"The amphoriskos is my responsibility."

"Don't talk about responsibility. There are people who are sick, people who are hungry, and children who can't go to school because they have no shoes, while you play in the dirt and look for old glass bottles."

Lily lagged behind him now and stopped walking. "You want me to go door to door, collecting pennies for the poor?"

"Better than escaping into the past." He turned around to face her. "You're as oblivious as a snowflake. With your brains, it's a waste."

"You think everyone has to cure the sick?"

"It would be a start." He pushed back his hair. "I care what happens to you. I don't want you running into harm's way for no reason."

"And if there is a reason?"

Rafi looked down the street toward the hospital.

"What about you?" Lily said. "You put yourself in harm's way."

"That's different."

"Because it's you, not me?"

"I have to get back to the hospital." He put his hands in his pockets, stepped off the narrow sidewalk and strode up the street.

She caught up with him. "I must talk to the police, give them information that might help the investigation."

"That's not what worries me." His face was turned away from her. "It's the trip to Sebastiye."

"I excavated the amphoriskos. I must find it. It's part of my report, my responsibility."

Why couldn't she tell him it was about her father?

He walked faster now, not looking at her. "Do what you think is best."

They trudged in silence, Lily on the sidewalk, Rafi in the street, looking at the ground instead of each other.

Lily thought about the appointment with the British police the next day. "Why do you call her Auntie Major?" she asked.

"It's all she talks about. My friend the major this, and my friend the major that."

"Is she really your aunt?"

"My father's sister." He stopped, looked at Lily without speaking and smiled. "Bet you were a terror when you were a child," he said after a while.

"Matter of fact I was. I always won whenever we had orange wars in the groves, girls against boys. We lobbed oranges at each other instead of snowballs."

"Orange groves?"

"In Pasadena, where I was raised. My father was Orville, my mother Mathilde. She was a proper Pasadena matron— marcelled hair, pearls. So when I came home with scruffy knees and orange peels in my hair, she would be outraged."

"Your father was Orville Sampson?"

Memories of her father eddied through her head. "He died when I was young."

"I'm sorry." He took his hands out of his pockets for a moment to gesture. "Orville Sampson. I've heard the name. Famous for something, wasn't he?"

"He—" Lily felt tightness in her chest. "He was a friend of Harding."

"President Harding?"

"Yes." Lily's answer was scarcely audible.

"I remember now." He eyed her speculatively. "He was involved in that oil scandal."

"He was a friend of Harding."

"I heard what you said." He scanned her face intently. "He killed himself when the scandal became public, didn't he? I was just a teenager at the time, but I remember my parents talking about it, something in the paper. . . ." His tone was hushed. "I'm so sorry."

"No need to be sorry. He was a wonderful man."

"I only meant—"

"I know what you meant. I loved him very much. I still love him."

"Of course you do." Rafi began walking again, scuffing fallen leaves aside with the toes of his sandals.

Lily strolled alongside him. "My father collected antiquities," she said. "He gave me an amphoriskos like the one from Kharub."

"You still have it?"

"We lost everything in the Crash." She looked down at the sidewalk, stepping carefully to avoid cracks in the pavement. "We seemed to manage at first. Then we ran out of money. My mother hung wash on the line at night after dark, so that no one could see that we didn't have servants. We lost the house, lived in a hotel on Green Street. My mother sold everything she could get her hands on to keep us going."

"She sold the amphoriskos?"

"Yes."

They stopped in front of the hospital. The beggar with the copper bowl was across the street, a book open in his lap.

"He never said goodbye," Lily said.

"Your father?"

Lily nodded.

"That's why you have to find the amphoriskos?"

She nodded again.

"You get to keep it? Finders keepers?"

"No. It belongs to the Department of Antiquities. We make a division at the end of the season, and Eastbourne gets to—got to—take some of the things back to London for analysis."

They stood next to the steps leading up to the hospital facing each other.

"I have to go," Rafi said finally. "Tomorrow morning at Patt's."

"For breakfast."

"At eight o'clock." He gave her a light peck on the cheek. His hands were still in his pockets.

All the way home, the conversation bothered her. Why doesn't he want me to go to Sebastiye? Why does he want me to stop looking for the amphoriskos? Or find out who killed Eastbourne, for that matter?

"He's being unreasonable," she said out loud, and a man passing by turned to look at her.

*   *   *

Back home, Lily went directly to the library. Eliot was at Lily's desk again. When she entered, he made an elaborate show of reading book titles.

"Tel Beit Mirsim?" Lily asked.

Eliot was red-faced. "Beth Shan."

"I don't have it."

"So I see."

"Try the library shelves. The site report section." She pointed toward the stacks. "DS 110."

"Yes. Of course. I didn't think of that." He backed away from her desk. "We probably have it at the British School. I'll just pop around the corner." He started for the door. "Sorry to bother you," he called back over his shoulder and slammed the door behind him.

*   *   *

In the morning, Lily reached Patt's by five minutes before eight.

Rafi was already waiting. His seat faced the door.

This morning, the coffee was almost drinkable. Often it was thick, the texture of sludge.

Bots they called it—mud. They ate in companionable silence. The rolls were crisp and warm enough for the fresh butter to melt into them.

He had just put down his cup and looked up. "There she is." He stood up and indicated a woman dressed in flounces and furbelows who sailed in their direction. "Auntie Major."

She carried a ruffled parasol, wore white cotton gloves and an enormous hat covered with blowzy pink roses. She descended on Rafi, arms extended as if to smother him with an embrace and a kiss.

He stepped back. "May I present Lily Sampson. Lily, this is my aunt, Mrs. Landau." He looked at his watch. "I have to leave now. I'm due at the hospital."

"Our appointment with my friend Major Fogarty is in half an hour," Auntie Major said. She looked like the drawing room of an English cottage at the end of a Sunday afternoon, slightly rumpled and padded with chintz. "My friend the major has an office in the Russian compound." Her dress was tight as a sausage casing.

She reached for Lily's hand, as if Lily were a child. "My friend the major will be waiting for us." She hustled Lily down the street, leading with her parasol. "I told him about your little problem."

"What problem?"

"You know. The threat on your life."

"What threat?"

"The one from the Nazi agent, of course. That day in front of the King David. My friend the major was quite concerned."

"What Nazi agent? Why did you tell him a thing like that?"

"You wanted to get in to see my friend the major, didn't you? Besides, that's what Rafi told me."

Burbling and cooing, she towed Lily down St. Paul's Road and up the steps to the Russian compound toward the elaborate white, onion-domed Cathedral. She said that she was pleased about Lily and Rafi; that her friend the major came from an important family in Sussex; that Rafi needed someone, and it was about time. She said her friend the major understood the Middle East well. She said Lily would adore her friend the major.

Lily nodded and grunted from time to time to indicate that she was listening as Auntie Major prattled on until they reached the block of government offices in the Russian compound.

"The law courts are in the Sergei Building." Auntie Major waved in the direction of a wide, two-storied building with a row of arched windows along its façade. "That's where my friend the major has his office."

Auntie Major smoothed the lines of her dress and cinched her belt before she knocked with the handle of her parasol. A man in a colonel's uniform opened the door part way.

"Dear Colonel Darnell. How nice to see you again." Auntie Major gave him a lustrous, expectant smile, accompanied by a lissome tilt of the head.

"I'm sorry, Mrs. Landau. This meeting is confidential." He looked past her and motioned for Lily to enter. "Please wait outside," he said to Auntie Major.

She leaned on her parasol and smiled again. "You don't understand. Major Fogarty expects . . ." she began.

"I'm sure you don't mind," the colonel said to Auntie Major. He led Lily into the office and closed the door. "Miss Sampson? You were Eastbourne's assistant?"

"I worked with him at Tel al-Kharub."

He pointed to a chair and sat down next to her.

A man with a trimmed British moustache was seated behind the desk. "Major Fogarty?" Lily asked.

He nodded. "Mrs. Landau said you wanted to see me?"

"I wanted to talk to you about Eastbourne."

Fogarty reached for a pipe and tobacco pouch on his desk. "What about Eastbourne?"

"He wasn't killed by bandits."

The major continued to fill his pipe, tamping down the tobacco and running his fingers along the bowl. "What makes you say that?"

"Eastbourne was bringing an amphoriskos from the site to the Rockefeller for the opening of the museum the day he was murdered. It's disappeared."

"And you think Eastbourne was killed for the amphoriskos?"

Lily nodded. "I think a laborer who worked at Tel al-Kharub stole it. A Samaritan named Abu Musa."

Darnell rose and started toward the door. "Young lady, there must be a thousand Samaritans. And they are all named Abu Musa."

"I plan to go to their village near Nablus," Lily said. "Ask around, see if I can find him."

The colonel moved closer to the door and tapped his hand against his thigh. "You do that, young lady," he said, reaching for the knob.

"And then there's Henderson," Lily said.

Darnell dropped his hand from the knob and started back toward the chair. "The American attaché? What about Henderson?"

"He was in Jerusalem the day of the riots. I saw him in front of the King David. I think Eastbourne went to meet him."

The colonel and Fogarty exchanged glances.

"Henderson?" asked Darnell. The major began to light his pipe.

"There was no mistaking him. He stood out—at least six inches taller than the mob around him. Sandy-haired, lantern jaw."

Fogarty drew on his pipe in great draughts, filling the room with smoke.

"Thank you for the information," the colonel said.

The sticky-sweet smell of tobacco smoke filled the room. Both men stood as a signal for Lily to leave.

The colonel walked with her to the door. "It's almost no use trying to find the killers." He opened the door and kept his hand on the knob. "Sad to say, the Mandate has many more pressing concerns."

Auntie Major waited in the hall, brimming with curiosity and indignation. "What was that about?"

"They just don't care," Lily said. "Too busy to be concerned with the murder of a British national?" She glared at Auntie Major. "Is that likely?"

"There's no reason why they made me wait out here," Auntie Major said.

"If I want to know what happened to Eastbourne, I'll have to find out for myself."

"After all," Auntie Major said, as they began to work together. "Major Fogarty is my friend."

"And why should I care who killed Eastbourne, anyway? It's not my job. I just feel sorry for Kate, that's all."

Auntie Major adjusted her dress again, pulling it down around her waist. "I can't let it bother me." She paused, took a deep breath and smiled at Lily. "Tell me about you and Rafi." The dress began to ride up again.

Lily stopped walking and faced Auntie Major. "The amphoriskos. That's my responsibility. Not who murdered Eastbourne."

Auntie Major narrowed her eyes and looked at Lily. "Young lady, you make no sense at all."

They had walked as far as the Palace Hotel on the corner of Mamilla. Auntie Major said, "Rafi tells me that you're going to Nablus with him tomorrow."

"We both have errands there."

Auntie Major seemed in the mood to gossip. "You two make a handsome couple."

"And furthermore," Lily said, "I don't just play in the dirt. Archaeology is important, too." She lifted her chin and gazed at the box tree on the corner. "No one can understand the future until they have viewed the past." That sounds like a quote from a textbook, she thought, and grimaced.

"I'm not at all sure I approve of the way you're behaving," Auntie Major said. "I live near here in Rehavia." She waved her arm in the direction of King George Street. "Why don't you come home with me and have a nice cup of real English tea?"

I can't stand another minute with this woman, Lily thought. She looked at her watch and shook her head. "Some other time. I have an appointment."

Lily left Auntie Major at the corner of King George and headed toward Ben Yehuda Street. "I enjoyed our little talk," Auntie Major said. "Shalom. TaTa. Give my regards to Rafi."

Maybe Rafi is at a morning break in Café Atara, Lily thought. I have to talk with him anyway about the curfew tomorrow. I may as well stop for a sandwich and coffee.

Lily passed a perfumery. I should buy a lipstick, she thought, and went inside. She came out of the shop into the bright sunshine a few minutes later, carrying a small packet containing lipstick and face powder.

Maybe Rafi is at that café near the hospital on Chancellor Road. Maybe he isn't eating lunch at all. She passed a beauty salon near the corner of Ben Yehuda and King George, then turned back. "I should get my hair done for the wedding tomorrow," she decided, and went inside.

For a moment the sharp odors of shampoo and lotion, of ammonia and acetone, stung her eyes. A bank of women doggedly perspired under hairdryers that looked like helmets from Buck Roger's world of the twenty-fifth century.

A young woman in a starched pink dress sat at a counter, with bottles of lotions and pots of cream displayed on the wall behind her. "May I help you?" she asked.

Lily sneezed. "I would like a shampoo and a set." She looked down at her hands. Her nails were uneven, her cuticles ragged.

"And a manicure." She held her arm out in front of her and spread her fingers. "Yes. A manicure."

The woman behind the counter picked up a white pen with a plume. "Would you like a facial today? We have a special on Mondays—facial, shampoo and set for only fifty mils." She waited, her pen poised above a yellow pad. "Your skin will be smooth and glowing."

Lily ran her finger along her chin and across her cheek to her temple. "Yes. Of course. That too."

* * *

Lily arrived late at dinner. Sausages of hair framed her face. She was pleased with the glamorous image she had seen in the beauty salon mirror until Sir William looked at her when she sat down and said, "Good God! What happened to you? You're made up like a corpse."

He launched another endless lecture, all the while dripping food on his jacket. He mumbled about pottery classification, the Czech Nazi Henlein, Galton's family resemblances. Lady Fendley interrupted now and then to wipe his chin or smooth his hair.

Lily, exhausted from her afternoon at the beauty parlor, the heat of the dryer, the face patting and chemical odors, listened to Sir William drone until the sound of his voice made her dizzy. She imagined Sir William, lecturing with a pointer in front of a huge clay pot, a caricature of a Toby mug shaped like the face of Henderson. His exaggerated jaw and deep-set eyes moved and shifted while the pot shouted orders in an incomprehensible staccato. She pictured them crammed inside an army tank that crawled, snakelike, along a hillside, while the fluid features of Henderson and the pot changed bit by bit, taking on the face of an anonymous gymnast she had seen in a film about the Olympics, then Henlein.

"Pay attention," Sir William said. "This is important."

"Of course it is," Lily answered.

Sir William mumbled on and on.

When she left them, Sir William and Lady Fendley were drinking coffee in the common room. Tired and irritated, Lily fetched Eastbourne's journal from her room and brought it downstairs to the library.

She sat in the large leather wingback chair at the far end of the room and opened Eastbourne's journal to the back pocket.

When she put the journal away earlier, she had folded the map carefully into the back pocket, beneath the plans and sections of buildings. It was now on top.

She propped her legs on the ottoman in front of the chair and spread the map over them.

She had seen the contour map somewhere before—without the checkmarks and zigzag lines Eastbourne had drawn on it. She remembered Kitchener's map, prepared for the Palestine Exploration Society in the 1880s. He had gone as far as the border between present-day Palestine and French-controlled Syria. "Kitchener of Khartoum," she said aloud, rolling out the last word like a parody of the voice of a stuffy British colonel.

She took Condor and Kitchener's British Ordinance map off the shelf. That was it. There were the same contour lines defining the hilltops in Eastbourne's photostatted copy. But Eastbourne had drawn a scroll along the boundaries with Lebanon and Syria, marked checks on the hilltops and joined them with jagged lines that looked like connect-the-dots from a children's playbook. Lily noticed that the marked hills were near the border and within sight of each other. But why? And what were the herringbone lines between them?

She put away the Condor and Kitchener, sat in the chair, spread the map on the ottoman and puzzled over it. She opened the journal to July 10 and turned the pages. There must be something she missed. She curled her legs under her and turned the pages. *July 15. One and a half kilometers north of Montfort.* She looked at the map again. There it was, marked with a check, a hill north of Monfort. Was he doing a survey of Crusader castles? The Ladder of Tyre on the coast north of Nahariya was marked, but Caesarea wasn't. Neither was Atlit. Latrun—the Crusaders *Le Toron des Chevaliers* built to defend the road to Jerusalem—had a small square.

What was Eastbourne looking for? And why had he entrusted the journal to her keeping? Someone wanted to know what was in the maps.

If whoever it is wants maps, I'll give them maps, Lily thought.

She found a piece of scrap paper and copied the coordinates of Eastbourne's symbols along the Lebanese border and the crusader forts, making it look like a list of telephone numbers. She found a copy of Crowfoot's *Early Churches in Palestine* on the library shelf, carefully erased Eastbourne's marks from the map and replaced them with checkmarks at sites of Byzantine churches in the Jordan Valley on both sides of the border between Palestine and Transjordan—at Beth Shan, and Madeba, at Jericho and Nebo.

She practiced forging Eastbourne's cramped handwriting, made a list of the sites she had marked and put it between the pages of the journal.

And then she leaned back in the large leather chair and contemplated the newly marked map.

Pretty good. She rested her head against the wing of the chair and idly turned the pages of the journal. Another meeting with KH on July 20th.

The doorbell rang and rang again. Lily put the journal and map under the chair cushion.

Rafi stood on the porch, holding out a rose, wearing an abashed smile. "Just finished at the hospital. I wanted to see you." In the entry hall, he handed her the rose. "About the curfew. We'll have to leave early tomorrow."

"I know."

"No. That's not the reason I came."

She bent her head to sniff at the rose and felt her hair brush against his sleeve.

"I wasn't very nice to you yesterday," he said.

He fingered the rose petals and ran his hand along her arm. "I didn't mean to criticize you."

She moved closer to him, and he stroked her hair. "You smell like a hospital," she said. He laid her head against his shoulder.

"I never want to argue with you." His hand ran along her back. "I was looking for an excuse to see you." He held her close. Her hands caressed his shoulders and she reached under his collar to feel the curve of his neck.

"It's all right," she said. She lifted her face when he bent down toward her, nearer, nearer, until she felt his breath on her, and she closed her eyes.

When they kissed, the skin along her spine prickled and the room began to waver. She leaned against him. Breathless and light-headed, she clung to him while he held her. She stroked the back of his neck, his shoulder.

They moved to the bench in the hall, sat down and clung to each other. They heard Sir William open his bedroom door upstairs and shuffle toward the bathroom.

"Tomorrow," Rafi said. He kissed the top of her head gently, put the rose in her lap, went out into the hallway and closed the door softly behind him.

Still trembling, Lily retrieved Eastbourne's journal from under the seat cushion and brought it upstairs.

This time, she put the notebook under the mattress near the foot of her bed. She found a piaster and a roll of adhesive tape, used a coin to open the back of the radio, taped her list of Eastbourne's coordinates onto the inside of the radio back, and screwed it in place.

"Tomorrow," she repeated as she fell asleep.

TWENTY

ॐ

LILY POINTED TO THE TOP of a hill. "That must be Sebastiye." It was two hours since they left Jerusalem. She looked up at the houses built against tumbles of fallen stones, scattered among ruins of ancient buildings and shattered columns. "Looks like the photos from the site report."

Rafi turned onto the bumpy track that led up the hill. Dust eddied around them. The station wagon sputtered, then died.

"We'll never get up there," Rafi said. He scrambled out of the car and propped open the hood. "The carburetor needs cleaning, the fuel pump is clogged, and everything makes noise but the horn."

"There's a little butterfly thing you have to wiggle," Lily said.

He held up his hands and waggled his fingers. They were streaked with grease. "I can't go to a wedding like this."

"There's a towel under the seat," Lily said.

With his hands still in the air like a surgeon who had just scrubbed, he tried to open the car door with his elbow.

Lily reached under the seat and pitched the towel to him through the open window.

"What's the rattle and bang in the back of the car?" he asked.

"Digging equipment. Picks, shovels, brushes. A folding ladder. And a dining canopy."

"In case you find a site somewhere and need to dig an emergency hole in the ground?"

"Exactly."

"Try the choke." He put the towel on the fender and reached under the hood again. "This car reminds me of a story."

"About the *Queen Mary*?"

"About a Texan who was visiting a kibbutz." He wiped his hands. "Turn on the ignition."

The engine whined; the wagon shook from side to side. "There it goes." He slammed the hood shut. "Anyway, this Texan said to the kibbutznik, 'Mighty nice little farm you have here, but my spread in Texas is so big that it takes a day and a half to drive around it.'" Rafi got back into the car and shifted carefully into low gear. "And the kibbutznik said, 'I used to have a car like that.'"

The wagon heaved, lurched and chugged up the hill.

Lily pointed out the remains of a crumbling structure where weeds grew from stubs of stone walls. "That's the palace of Omri the king of the Israelites. The town's built over ruins of their royal city, Samaria. Harvard dug here before the war, then the British in the twenties."

Five or six men in vivid striped cloaks and baggy pants tied at the ankles smoked hookahs, leaning against an ancient foundation in the shade of the wall of a house built of scavenged ashlars. "Over there, where the men are sitting, is the Temple of Augustus, built for him by Herod."

Two of the men sat in chairs; the others squatted on the ground. They spoke in low voices, arms sweeping the horizon, their bright turbans swaying with each nod of their heads. One of them called out to a man who came through the courtyard.

After a bawdy laugh, he, too, sat down and grasped one of the pipes.

"Wedding must be over there," Lily said.

Rafi parked in the shade of a carob tree. "Not under this tree," Lily said. "Carob sheds this time of year."

Rafi backed up the station wagon and it rattled into the shade of a building. "That must be the groom's house. My patient said you can't miss it. He said men and women celebrate separately."

"I'll find the women. Keep your ears open for any talk about Abu Musa."

Rafi reached for the door handle. "Meet me here at three o'clock. We have to leave early so we can make it back to Jerusalem before curfew."

He turned off the ignition, set the brake and listened to the car gasp and knock. "Cheap gas. Idles too fast, too." He got out and went around to Lily's side. "They call this the Red Day of the wedding. The fourth day. I've no idea why."

A large stone bathhouse, the rooftop studded with rounded domes inlaid with thick bubbles of green Hebron glass, stood beyond the pillars of an ancient ruin. Women came and went from there, crowding around the door. Lily strolled up to the bathhouse and looked inside.

Lit by a ghostly green light from the skylights, women, all talking at once, clustered around tables and peered into baskets overflowing with striped cloth, dishes and bowls, kitchen gadgets, and copper pots. Jewelry clinked as the women moved. Rhythmic music, throaty singing, clapping of hands, and an eerie, throbbing, cry flowed from another room.

A soft voice sounded in her ear. "Welcome, welcome. I speak English." Lily turned to see a matron wearing a long white cotton dress woven with green, red, and yellow stripes and tied with a broad sash.

"You look at my dress." The woman stroked her red-and-yellow satin chest panel. "Here we do not embroider. We have special cloth. Very good. Very expensive." She wore a bonnet decorated with antique coins and covered by a white gauze veil that fell down her back; on her arms, silver bracelets; around her neck, gold and silver chains and glass beads strung with magic eyes and the hand of Fatimah.

"Come. Come. We go to the wedding." She grabbed Lily by the hand and made a path to the door.

"My name is Yohevet, like the mother of Musa in the Holy Book." She gestured toward the baskets. "Wedding gifts from the groom's family." She thumped her chest, and the beads jiggled and tinkled.

The heat of the room, the crowd, the noise were oppressive.

Yohevet indicated a woman fingering a dress with a nod of her head. "That one is saying, 'Not good enough.' She lies. I buy the cloth myself in Medjel. I watch them weave and dye. The best silk and cotton."

She gestured toward another, holding up jewelry to the light. "She say the wedding will put him in debt for the next ten years. Is true. It cost more than five years of oil from all the olive grove." She shook her head and sighed. "Come. We eat."

The town gossip. She'll know about Abu Musa, Lily thought.

Yohevet led Lily into an open courtyard lined with tables— tables piled with fruit; with pastries of savory chopped meats; with saffron-colored cakes, sticky with honey. Smoke from braziers of charred meat hovered in the air. Lily tried to snake her hand between two women in the throng around the table to reach a pastry.

Yohevet jammed one into Lily's hand. "You like? Is special. I make myself. With minced meat and sumac." She pounded her chest again, then stuffed another tidbit into Lily's other hand.

Lily bit into one and savored the crisp texture of the flaky pastry, the pungent taste of sumac. A woman leaving the table knocked against Lily's elbow as she lifted her hand for a second bite. The delicacy fell to the floor.

Yohevet said, "Come. See the bride." And she beat her way back through the crowd, dragging Lily behind her through the stifling crush.

In the next room, a fourteen-year-old sat on a carved chair like a queen on a throne, with cushions and rugs and quilts piled around her. The girl wore bright patterned pants with a long sash wound around her waist. A coat, striped red, black and yellow, draped gracefully over her head like a veil, fell around her neck and down her back. Necklaces and earrings trembled among braids that peeked out from under the coat.

"Her new husband's coat," Yohevet said. "Now he protects her."

"She's just a child," Lily said.

"No, no. I examine myself. She is woman."

Mothers led little girls by the hand to the bride. They touched her dress with awe, bowed before her, and brought their fingers to their foreheads in deference.

At the far end of the hall, a woman beat a tambour and another sat next to her on a low stool, playing an instrument that resembled a guitar. "An oud," Yohevet said.

A high pitched trill vibrated from women on the bride's side of the room, reverberating back and forth in the crowded space from one side to the other.

"To keep away evil eye," Yohevet said.

Bangles jangling, jewelry clinking, they clapped their hands in rhythm to the music. The groom's family began to sing in a minor key, melodies that seemed to echo unrequited longing.

"*Dodi li,*" they sang and clapped their hands.

"A love song of King Solomon from our Holy Book," Yohevet said.

They danced to the sensuous rhythm of the tambour, to sentimental laments plucked from the melodic oud. Their silver hair ornaments dangled from false braids and swung with the cadence of the music.

The overpowering smell of jasmine water and attar of roses, the smoke from lamps that lit the room, mesmerized Lily. She began to sway with the rhythmic throb of the tambour and the nasal whine of the singers.

"*Dodi li,*" they sang. They were answered with trills and songs from the bride's side of the room.

The music swirled around Lily; the dancers twisted and gyrated. The shrill warbling of ululation rang in her ears.

"*Dodi li,*" Lily sang, "*v'li dodi,*" and clapped her hands. *I am my beloved and my beloved is mine.* Lily's feet moved in time to the music, her shoulders and hips whirled and pivoted. *He feedeth among the lilies.*

The women passed copper dishes from hand to hand, dipping their fingers, wetting their palms, rubbing amber liquid into their hair.

"This is the night of the henna," Yohevet said. "Tonight, we make everyone beautiful, but most of all the bride."

Lily looked down at her own hands, with the bright red polish of yesterday's manicure, and at the women seated cross-legged on the floor, with their red palms and auburn-streaked hair, giggling like little girls as they groomed each other. Different countries, different customs, she thought, and sat on the floor next to Yohevet while the copper pot passed toward her slowly from one woman to another.

What did the woman say? Yohevet is the mother of Musa? "You are the mother of Musa?" Lily said to Yohevet while they waited.

She clicked her tongue against her teeth. "Yohevet."

"You know Abu Musa?"

The woman shrieked. The clapping and trilling stopped and the sound of singing trailed away. Yohevet held the henna dish in the air without moving, her face blank and cold. "Who?" Yohevet spilled henna on Lily's skirt and glared at her.

"Abu Musa. You know him?"

The bathhouse became silent. The women formed a circle around Lily, as if to cut her off from the rest of the room. One by one, they lifted their left hands, their palms red with henna.

"*Hamsa b'aynik,*" one of them said. Five times in your eyes— the curse to avert the evil eye.

A woman pushed her way through the crowd and stood before Lily, her arms across her chest, her nostrils working in anger, her dark eyes burning into Lily's face, a guttural tirade spilling from her, swelling the veins in her neck.

"She say you may not say that name at her daughter's wedding. An evil man. A wicked man. We celebrate for joy, and do not call on the name of a devil." The mother of the bride tossed her head with contempt. "She say you are not welcome here. You will leave this wedding. You will leave this house."

They cleared a path for Lily and she walked slowly to the door, her wet skirt flapping against her knees.

She stood in the shade of the carob and looked back toward the bathhouse. The ground beneath her feet was thick with litter from the tree: fallen leaves, acrid-smelling red blossoms, and rotted pods that were moldy from the dew. After a while, she heard a tentative ululation, and then an answering trill. The singer's voice began to intone a love song. By the third verse, Lily heard the rhythmic click of cymbals and the beat of the tambour drum.

She looked down at the stain on her skirt, leaned back against the tree and waited for Rafi.

TWENTY-ONE

RAFI SWERVED AROUND sun-hardened grooves left by wheels of donkey carts.

Lily pointed to the mountains shimmering in the distance. "That's Mount Gerizim, the holy Samaritan Mountain. The other is Mount Ebel."

The equipment in the back of the station wagon clattered with each rut in the dirt track. Dust billowed behind them.

"So," Rafi said. "You're *persona non grata* in Sebastiya. You and Abu Musa."

"It's nothing to laugh at." They hit a furrow and Lily bounced in the seat.

"About Abu Musa," Rafi said. "I think he tried to seduce the bride. And raped a girl in Ramallah."

"Are you sure?"

"My Arabic isn't all that good. But that's what I think they said. The girl in Ramallah—her brothers killed her."

"For being raped?"

Rafi nodded and gunned the engine. They hit another bump, and Lily held onto the strap over the window.

"Drive carefully. It isn't safe here." She stared at the road in front of them, at the gray stone houses of Nablus that floated on the top of the hill visible between the shifting outlines of the mountains. "The newspaper says police are searching the whole area."

"Patrolling the terror triangle." Rafi said. "Nablus. Tulkarm. Jenin." He dodged another pothole, tilting the car and slanting Lily toward him. She stroked his arm and he grinned at her, reaching for her hand. "Rough roads have compensations."

"You suppose Abu Musa really did that? Raped a girl?" she asked.

"Who knows? I'll find out from my patient."

"He won't tell you."

"I'll be more subtle than you were back there at the wedding. Dissimulation is the key."

"You'll lie?"

"I told you once, I don't always tell the truth." When turned toward her, the car veered. Lily slid against him again.

"I'll miss this when we reach the paved road in Nablus," he said.

"Watch the road," she told him.

They jolted along the rutted track and Lily careened against Rafi, swayed toward the door, and slammed back in the seat. He concentrated on the jagged surface, meandering over the track to avoid dips and troughs, until the car rattled over another gash in the dirt.

They were halfway to Nablus, almost as far as Deir Sharaf, when Lily saw the row of massive stones obstructing the road. "Looks like an ambush!"

Large boulders on either side shut off access to the shoulder. Footprints and telltale gouges—scratched across the road by rocks lugged into place to block their passage—slashed the ground.

Rafi slowed. "You're right."

He stopped the car and threw it into reverse. The station wagon bucked, groaned and stalled.

"Oh, God." Lily said.

"Don't give out now," Rafi muttered to the steering wheel. He patted the knob on top of the gearshift. "You know how to turn over. You've done it before." He let out the clutch slowly. "Get us out of this, and I'll buy you a new horn."

The wagon lurched, gasped, heaved and backed along the track, gathering speed. Rafi stroked the dashboard.

"Good girl," he said as he grasped the gearshift again, and turned the car around.

He turned to Lily "We have to go through Tulkarm."

Lily shook her head. "Tulkarm's too dangerous."

"And this isn't? Bandits hiding behind a roadblock?"

"We don't know what we're getting into there. Nobody's following us. Maybe no one was there."

"They're there, all right. Waiting for the next damn fool to get out of his car to clear the road."

"We don't have anything of value. They can see that."

"Doesn't matter." The steering wheel shimmied in his hand. "They'd kill anyone for two piasters."

The folded hills on either side of them were green with orchards. They drove through rolling countryside where villages dotted the hilltops and stark, gray-white rocks stood like sentinels in fields scarred by goat paths. Stone walls of terraces hugged the steep slopes like steps of a great Olympian stairway.

They hit another bump. Lily bounced. Her head almost hit the roof of the car. "Let's hope we'll make it as far as Tulkarm."

A boy in a striped vest, a turban wound around his head, tended a flock of sheep that moved slowly along the track in a cloud of dust. The boy drove the herd with a long stick while two mangy dogs ran around the animals, snapping at their heels when they strayed.

Rafi careened around them, through a dry ditch at the side of the road, the dogs snarling at the wagon, leaping at the fenders and doors. The boy watched with dark, impassive eyes.

They sped and bumped along the corrugated road, the dogs barking in their wake, until the flock was out of sight.

They were almost as far as Tulkarm when the station wagon sputtered, wallowed and shuddered to a stop.

Rafi sighed and looked at Lily. "Your car has palsy." He got out and kicked the fender. "Bad car."

He sat on the running board, shaking his head. "This car is nothing but a *tarrantah*."

"*Tarrantah*?"

"Means jalopy. The word came into Hebrew from the French by way of Russia."

"How—?"

"When Napoleon invaded Russia, the camp followers came along with the army. Russians would ask the women how old they were, and they would say '*trente ans,*' thirty years. So in Russian it came to mean anything old and worn out."

After a while, he stood, went to the front of the car and pulled open the hood.

"The engine is full of grit. We're stuck."

"What are we going to do?"

"I need something to clean it out. Maybe I can prime it."

Lily went to the back of the wagon to open the tailgate. "There's water in the cooler and gasoline in the jerry can. Will that help?"

"Maybe. Maybe. Give me the gasoline. And that rag we had before."

"Towel."

Lily waited near the verge of the track, feeling the wind change as the afternoon breeze came off the sea. "Hurry up. It's almost four o'clock."

"Not to worry." Rafi's voice resonated under the hood. "We'll make it in time." He lifted his head and wiped his hands. "I almost have it."

Lily paced the side of the road, glancing back at Rafi. He ran his tongue along his upper lip. His forehead wrinkled in concentration. She wandered past a weedless patch of fresh dirt, sunken lower than the surface of the surrounding soil, and felt a draft of cool air blow against her ankles.

"I think this may work," Rafi said, ready to close the hood.

Lily knelt on the ground, passing her hand over the surface of the depression. The cool air was still there, coming from somewhere underground. She stood up, went to the back of the wagon, took out a pickaxe, a shovel, and a roll of string wound around four surveyor's pins and dropped them next to the patch of dirt.

She put her hand close to the ground, felt for the direction of the draft again, used the pointed edge of a mason's trowel to sketch a rectangle around the patch and jammed the surveyor's pins into the corners of the square she had outlined, stretching the string from pin to pin.

"What in hell are you doing?"

Lily reached for the shovel and began clearing away loose dirt. "There's something here."

"What are you talking about?"

"Something's buried here." She knelt down and scraped with the side of the trowel in quick, steady strokes. "The soil is loose. Freshly dug in the last few weeks."

"Leave it alone. It could be a dead body. Or a sick animal."

"It's not here long." She brushed aside a cigarette butt, brown and desiccated from the sun, then picked it up again, rolling it between her fingers. The paper crackled, and the tobacco spilled out. "My guess is two weeks."

She picked up the shovel and began digging. "If it were a dead animal, there would be a smell. Somebody hid something here. In a cave."

"What do you mean, a cave?"

"I can feel cool air coming from a hole under the ground." She stretched out her hand and passed it over the surface. "See for yourself."

Rafi knelt down and spread out his fingers. He looked baffled, wiped his hand and tried again. "What do you expect to find?"

"Pirate treasure, of course. Grab a pick and shovel. Make yourself useful."

He stood up. "We don't have time for this. We won't get back to Jerusalem before the curfew. We can come back tomorrow."

"That'll be too late. We've already left tracks. They'll know whatever it is has been spotted. Dig."

Rafi lifted a shovel out of the back of the wagon and moved some soil halfheartedly. "I think you're crazy."

"Try to stay inside the square marked with the string. And keep the side walls straight."

"Why?"

"Otherwise, it'll collapse. The whole thing will fall in on us."

"Helpful hints from the professional ditch-digger."

Lily worked quickly, filling the shovel and tossing the dirt outside of the square in a rhythmic motion.

Rafi stepped back. "Be careful. You're getting dirt on both of us."

"Shut up and dig."

* * *

With both of them digging in the loose soil, it went fast. By the time the long shadows of late afternoon etched the ground and cool breezes came off the ocean, the hole was almost chest-deep.

"Not much further now." Lily leaned down and held out her hand. "You feel the draft?"

Rafi reached toward the bottom of the square. "It's coming from over there."

"Get a whisk broom. And the little ladder."

He tossed the brush he had retrieved from the station wagon into the square, jumped in after it, and propped the ladder against the sidewall. She felt for the draft again, scraping with the trowel, then swept the surface with the whiskbroom.

"There it is," Lily said. "You see the top of the cave?" Lily traced along an edge of stone at the side of the square with her hand. She brushed again and stepped back. "Wooden boxes. Big ones. Crates more than three feet long."

Rafi jumped into the hole and wiped at a box. "Something's printed here. Stenciled on the side." He stepped back and cleared away more dirt. "Holy Moley."

"What?"

"12 *Shutzen*. 98 *Mauser*."

"What's that?"

"German rifles. Probably hidden by the Mufti's men. Precisely what the patrols are hunting for."

Rafi climbed out of the square and went back to the station wagon. He emptied tools and supplies from back of the wagon and dumped them on the ground. "Help me with this."

"What are you doing?"

"Clearing a space for the rifles."

"Who's crazy now?"

"We'll cover them with the tarp from the dining canopy. With the tools on top, no one will know they're there."

"I'll know. What if we're stopped?"

"We can't just leave them."

"It's almost six o'clock," Lily said. "We can't get back to Jerusalem before the curfew."

"We're not going to Jerusalem. We're going to Netanya."

"What's in Netanya?"

"A basement."

Rafi jumped back into the square and cleaned off a crate. He tugged at it, pulling first one side, then the other. "This must weigh a ton."

"You can't do that. It's too heavy."

"If I can get some leverage, I can get it out of the hole." He knelt down and pulled the long wooden box onto his shoulder. When he tried to stand, the weight shifted and slid toward the ground. He grunted and reached down to steady it.

The veins in his neck stood out. "Help me with this, can you?" His voice was strained.

Summoning all the strength she could, Lily pushed at the side of the crate to balance it on Rafi's shoulder.

"Why am I doing this?" she said. "You'll get us both in trouble."

Rafi went up the ladder one rung at a time. "Oh, God. This'll break my back."

He carried the load to the station wagon, dropped it behind the back seat with a clang and leaned against the tailgate, grunting and struggling for breath.

"My, you're strong," Lily said, laughing.

"Oh, stuff it." He tugged at the crate and wedged it into the space behind the seat. "We can't fit more than one box in here. We have to come back tomorrow with a truck."

"What do you mean, 'we'? This is the second time you got me mixed up in something like this. Third strike, you're out."

A cloud of dust approached from one of the hilltop villages, and as it came nearer, Lily made out a mule-driven cart, driving toward them along the sinuous path that led back and forth along the hill from the village to the road.

"Hurry up. Someone's coming," Lily said.

Rafi jumped back into the hole and picked up the whisk-broom again. "A desperado in a donkey cart?"

"He could be one of the Mufti's men. For God's sake, what are you doing?"

"Looking for ammo." He kept brushing. "Here it is." He tugged at a carton. "500 *Einsteckmagazin*; 8 mm."

"Hurry," Lily said.

The cart swerved back and forth along the path to the road as it lumbered down the hill toward them.

"We'll make it before he gets here." Rafi jammed the ammo into a space in the back of the car beside the crate of rifles and covered both with the tarp of the dining canopy, then piled the digging equipment on top and slammed the tailgate shut.

"There. No one can tell." He climbed back into the car. "Let's go."

The mule cart was less than fifteen feet above them. They could see the angry scowl of the *fellah* as he pulled the mule around another turn in the path. Rafi turned on the ignition, carefully let out the choke. The motor rocked. The car bucked and trembled and staggered forward. The mule brayed in fear. It backed against the cart, tumbling cart and driver onto the terrace.

"I told you we'd make it." Rafi patted the trembling steering wheel affectionately. "We'll be in Netanya by six thirty."

"The curfew is at six. We'll be stopped."

"We'll burn that bridge if we get to it."

Lily could see the *fellah* in the rear view mirror, running down the road after them.

"Where are we going in Netanya?"

"Leora's house. Leora and Gadi."

"Who are they?"

"You met Gadi. In the taxi to Jerusalem. When you were on your way to the opening of the Rockefeller."

"That time the guns were Lugers."

"You did this yourself. You're the one who found the cache."

"You're not going to get me embroiled in this."

"You're already involved."

"Why are you doing it?"

"Let's just say I am my brother's keeper."

"That's no excuse. You'll get us both in trouble."

He turned to face her. "We can fight the Nazis here, now, or later on the streets of Chicago. Which do you prefer?"

"People who feel that way go to Spain and join the International Brigade. Just send some tinfoil and scrap metal to the Loyalists."

He shifted gears and swerved around a rut in the road. "When I was a child, my mother kept a little tin box in the house for pennies to buy land from the Turks in Palestine. One evening— I was only about eight or nine—Louis Brandeis came to Chicago to give a speech. He had just been appointed to the Supreme Court. He came to dinner at our house."

Rafi paused. His eyes clouded as he evoked the memory. "My aunt, Avi's mother, came down from Milwaukee with her friend and they talked all evening, about his struggle to get working women the minimum wage, about the Balfour Declaration. I didn't understand what they talked about. I fell asleep at the table and someone carried me to bed."

"But you remembered it all."

Rafi nodded. "I'll never forget that night, everything about it. Crumbs and poppy-seeds scattered on the plates; seltzer bottles; cut-glass goblets; reflections from the chandelier, like little rainbows on the white tablecloth; a bowl of green gage plums that made my mouth pucker."

"What happened?"

"As soon as the war ended, my aunt came here. The British had just taken over. My aunt and uncle joined a kibbutz. They had tough times. She was pregnant with Avi. They had nothing, lived in a mud hut while they built the kibbutz with their own hands, the children's house first."

"And her friend from Milwaukee?"

"Golda? She followed a few years later. Got involved in politics, in this committee and that. The right to be hired as a fruit picker, minimum wage, all the things that she and Brandeis talked about that night. I never met a woman with such determination and energy. She's like a steam-roller."

"And now you smuggle arms on your summer vacation. What are you going to do with the rifles?"

"Leora and Gadi have a root cellar."

"They live in a kibbutz?"

"They have an orange grove. On a bluff overlooking the sea. With a little truck garden."

"And you'll hide the guns in the cellar."

"A root cellar in the chicken house."

"Chicken soup with a vengeance."

"Why not? Chicken soup is the universal panacea." Rafi turned to her and smiled and they hit another bump.

"Watch the road," she said.

* * *

An armored car blocked the road ahead of them. A soldier in a red beret leaned against it, waiting.

"Oh damn," Lily said. "A British patrol."

As they came closer, the soldier moved to the center of the road and signaled for them to stop.

"See if your blond hair can get us through this one," Rafi said.

TWENTY-TWO

LILY SMOOTHED HER DRESS, wiped her face and rolled the window down as they pulled up to the barrier.

"Officer," she said, as breathlessly as she could, "I'm so glad we found you." She smiled, took a breath, and went on sounding agitated, her tone pitched high and tremulous. "Three men. Back there," she waved vaguely in the direction of the road. "They buried some boxes." She held out her arms like a fisherman describing the one that got away. "Big boxes. In a cave, near Tulkarm."

The soldier looked first at Lily, then at Rafi, and glanced at the equipment in the back of the wagon.

Rafi leaned forward. "Boxes maybe three feet long. They looked heavy."

Lily noticed Rafi's soil-smeared shirt and her own dirt covered arms. "We're doing an archaeological survey. For the Department of Antiquities. We put in test trenches near Atara. No luck." Her voice rose half an octave and she spoke more rapidly. "We were coming home. That's when we discovered them."

"Madam," the Englishman said.

"They ran back to the village when they saw us."

"Madam," he said again.

Lily pointed to the road behind her and kept talking. "Near Nur-e-Shems, or Danibeh." Her voice shook and increased in tempo. "We thought it was a funeral. But it wasn't."

"Please, madam," the soldier said, "calm down."

"I'm all right." She ran her fingers through her hair and looked at her hands. "My. I'm covered with dust." She turned to Rafi. "What did the writing on the side of the boxes say?"

"Mausers. They were burying Mausers. It looked like an arms cache."

"You saw this?" the soldier said.

Rafi nodded. "If we hurry, we can get back there before they get away."

"How many men were there?"

"Three or four," Rafi said. "At least a dozen boxes. As long as rifles."

"Can you show me where this is?"

"I'll take my wife home and meet you back here." Rafi said. "There may be trouble. No place for a lady."

"Right. We'll need reinforcements," the Englishman said. "Meet me at the police post in Netanya. We'll take an armored car and a couple of supernumeraries. Can you handle firearms?"

"We have to get back there before they move the stuff again."

"Right."

"I'll hurry," Rafi said. "They may get away." And he started the wagon and drove in the direction of Netanya.

"Your wife?" Lily said when they were back on the road.

"Why not? We make a good team."

"Is this a proposal?"

"It could be."

"You're married to Ora. The girl with the giggle."

"Only on Tuesdays and Thursdays."

The road was smoother now, and they sped along the macadam. "I'll drop you off at Leora and Gadi's. Tell them to put the Mausers and ammo with the rest of the weapons in the root cellar. Under the onions and potatoes."

"Where do they get the other weapons?"

"From friends. Gadi has a shop in Netanya. A linen shop. He goes to Belgium twice a year to buy tablecloths and lace."

"He must have a good business."

"He goes mostly to see friends. They give him gifts."

"Chocolates?"

"Chocolate gives him hives. So they send other things. Special delivery."

"To the beach? At night?"

Rafi nodded.

"What about Ora?" Lily asked. "Does she go along?"

"She lives in Hedera."

Lily had been there once. It was another small, isolated beach town, north of Netanya. "She has a linen shop too?"

"A gift shop. Delft. Bohemian glass."

"And her friends send her gifts from Holland and Czechoslovakia?"

"Not for much longer. She'll close the shop after Hitler takes over Bohemia."

"Then it will be the Mufti's turn to shop for cut glass."

"Exactly."

"You won't be able to go back tomorrow and get the rest of the guns after all," Lily said.

Rafi reached for her hand. "If we get back to Tulkarm in time, the Mufti's men won't be able to use them, either."

The road leading into Netanya was smooth and paved; close to town, the air lifted and wafted toward them with the soft tang of the sea. They passed the police post, stark and rigid as a

prison, at the edge of town and drove down the main street of
the little resort.

Couples strolled along a promenade or rode in horse-drawn
carriages that clop-clopped gently along a broad avenue. Roses
blossomed in the center divider and bright flowers bloomed on
either side of the street—beneath the trees, in front of the shops,
along the walks of *pensiones* with broad porches where people
sat drinking tea.

Rafi pulled the car off the road into an orange grove and
bumped along in tall weeds toward a white stucco house on a
bluff. Faded green paint flaked from the window frames and a
wooden door. Two bicycles rested against the side of the building.

He went toward the house and Lily followed. A woman in a
flowered cotton dress answered Rafi's knock. Her face, her arms,
her neck were covered with freckles. A single, long, ginger-col-
ored braid reached halfway down her back.

"Gadi here?" Rafi said.

"In the orange grove."

"Tell him to empty the station wagon and park it out of
sight, in the back. I have to get to the police post as quickly as
possible. I'll borrow a bicycle. Lily will fill you in on the de-
tails."

He started down the road and turned back again. "I forgot," he said, got off the bicycle, leaned over and kissed Lily on
the forehead. "I'll be back soon."

"You're Lily?" Leora said after he rode away.

"And you're Leora."

"Rafi talks about you all the time."

Lily felt herself blushing. "Good things, I hope."

Leora smiled and looked out at the grove toward the station
wagon. "What's going on?"

Lily told her about the cave filled with German guns, about the boxes with rifles and ammo in the back of the station wagon, about the encounter with the British patrol. "Rafi said to hide the rifles in the root cellar. The Brits don't know we have these. Rafi is leading a police patrol back to Tulkarm to recover the cache, maybe catch the gang with the guns."

Leora listened carefully, nodding and smiling.

"I like you," Leora told Lily when she came back from speaking with Gadi. "You'll be good for Rafi."

Everyone's a matchmaker, Lily thought.

Leora stepped back and examined Lily. "You look a mess," she said. "Wait here."

She returned with a bucket, a towel and two bars of soap. "This one's for your clothes." She held out a chunk of white soap. "And this one," she brought the wrapped bar up her nose and savored the aroma, "is for you." A whiff of jasmine wafted from the soap.

A dark red silk robe smelling faintly of lavender and mothballs was draped over her arm. "You can wear this while your clothes dry."

"It's beautiful," Lily ran her fingers along the smooth surface of the robe. The silk was as smooth as cream. "Are you sure?"

"Gadi brought it back from Europe. It's the wrong color for me. Makes me look like a spotted hen." She handed Lily the bucket. "The shower is down that hall, on the right."

* * *

Lily stood in the hot shower, soaped the dirty clothes as she peeled them off, scrubbing one piece at a time, dropping it in the bucket filling with water and stomping on it until she thought it was clean.

She unwrapped the bar of perfumed soap that Leora had given her and rubbed it back and forth against the sponge, releasing the sweet scent of jasmine. She squeezed the sponge. Bubbles spurted out, glistening on her arms and breast and clinging to her skin with milky softness. She slicked it gently against her shoulder, humming to herself, remembering Rafi's fingers reaching out to stroke the curve of her neck.

* * *

In the kitchen, Leora was cutting cucumbers.

"Can I help?" Lily asked.

"All done. We'll have supper after Rafi gets back." She tilted her head and looked at Lily. "That looks good on you."

Lily lifted the bucket of wet clothes. "Where can I hang these?"

"The wash line is just past the rose garden, near the stairs to the beach."

Lily went through the house to the garden and felt the faint evening breeze caress her skin. It carried the scent of roses and the sea. Off to the left in the orange grove, Gadi was washing the station wagon. He paused to look at her walking among the roses, waved and turned back to the car.

Lily hung the clothes on the line at the far end of the garden. Beyond the road, the sky over the hills was already darkening. She walked around the rose beds, bending down to breathe in their perfume or to stroke velvet petals of a long bud.

She found steps that led down to an isolated cove, hidden from the garden, where dune grass bent and wavered in the evening breeze and the golden sun, low on the horizon, dappled the sea.

In the cove, she walked barefoot along the beach, the silk of the robe caressing her like a second skin. Wet sand crunched under her steps, and she dug into it when the surf lapped against her feet, squeezing the slurry of sand and water between her toes.

She paused at tide pools to watch the edge of the sea roil among the rocks; watch dentalium and cowrie tumble, water-washed in the foam; watch sand crabs wink at the rim of tiny breakers and sea anemones waver and undulate in the current.

She waited impatiently for Rafi to come back, to hear what happened at Tulkarm, listening for the tenderness of his voice.

She watched the sea inch up the beach, the cool water licking at her toes, advancing and receding, each time a little higher on the strand. She stood at the edge of the water, until she became a creature of the tide, feeling it billow back and forth, moving against the arch of her foot, caressing her ankles. She felt the sea retreat, pulling grains of sand back to the surf from under the soles of her feet.

She glanced back at the bluff. Rafi appeared at the top of the stairs. He came down the steps toward the beach, and she went to meet him, to ask what happened. "Did they . . ."

He stroked the side of her cheek, and she leaned into the fold of his arm.

"It went without a hitch," he said.

She felt his hands trace her neck, felt the silken robe slip from her shoulders, felt it fall from her arms onto the ground, felt his hand along her back, felt the texture of his chest and shoulders, the curve of his neck. He kissed her cheek, her chin, her eyelids, the curve of her neck, and she felt the flow of skin against skin, smooth as water rippling in the wind. She leaned into the taste of him, the smell of him, while the sea pounded in her ears, and they clung together on the beach, bathed in the golden sunset, while the night overtook the sky.

TWENTY-THREE

LILY WATCHED RAFI'S HANDS at supper, imagining them stroking her shoulders, reaching along the curve of her back. "We got there just as they were moving the guns." She watched his lips as he talked about the police expedition to Tulkarm. "Police arrested four men. They'll be sentenced to hang. Tomorrow the military command will bulldoze their houses. That's standard punishment for terrorists."

He has a beautiful mouth, his lips flexible and strong—and the line of his jaw—

"They'll be released," she heard Gadi say. "There's always some excuse to free those brigands—not enough evidence, they were burying a dead donkey—anything will do."

She watched Rafi butter a roll. "They claimed that they were digging up the arms to turn them in to the British authorities. A *fellah* told the police that I took a box of rifles, that I was the one who had buried the guns." He paused. "Please pass the cheese."

Lily's fingers lingered on his forearm when she handed him the plate. "The one who chased us?"

Rafi nodded.

"You think the Brits will bulldoze the Strauss Hospital?"

"Of course," Rafi said. "And the American School. They're onto us."

"Oh stuff it," Lily said.

Gadi speared a slice of tomato with his fork and waved it in the air. "You're in the clear. No one in the English-speaking community smuggles arms. Everyone knows that."

"And a good thing too," Lily said.

*　*　*

In the morning, Rafi took the station wagon to a garage in town. Lily and Leora had brought their coffee out to the bluff, where Lily sat on a bench overlooking the sea, her skirt spread around her, a smile on her face.

Children's voices, high pitched and laughing, drifted up from the cove. Lily's newly washed clothes were crisp and bright and smelled of sunshine and fresh air. She felt the sun brighten her cheeks, felt its warmth on the soft down of her arms, and she tilted her head back, throwing out her arms to embrace it all. Dawn had washed the world and the morning danced under a cloudless sky.

*　*　*

Lily and Rafi arrived at Chancellors Road in Jerusalem in late afternoon, in time for his shift at the hospital. She drove to the American School through the narrow lanes behind Mea Shearim. Bearded men in black suits pressed against buildings waiting for Lily to pass. Tired housewives lumbered along the pavement.

Boys with long side-locks and milky-white skin, miniature adults in black cloaks, somberly kicked a soccer ball. The ball hit the station wagon with a thump. The boys stopped the game, waiting silently for the station wagon to pass as it bumped over the cobbles. The side-curls gave the boys a look of sadness, like basset hounds.

A woman blocked the way. Lily sounded the horn. The woman, a black scarf tied over her shaven head, her shoulders drooping from sacks of groceries, turned around, glared at Lily and continued trudging down the middle of the road.

Lily parked the wagon in the back of the garden and ran up the steps to the portico. Lady Fendley sat at the desk in the office and called to Lily as soon as the door opened. "You were gone a long time for just a wedding." It sounded like an accusation. "There are all sorts of messages for you."

"The car broke down."

"You should have called." Lady Fendley put down the pen and drew in a breath. "In these times!" She shook her head and wagged her finger—as Lily's mother had done when Lily had come home late—then ticked off messages one by one. "Kate wants you to bring the wagon back down to Kharub." She turned down her index finger. "Someone named Jamal said he has tomorrow off and can go with you to Beit Jibrin. You going there? It's morbid." She was up to her ring finger. "And your friend Avi called. Something about an amphoriskos."

"I'm sorry. Next time I'll call." Lily started up the stairs. "What about the amphoriskos?"

"And Eliot came by," Lady Fendley called after Lily. "He was looking for the site report from Tell Abu Hawam. It wasn't at your desk. He said you took it upstairs. I had to get the extra key so that he could look on your desk."

"In my room?"

"You shouldn't take books upstairs unless you leave a note on the shelf," Lady Fendley said.

"But I—Never mind," Lily said and hurried up the stairs to unlock her door.

The desk was in order, but her closet door stood open. The coverlet lay smoothly over the foot of the bed. Lily reached under the mattress where she had hidden the journal and pulled it out.

The drawings of plans and sections fell, loose, onto the floor. Lily remembered folding them carefully into the pocket at the back of the journal before she slid it under the mattress. The list of sites she had forged in Eastbourne's handwriting was gone.

She unscrewed the back panel of the radio. The coordinates she had copied were still there.

Lily put the maps back in the folder and spread the plans on the desk. This time she focused on the sheet with drawings of small, round semi-subterranean structures with slotted, high windows and thick walls; plans of larger, square edifices with even thicker walls, casemates and turrets, similar in plan to ancient fortresses; and cross-sections of wide concrete culverts. A detailed illustration of a turret included plans for a revolving steel cupola, that could disappear and be raised or lowered by a lever and counterweight.

Lady Fendley's voice called from the corridor. "Are you in there, Lily?" She knocked. "Telephone for you. Your friend Avi."

Lily folded the map and plans, put them in the pocket of the journal, placed it in the desk drawer and headed for the phone in the upstairs hall.

Avi's voice was almost drowned out by the rattle of dishes and the sound of running water in the background. "I'm in the kitchen," he shouted, "and can't hear very well. You have to yell." He told her he had heard that someone brought a blue glass amphoriskos to an antiquities dealer in Tel Aviv.

"I have to bring the wagon back to Kharub tomorrow," Lily said.

"I could meet you at the tel tomorrow afternoon, say four-thirty. We could drive up to Jerusalem together, go to Tel Aviv the next morning early."

"Great. See you tomorrow," Lily said. She put the telephone back on the table, then picked it up again. "Thanks," she shouted into the mouthpiece and hung up.

She went back to her room to find Jamal's number at the Austrian Hospice, and left a message for him to meet her at Damascus gate the next morning at nine a.m.

*   *   *

Jamal was waiting for Lily in the morning. He ran across the road from Damascus Gate in the face of traffic, and climbed into the seat next to her in the station wagon.

The road south to Bethlehem curved along the crest of the ridge. They drove through the German Colony with its staid Bavarian villas trimmed with green shutters and pots of red geraniums. They passed the stone houses of Bakaa with their flat roofs and wide, vaulted porches; passed row on row of long stucco buildings at Allenby Barracks.

Jamal slumped in his seat, chewing on the cuticle of his thumbnail, his eyes large and staring at the dash

"What's wrong?" Lily asked.

"I don't like this. I don't feel comfortable going back there. Maybe we should turn around and drive back to Jerusalem."

The road crossed through the Judean Hills, covered with stone terraces, green with olive trees and grapevines. An ancient cinder-cone from a long dead volcano stood out against the golden hills of the Judean desert that cradled the blue mist of the Dead Sea.

"I told Kate I would bring the station wagon down today," Lily said.

"How will you get back?"

"Avi will drive me."

"Avi again," he said, and examined his thumb, running a finger along the edge of his nail.

"Avi's a nice boy."

Ahead of them, Lily saw the church steeples and spires of Bethlehem. Just before they reached the kibbutz of Ramat Rahel, they came to a pillbox. Narrow slots below the conical roof squinted at them like eyes in an angry mask. It looks like the circular structures in the drawings in Eastbourne's journal, Lily realized with a jolt. Why would Eastbourne have plans of modern military installations?

Why not? Yigael Sukenik, son of the chair of the Department of Archaeology at Hebrew University, was researching warfare in Biblical times and doing a survey of ancient Judean fortresses. "If we ever have an ancient war," Sir William had once said of him, "Yigael will make a perfect general."

Lily waved her hand in the direction of a kibbutz. A stone wall enclosed a water tower, some barracks-like buildings, and weed-covered knolls. "That's Ramat Rahel," Lily said. "Those mounds are probably the remains of a Judean fortress from over twenty-seven hundred years ago."

"Canaanites were here before that."

"Canaanites?"

"My ancestors."

"I thought you were a Philistine."

"Both. Canaanite and Philistine. This is the home of my ancestors. That's why it's called Palestine. Others come and go, like guests. Brits, Turks, Romans, Jews. But we were always here. And we will be here forever."

"So you agree with the Mufti?"

Jamal clicked his tongue against his teeth and gave a quick

shake of the head to indicate 'no.' "I understand him," Jamal
said. "I don't agree with him. I don't like violence."

"You back his opponent, Khalidi?"

He clicked his tongue again in a gesture of denial. "Palestinians have a hundred factions, each with a different point of
view. It's all a matter of perspective."

"That's what Avi says."

"Avi again." He went back to biting the edge of his finger.

Lily had already passed Rachel's Tomb near the entrance to
Bethlehem and Shepherd's Field with its terraced olive groves.
She drove through the narrow streets of Bethlehem.

"It seems to me," Lily said, "that the Mufti has caused economic disaster for Palestinian Arabs. His men kill anyone who
won't go along with his dictates—farmers who sell land, mer-
chants who don't join the strike."

"He says if we don't act together, we'll lose the land."

"You agree?"

Jamal sat rigidly in his seat, absorbed in private thoughts.
He stared straight ahead, toward the Bethlehem market.
Franciscan monks in brown habits carried baskets filled with
fruit. Lily glanced at Jamal. His cheeks were suffused with an
angry glow, the wings of his nostrils dilated.

A fly came in through the open window next to Jamal, buzzed
around his head, and flew out the back window.

"Haven't you ever wondered what a fly sees with all those
lenses in its compound eye?" Jamal asked. "Humans have two
eyes, and see in three dimensions. The fly sees a hundred pic-
tures. What does he see that you and I can never grasp? Can he
understand more than we do?"

Greek Orthodox priests with black robes and rigid hats like
crowns draped with cloth passed in front of them.

"Where are the tourists?" Lily asked.

"Who?" He looked around, at coffeehouses where old Arab men played shesh-besh and smoked; at laden donkeys struggling along the cobbles. "Too early in the day."

They drove through the empty expanse of Manger Square. Souvenir shops surrounded the Church of the Nativity, with its low entrance door. Proprietors of the shops sat in arched doorways on low stools, arms crossed across their chests, smoking hookahs, sipping coffee, waiting for customers to buy their mother of pearl rosaries and olivewood camels. They called out, "Welcome, welcome," to Lily as the station wagon crawled along.

"I always get lost here," Lily said.

"Keep going," Jamal told her. "Hebron is straight ahead."

He was silent as they drove on. Hill villages with stone houses and flat roofs surrounded by rough fieldstone walls looked down on the road. On either side of them fields were green with vines and fig trees; men and boys winnowed wheat with pitchforks; women sifted flour in flat baskets, donkeys pulled large rolling stones to crush olives.

Every man under his vine and fig tree, Lily thought.

"I don't like the Mufti," Jamal said after a while. "Violence in the name of patriotism is still violence. I think he's despotic, maybe a little corrupt. He took money from the Waqf—the widows and orphans fund—to buy arms."

"Why do people put up with him?"

"You know the Bible?" Jamal asked.

"I use it sometimes in my research. For historical references."

"You know the part in Deuteronomy where Moses promises that in Canaan, Israelites will have cities that they didn't build, cisterns they didn't dig, vineyards and orchards that they didn't plant?"

"I don't recall exactly."

"Take my word for it. It's there. That's what Palestinians fear the most. To be exiles in their own land, laborers in their own groves."

"But Jews don't steal the land. They buy it."

"That's why the Mufti doesn't let people sell."

They passed the burned-out houses of the Jewish settlements north of Hebron. Jamal turned in his seat to look back at them. "The Mufti's men killed my uncle. There's blood between us."

"Your uncle sold land?"

"Near 'En Kerem."

"To Jewish settlers?"

"It was his to sell."

The road went through Hebron, where Abraham built his altar and buried his family. "According to legend," Jamal said, "the stones of the Cave of Machpelah, Haram al-Khalil, were laid by djinns under orders from Solomon. You believe it?"

"I believe they were laid by Herod, with the help of taxes and enforced labor."

"Like your friend Avi says, it's all a matter of perspective." Jamal looked down at his hands and picked at his fingers. "I remember a Bedouin workman at the tel who had tuberculosis. I tried to get him to the hospital. He insisted that his cough came from an evil djinn, commanded by one of his enemies. I tried to explain about bacillus in his lungs. He said I was naïve and gullible."

"Oh?"

"He asked if I believed the story that at the North Pole, the sun didn't set in the middle of summer and didn't rise in the middle of winter."

"Yes?"

"He said I was foolish to believe it. Because people who live at the North Pole couldn't celebrate Ramadan, and Allah would never permit it."

"Does your Bedouin observe Ramadan even in summer in the desert?"

Jamal nodded. "Even on the hottest days of July, he doesn't eat or drink water from dawn to dusk for the entire month. But he smokes cigarettes."

"Isn't that allowed?"

"The Arabic word for smoking is the same as that for drinking. When he smokes, he hides in his tent, so Allah cannot see him."

Lily grinned. "Surely Allah has more eyes than a fly. Even a fly has a hundred eyes. You said so yourself."

They continued down the road, past the souk.

"Keep going, keep going," Jamal said.

They drove past glass factories with open-air furnaces and glass blowers forming bowls and vases and lamps in jewel-like colors, past shops festooned with glass bracelets and beads.

"Turn to the right there, after that house." Jamal pointed to a stone building just ahead. "The road's paved with gravel for a while and then turns into a dirt track."

The track narrowed after about a hundred yards. Lily drove slowly over the rutted road, her hands tight on the steering wheel.

Jamal fidgeted in his seat. After about twenty minutes he said, "We're coming up on it soon." A little later, he pointed toward a pair of boulders on the side of the track. "They were hiding behind those rocks. Three of them. We came up from the other side. We were attacked just beyond there."

Lily turned off the engine and got out of the car. Multiple tire tracks and footprints scarred the ground. The stench of a dead animal hung in the air. She shuddered.

Jamal walked past the boulders. "They jumped out from behind that rock and told us to halt. They leveled their rifles at him and shot him point blank."

"The newspaper report said that he was shot with a revolver."

He shook his head. "They used rifles. Two were armed. I don't know about the third—he hung back. I told that to the police." Jamal looked at his watch. "I don't have much time."

Lily examined the ground, trying to imagine Eastbourne facing his murderers. Was he frightened? Was he defiant? "Exactly where did you stop?"

He walked a few paces in the direction of Beit Jibrin. "Right about here. They ordered Eastbourne out of the car and told me to drive on to Hebron. I heard the shots as I drove away. There's a terrible odor here."

"Did you see them shoot him?"

"I looked back. He was stumbling along the track, and then they shot him again."

Lily felt a sudden surge of anger toward Jamal. "Why didn't you go back?"

"I was only one person and they had guns." He shifted uncomfortably, looked at his watch again. "I'm on call tonight."

Lily searched the ground carefully. It showed evidence of heavy traffic—footprints that overlay one another, wheel marks from carts and lorry tires. At a point about five yards further on, there was a jumble of marks from sandals, boots, and at least three different pairs of shoes near a dark stain on the ground. Eastbourne's blood, Lily thought. One set of footprints near the stain meandered unsteadily. Eastbourne's steps.

Lily wandered over the ground, expanding her inspection of the area, searching for signs of the amphoriskos. As she neared the boulder, the smell became overwhelming. "There's a dead animal here."

"I have to leave. It's just garbage. Someone probably picnicked here."

Lily walked back toward the rock. The smell was stronger now. The freshly dug, uneven surface of the ground was pocked with small rodent holes and animal tracks. Lily bent down to look at a small bone lying loose on the ground. The odor, unpleasant and almost overwhelming, triggered an atavistic fear and revulsion. She picked up the bone. The sinews were almost dry and still attached. The bone was still fresh, scarred with small parallel scratches where rats had gnawed it.

Jamal held a handkerchief to his face. "It's a chicken bone."

But it wasn't and Jamal knew it, Lily thought.

"Left over from a picnic," he said.

"This is human bone." He knows that. "A metatarsal. Someone was buried here. Recently. We have to report it."

Jamal looked at his watch again. "There's a police post about five minutes further on at Beit Jibrin. I don't have time to go with you." He walked back to the car for his bag. "You go ahead. I'll find a ride." He started walking up the track toward Hebron.

"But you—"

"I'll get someone in the village to take me to Hebron so I can catch a bus. Don't worry. I speak the language."

Lily hesitated.

Jamal waved "You'll be all right. It's not far."

Only five minutes, she thought. Closer than Hebron.

She got in the car and started toward Beit Jibrin.

TWENTY-FOUR

THE RANK SMELL OF DEATH stayed in her nostrils as Lily shifted the car into first gear. She felt the tires grab the dusty surface of the track. Distracted, she drove automatically, bumping over furrows and troughs.

Her mind churned with questions about the burial behind the rock. What connection did it have to Eastbourne's murder? Why was Jamal so anxious to get away?

The ruins of the Crusader Church of St. Anne on the hill above Beit Jibrin loomed in front of her. With Beit Jibrin so close, why did Jamal drive to Hebron the day Eastbourne was killed? Hebron was more than twenty minutes away.

Bandits. Were they really bandits? Lily wondered if Jamal could have saved Eastbourne if he had tried, could have skirted back? Eastbourne still may have been alive when he left. Maybe not. Two shots, Jamal had said.

* * *

The police post turned out to be a small concrete building. A Union Jack flapped from a pole in front. Inside, a constable sat at a desk, a cup of tea next to his elbow.

217

"Can I help you, miss?" He looked up at Lily from the book he was reading and smiled as if they were old friends. "Why, it's the lady archaeologist."

Lily peered at his sandy hair and ruddy face, trying to recall if she had seen him before.

"Remember me?" he asked.

It was no use. All ruddy-faced Englishmen look alike. "Of course I do," Lily said.

"At the road block? The day you drove up to Jerusalem for the opening of the Rockefeller?"

"Oh." The day she met Rafi. "Of course. The man from Colchester. Interested in Roman ruins."

He spread the book, spine up, on the desk and gave her an encouraging smile. "What can I do for you today, luv?"

"I found a dead body."

"Oh?"

"On the Beit Jibrin track. Buried behind a rock, near where Eastbourne was killed."

"You're quite sure, now?"

Lily nodded. "In a shallow grave."

"If it is buried, like you say, how do you know—?"

"Animals burrowed into it and brought bone up to the surface. Human bone."

"What makes you think it's human?"

"I know, that's all."

"I see. Archaeologists know those things." He took a sip from the cup. "And now you want to dig it up?"

"It's not an archaeological site. Not a regular grave either. Too shallow, too recent."

"You suspect foul play?"

Lily nodded again.

"And you want us to investigate?"

"Yes."

"We have our hands full as it is without going out to look for trouble." He sat down at the desk and reached for the book. "Digging up every corpse in Palestine."

He seems to have time today, Lily thought. She twisted her head to read the book title. "What are you reading?"

"Just a novel. A detective novel by Margaret Sotheby."

Lily read the title out loud. "*The Body from Baghdad.* Dame Margaret is a friend of mine, you know."

"Of course she is, luv. And now you think you found a body. Like the archaeologist in the book."

"It's not like that at all. The body was hidden behind a rock, covered with dirt."

He closed the book this time and pushed back the chair. "All right. It's a dull morning. Suppose you take me there, luv."

Lily thought of the smell, the rat-gnawed metatarsal, and the dark stain left by Eastbourne's blood on the dusty track. "I can't go back to that place."

"Isn't that what archaeologists do? Dig up dead bodies?"

"I don't deal with the wet dead."

"Wet dead?"

"Fresh cadavers. I only work on skeletons at least five hundred years old—clean and dry. Just skeletons."

"Same thing, luv. A body is a body."

"No, it's not. A skeleton is data. But a dead body is—"

"Carrion?"

"Exactly. I have an appointment at Tel al-Kharub."

"That's where you dig?"

"I did. We're closing down the excavation."

"You worked with Eastbourne?"

"Yes."

He stood up again. This time, the amused smile was gone. "My sympathies, ma'am." He looked at Lily speculatively.

"Were you one of the investigating police?" she asked.

"I handled the team of bloodhounds. We tracked a scent as far as Kharass. Turned out to be a false trail." He looked away for a moment. "Where did you say this body is?"

"Near where Eastbourne was killed. You can't miss it. Just follow your nose, officer."

"Meriman's the name. Sergeant Meriman." He sat down at the desk, opened a drawer and brought out a pad and pen. "I have to write out a report, ma'am. Name?"

"Lily Sampson."

"Address?"

"American School in Jerusalem. 26 Salah-edh-Din Street."

"You have a telephone?"

"One three one."

"Location of the disturbance?" he said, looking up. "Beit Jibrin track, behind a rock." His pen scratched along the page. He scanned his watch. "Eleven-thirty." He stopped writing and read the paper over. "That's all for now."

"I can go now, officer?"

He smiled at Lily. "You'll still have to come back. If we find anything, you'll be a witness. Have to make a statement."

Lily moved toward the door. "This afternoon. In about an hour and a half." She hurried to the door and waved at him over her shoulder. "See you later."

* * *

Where the camp had been, the hill was bare, the earth scarred with tire tracks, postholes from vanished tents, and old footprints. Nothing grew on the hard-packed ground, not even weeds. The corrugated tin walls of the dig house kitchen remained. That too was being dismantled, the roof already gone.

Kate stood next to a hired lorry, directing Bedouin workmen who were stacking boxes on the flat bed of the truck. "Cartons with blue labels go on that side," she said, gesturing to the right. "Orange labels on this." Her voice was authoritative.

Nothing about Kate was the same. Even her posture had changed, the apologetic droop of her shoulders gone. She seemed taller. I never realized how much she shrank in Eastbourne's shadow, Lily thought.

Kate paused when Lily drove up. "You brought the wagon." She smiled at Lily. "I'll miss working here." She looked around as if she still saw the absent camp, the dining tent and the pottery shed.

"It looks denuded," Lily said. "Like a man with too close a haircut."

"So sad." Kate gestured with a nod of her head toward the ghostly corrugated walls. "Park over there, behind what's left of the dig house."

Kate signaled to a workman. "Be careful with that. Don't stack the cartons more than two deep." She turned back to Lily. "We'll be finished packing tomorrow. Help me check the inventory of boxes. The registry is on the front bench of the lorry, passenger side."

Kate picked up a clipboard from the top of a stack of boxes and climbed into the truck bed. "How will you get back to Jerusalem?" she asked Lily.

"Avi will meet me here this afternoon. About four."

"We'll be done long before that." Kate pointed to the area next to the dig house. "I put aside two more boxes of material from the tombs for you. Over there, next to the dig house. When you finish your dissertation, ship the whole lot to me at the Institute of Archaeology, University of London."

In a little more than an hour, they finished the inventory of boxes stacked in the truck. There was a rhythm and satisfying comfort in the mindless busy work, Kate calling out numbers of artifacts from labels on the side of the cartons, Lily checking them off in the registry.

"That's it for today," Kate said and slapped her hands together in a gesture of finality. "*Helas. Basta.* Beacon Pharmaceutical will be here in the morning for the lorry and the wagon." She climbed down from the truck bed. "You'll come to the house for tea?"

"I have to go back to the police post at Beit Jibrin," Lily said.

Kate leaned forward. Her hand clutched Lily's arm. "They found the killers?"

"It's not about Eastbourne. I found a body."

"What kind of body?"

"I don't know. They're recovering it now. I have to go back to give a statement."

"Better drive the wagon to Beit Jibrin. No other way to get there. Bring it back and leave the keys under the seat."

"Will all this be safe—the cars, the material in the boxes? It won't be stolen?"

"Thieves aren't interested in sherds and scraps. Most of the whole pots were shipped to the Rockefeller. I gave the foreman of the Bedouin a few pounds to guard all this." She indicated the camp, the tel, the boxes with a sweep of her arm. "It's all safe, such as it is," she said. "They'll keep an eye out for Abu Musa." She paused. "Some things are gone. Like the amphoriskos. You found it yet?"

Lily shook her head and clicked her tongue against the roof of her mouth like an Arab. "I heard a rumor that someone sold it to an antiquities dealer in Tel Aviv. I'll check it out tomorrow."

Kate reached for Lily's hand. "This is goodbye for now, then. Little Geoff and I are going up to the British School Thursday evening and sailing for England Friday morning."

"You're leaving?"

"I have packing to do in Ashkelon. Put a note on the lorry telling Avi to wait in case you're not back by four."

"I'll be here long before that."

"You never know with the police." Kate still held Lily's hand.

"Will you be all right," Lily asked, "when you're back in England?"

"I'll get on. I took a flat in Bloomsbury, on Gower Street. Beacon Pharmaceutical gave me a stipend to work up the material for the site report." Now she clasped Lily's hand between both of hers. "And Sir William arranged for the Egyptian Exploration Society to hire me on. At the University of London, for a course of lectures on the Archaeology of Palestine, and as Keeper of Antiquities for the Fendley Collection."

"And little Geoff?"

"He goes to public school. Geoffrey received a consulting fee of five thousand pounds from somewhere, the week before he died. Used it to set up a trust fund for little Geoff's education. His patrimony." She pumped Lily's hand up and down. "It was good working with you. See you next summer in London to work on the site report."

Kate strode to her battered Austin. Lily stayed on the desolate hill, watching Kate's car until it was out of sight.

* * *

"I'm sorry, ma'am," Meriman said, "but you'll have to view the body. It's required by law. We need to know if you recognize whoever it was. Being an archaeologist, maybe you can help."

The stench permeated the police post. Meriman took two handkerchiefs and a small bottle of lavender water from the desk drawer, sprinkled some of the lavender on one of the cloths and handed the other to Lily with the bottle. "You might need this." He hesitated. "Sorry, ma'am," he said again. "It's the law."

He led her down the corridor. When he opened the door, she staggered back, assailed by the overwhelming stench that filled the room.

A body with an embroidered white dress lay on a table. "Oh my," Lily said and backed toward the corridor.

Maggots billowed around the neck, over what had been the cheeks, and festooned the dress, undulating and fluttering on the red embroidery. The dress seemed to shimmy as if it were alive.

"Oh my," Lily repeated, closed her eyes and turned her head.

"So sorry, ma'am."

Lily gagged and leaned against Meriman. "It's a wedding dress. From Ramallah."

"How do you know that?"

"Red embroidery on white linen and silk. The design—rosettes—is from Ramallah. Each village has its own pattern."

"A wedding dress? We thought it could be a man. But it's hard to tell. The body is in bad condition. In this climate, with the bugs and rodents…" His voice trailed off. "I hate to ask you this, ma'am. Could you go closer? See if you recognize the deceased?"

She took a deep breath. The effluvium of decay overwhelmed her with primal fear, invading her senses, forcing her back against her will.

"I'll try." She shook a few drops of lavender water on the handkerchief, covered her nose and mouth, and stepped forward, controlling the urge to run from the building.

It was impossible to tell what the body had been in life. The cheeks were gone. Maggots swarmed and jostled in the eye sockets and over the brows, a pulsating mask that flowed like pointelles in an Impressionist painting come to life.

But the mouth, set into a gelatinous rictus, had Abu Musa's unctuous smile. There was no mistaking it—the brown teeth, broken left incisor, missing lower incisors, and gaps where the right canine and first left premolar should be. Alive with maggots crawling and squirming and tumbling over one another, it was Abu Musa's face.

Lily retched. She felt the bile rise in her throat and stumbled outside.

Sergeant Meriman followed. "You all right, miss?"

"I know him," Lily said. "He was one of the workmen at Tel al-Kharub. Abu Musa."

Meriman looked surprised. "Abu Musa?"

"You know the name?"

"Why should I?" He took Lily's arm. "You need a drink. We both need a drink. Come back to my office."

* * *

Meriman took another sip from the teacup on his desk. His breath had a whiskey smell. "Something to calm the nerves," he said, and reached into the desk for a bottle of Dewars and a glass. He poured two fingers of Scotch and handed it to her.

"Drink it down. It will do you good."

Lily's hand shook as she brought the glass to her lips.

"You're too upset to drive right now," Meriman said. "I know a little pub, on the seashore near Ashkelon. Why don't we go there? It will give you time to relax. Come along." He took her arm and led her outside. "Ever been in a Q car?" He gestured toward a vehicle parked at the side of the police post.

"It looks like an ordinary panel truck."

"That's the idea. We use them on patrol." He knocked against the side panel with his knuckles and produced a heavy thud. "You're safe in here. Armor-plated sides. Terrorists think it's a commercial van. When they attack, we meet them with rifle fire."

* * *

They pulled up to a small building with a gas station on one side and a lunchroom on the other.

"Charlie has fish and chips. And cold beer," Meriman said.

The door was open. Beyond the scattering of small linoleum-covered tables and straight-backed chairs, a small, dark man sat behind a counter, a newspaper spread out before him. It was difficult to think of the place as a pub.

"Hello, Charlie. No customers today?" Meriman called to him. The man folded the paper. "Any good news?"

"Hello, constable. There's never good news in this bloody country."

"Charlie here is from Bombay," Meriman said to Lily.

"Madras," Charlie said.

Meriman shrugged. "Same country."

"Not really."

"Give us two of your nice cold American beers."

"I only have Stella beer today."

Meriman pulled out a chair and sat at one of the tables. "Stella, then. It'll have to do."

The waiter brought two bottles and two chilled Pilsener glasses beaded with cold water from the icebox.

Meriman tilted the Pilsener glass and poured the beer slowly. "Have a beer?" he said to Lily.

"I don't drink."

"Religious reasons?"

Lily decided that was as good an excuse as any. She composed her face into the smug mask and resigned air of the truly holy. "Yes," she said.

"You want a tea?" Charlie said.

Lily nodded.

"Nothing like a cool beer on a warm day." Meriman savored the beer and sighed contentedly. "My mates drink it warm, but I like it American style, kept in an icebox." He took another long draft. "No offense," he said.

"We can't stay too long," Lily said. "I have to be back in Jerusalem before the curfew."

"Not to worry. Curfew's called off. We found what we were looking for. Cache of arms near Tulkarm."

"Imagine that," Lily said.

Meriman held the bottle in his hand, and studied the label—a drawing of two camels in front of the pyramids. "Stella Beer," he said. "Egyptian. My father told me about this beer. He was stationed in Cairo during the war." Meriman poured the second bottle into the glass.

"Two more beers, Charlie," he said. Charlie had already opened them and was carrying the bottles to the table on a tray.

"My father told a tale about this beer. It tastes awful, you know. He said he sent a sample to a local chemist to find out what was in it. The report came back that his horse had kidney stones." He chuckled and sighed.

By now, he was drinking straight out of the bottle.

"Who do you think killed Abu Musa?" Lily asked.

"I haven't the slightest. The whole bloody place is full of armed brigands. It's like your American Wild West. And I'm supposed to keep order." He lifted the bottle with a broad gesture that encompassed the bar and the world outside. "In this whole bloody place." He shrugged and a few drops of beer spilled on his sleeve. "It can't be done."

He took another pull at the beer. "Not going to waste time on it. He's only another bloody wog. They have all sorts of vendettas. He could have looked cross-eyed at somebody's sister, for all I know."

"But whoever killed him stole the amphoriskos."

"The what?"

"A blue glass vial. It's missing from the excavation. We think Abu Musa stole it."

"In this bloody country they'll kill for a shilling, much less a piece of old glass."

Meriman finished the beer and put the bottle down. "Don't you worry your pretty head about it," he said. "Have another beer." He signaled the waiter.

Meriman's face was flaccid, his eyes drooping and unfocused. There were four empty bottles in front of him now. He arranged them in a square, two on a side.

"Two more beers, Charlie." Meriman looked across the table at Lily. "It's warm today, isn't it?"

He sighed again. "Things are seldom what they seem. At first, I was happy to be posted here. I thought it would be more romantic, more exotic. East of Suez, and all that. The Holy Land. But it's not, you know. Englishmen sell out their own country here for five thousand pounds."

"How is that?"

He paused dramatically, sipped from the bottle and put it down again. "Can't tell you that, luv."

What was it Kate had said? Eastbourne got a consulting fee, five thousand pounds. Was it Eastbourne? "You're right. It is warm today," Lily said to Meriman. "Certainly makes you thirsty. Two more beers, Charlie."

"You sure?" Charlie asked.

Lily reassured hum with a smile. "Please."

The drawings in the pocket of the journal, Lily thought. A line of forts—and along the border, the Tegart lines.

"It was Tegart's idea, wasn't it?" Lily said. "Forts to control the gun running and terrorist activities. Keep the avenues open between Jerusalem and the Suez Canal in case of war." She took

in her breath. "Eastbourne was supposed to scout out the locations."

Meriman leaned forward confidentially, tipping a little beer
on the table and blinked. "How-d'ya find out?"

"Same way you did," Lily told him.

"The Arab who came to the police post with a story about
Eastbourne meeting Nazis in Jerusalem?"

So that was it. The Mufti is working with the Nazis, Jamal
had said. There's blood between us. Don't ride with Eastbourne
to Jerusalem, Jamal had said.

"Jamal," Lily told Meriman.

"Don't know his name. The cook, he said he was."

And Jamal, not Eastbourne, had left the notebook in her
tent.

Meriman grunted, shook his head and lifted the bottle again.
"Your friend Eastbourne sold the whole thing, kit and caboodle,
to the Nazis." He put down the bottle with a bang. "Had to
scrap the entire idea. We started some forts, like the one at
Latrun. Had to turn them into police posts."

"That's why Eastbourne had to be killed, isn't it?" Lily said.

Meriman's head rocked unsteadily up and down in agreement.

"The newspaper report said that you tracked a scent to
Kharass and found a revolver hidden in a wall," Lily said.

"Lily, is it?" He lowered his vice to a conspiratorial whisper.
"Eastbourne wasn't killed by a revolver, Lily. He was shot with
an Enfield rifle."

"A British weapon?"

"My job was to lay a false trail and take the bloodhounds in
the wrong direction so the newspapers could report that he was
shot by armed bandits from one of the villages." A tear lingered
in the corner of his eye and ran down the side of his nose.

Oh God, a maudlin drunk, Lily thought. "You know who
shot him?"

He fingered the bottle and nodded. "A Jewish supernumerary. One of those religious types, the kind with the black fedoras. We set it up so that three men dressed like *fellahin* would waylay the station wagon. We knew the route Eastbourne would take. Hired a workman from the tel to identify him, make sure we got the right man. The rest was easy."

He leaned back in the chair and closed his eyes. "The supernumeraries told me that the workman went through Eastbourne's pockets afterward, stole money from his wallet."

"Abu Musa?"

"Don't know, luv. Never met him."

So Abu Musa took the amphoriskos. But what did Henderson and Dame Margaret want with it?

Meriman placed three more bottles on top of the four that already sat in front of him. Slowly and carefully, with his tongue sticking out of the side of his mouth, he tried to balance one more on top of those. "I'll make a pyramid of pyramids," he said and began to chuckle. "See?" He held the bottle out to Lily. "Pyramids on the labels." He knocked his elbow against his pyramid and it tumbled, spilling beer across the table.

Lily looked at her watch. It was almost four. "I have to get back."

He didn't hear her. He was already asleep, face down on the table.

"I'll help you pour him into the lorry," Charlie said. "This isn't the first time."

Lily searched Meriman's pocket for the keys. "Passenger side," she told Charlie.

She started the truck and headed for Beit Jibrin. All the way back, Meriman slumped beside her, his eyes closed, his head lolling, his mouth hanging open. After a while, he began to snore.

She parked the Q car in front of the police post, started to get out but sounded the horn instead. Even from here, she thought, she could smell Abu Musa.

An Arab supernumerary opened the door of the police post and walked toward her, smiling. "He's at it again. He drinks as a Sphinx."

"He what?"

"Isn't that the expression?"

"Drunk as a skunk."

The supernumerary shrugged. "He does this all the time. Passes out in the lorry. Sometimes he doesn't make it home."

Lily handed him the keys. "You can take care of him?"

He nodded and grinned at her. "I always do."

She got into the station wagon, started the motor and drove back to Kharub.

TWENTY-FIVE

ALL THE WAY BACK TO KHARUB, the vision of Abu Musa's eyeless grimace haunted her. Lily coaxed the station wagon up the bald hill to the site. For the last time, she thought.

Avi's lorry was parked squarely in the empty field. He sat on the running board by the open door, leaning back against the seat.

The dining shed was dismantled, its corrugated tin sides stacked neatly next to the rented truck. Lily parked the wagon on the other side of the truck.

Avi stood up. "What happened?" He gestured toward the bed of his lorry. "I put your boxes in the back. Let's go. We have to be in Jerusalem before curfew."

Lily climbed into the passenger seat. "Curfew's over. Meriman told me."

"Who's Meriman?"

Lily told Avi about finding Abu Musa's body, about going to the police station to identify it. "I asked about the amphoriskos. No sign of it."

"You smell like a brewery," Avi said. "Spent a lot of time with Meriman, didn't you?"

"We went to a pub in Ashkelon. Not much of a pub. He got drunk, I had to drive him back."

Avi let out the throttle. The motor turned over. "I heard that Abu Musa raped a girl in Ramallah the day before her wedding. Her brothers killed her."

"That explains the wedding dress Abu Musa was wearing when they found him."

"Did they do anything else to him before he died?"

"Like—?" The stench, the rat-gnawed cheeks and arms were bad enough. "I don't know. The body was too far gone to tell."

Avi backed the lorry and turned it around. "You remember the day after Eastbourne's funeral, when someone shot at us in front of the King David?" They bumped over the field toward the road. "They may not have been after you. It was probably Abu Musa."

"How do you know all these things?"

"This is a small country. If I didn't mind everybody else's business, I wouldn't be doing my civic duty."

"You were right about something else."

"Oh?"

"Eastbourne was a spy."

"And that's why he was killed?"

Lily nodded. "He . . ." She hesitated. Speak only good of the dead. The rest of it, the maps in the journal, the five thousand pounds that Meriman spoke about, could wait for another time.

Avi shifted gears and the lorry groaned up the hill. "You think Eastbourne sold the amphoriskos? He was strapped for money."

"I think he sold more than the amphoriskos," Lily said.

* * *

In the morning when Lily brought her breakfast into the garden, Avi was already waiting.

"It's getting late," he said. "It'll be hot and sticky in Tel Aviv today."

The lorry careened down Jaffa road, past the warren of nineteenth century stone houses of Nahalat Sheva.

"Take it easy," Lily said.

"Sorry."

The streets smelled of dampness and kerosene.

"Something bothering you?" she asked.

"No. Yes."

The shops at Ben Yehuda Street and King George were still shuttered.

He shrugged "Maybe I just got up on the wrong side of the bed."

"Where do you stay in Jerusalem?" Lily asked.

"With Auntie Major. She told me all about you and Rafi in Netanya."

"Your Auntie Major has the brains of a tiddley-wink. I hope it's not hereditary."

"Why? You planning to have my child?"

"Not yours."

"Rafi's?"

"Avi . . ." she began and then thought better of making an excuse.

The street narrowed. They bumped along the cobbles. Avi drummed on the steering wheel, the lorry crawling behind donkey carts and porters who bent under the weight of chests and boxes that clogged the road.

"What did you call Auntie Major before she met Fogarty?"

"The *Mezuzah*."

"The little prayer scroll rolled inside a container that they nail on door jambs?"

Avi nodded. "'You shall write them on the doorposts of your house and upon your gates.' Religious people kiss them when they go into a house."

"*Mezuzah?* Because she was religious?"

"No. Because everybody kissed her."

They slowed when they passed Machane Yehuda, the Jewish market where hawkers cried out prices of fruits and vegetables. Fat women in dark dresses, heads covered with scarves, lumbered through stalls shaded by burlap. Their arms were filled with sacks that brimmed with flapping chickens and the green tops of carrots.

Avi gestured in the direction of a hospital surrounded by a wall that enclosed a cow pasture. "That's Shaare Zedek," he said. "The cows give fresh milk for patients. Old Dr. Wallach rules the place with an iron hand. He came from Germany in 1890. This was wilderness then. That's why the wall. Protection from bandits.

"Down in the basement, there's a room full of automobile batteries that provided electricity until Wallach got a generator. The Turks surrendered to the British right there on the balcony. Because of Schwester Zelma. You heard about her?"

Lily shook her head.

"Head nurse at the hospital. Came here maybe thirty years ago. When the Brits took Jerusalem, General Allenby arrived on foot, like a pilgrim. Schwester Zelma met him on the road with a cup of tea. When I am mortally wounded in the service of the *yishuv*, bring me to Schwester Zelma."

"You joined the *Irgun?*"

"Not yet. And if I did, I couldn't tell you."

They left the city, driving rapidly downhill, through hairpin turns. The houses of Deir Yassin clustered on top of the hill above the road. Terraced orchards lined the hillsides. At each curve, Lily held onto the door and stomped on the floorboard of the lorry, reaching for a brake that wasn't there.

They drove around the Kastel. She looked at the sheer drop to the valley below and stamped her foot against the floorboard again.

"Dangerous curve. People go off the road here," Avi said, turning toward her. "Especially when it's raining."

"Don't look at me," Lily said. "Watch the road."

They drove in silence for a while, through Bab al-Wad. Calcareous and rocky earth was dotted with Aleppo pine seedlings.

"Reforestation," Avi said. Pine trees three or four feet tall were planted in pockets of dark brown soil. "The great forest of Jerusalem. I don't know if anything will take. The hills are so eroded even the ribs of the earth are showing."

They passed the ruins of a watchtower. A single wall stood like a sentinel above a tumble of rocks on the bare hill. On the left was a small stone house where a weatherbeaten sign announcing food and lodging flapped above the door.

"You shouldn't travel alone on these roads," Avi said. "It isn't safe."

"I don't."

"That's right. You went with Meriman to Ashkelon, with Jamal to Beit Jibrin, with Rafi to Netanya. A regular *mezuzah*."

"It's really none of your business."

"And to the German Colony with Henderson. I forgot that one."

"That's in Jerusalem."

"It was a foreign country," Avi said.

Lily bristled, remembering the Nazi flag that hung from the balcony of the Austrian consulate. She crossed her arms and looked out the window at the rock-strewn hills.

"I'm sorry," Avi said after a while. "Don't mind me. I had a terrible dream last night. I can't shake it."

"What?"

"I was in terrible pain. At a funeral. Everyone was crying. It didn't make sense. I don't know what it means."

"Whose funeral?"

"I don't know. But it left me with this awful feeling. Like something bad is about to happen."

"Like what?"

"I don't know. Just that it's bad."

Lily waited for him to say more. "You want to go back?"

"No. It's just so strong." He shook himself. "Probably just coming down with a cold." He squinted at the road through the bug-spattered windshield and kept driving.

"That's Latrun over there," he said and pointed toward the ruins of a Crusader church and tower on a hill above an Arab village. "Next to Imwas. The Brits built a police post there."

Latrun had been marked on the map. "I know," Lily said.

*   *   *

The minarets of the Great Mosque of Jaffa stood out against the sea on their left. The lorry inched north toward Tel Aviv along the crowded street, wedged between carts and vans, cars and wagons. Everything stopped for a flock of sheep meandering down the middle of the road, goaded by an old shepherd with a long stick that had a strip of cloth tied to the end.

"The clock tower says two o'clock," Lily said. "We weren't on the road that long."

"Ignore it. It's always two o'clock at the Jaffa souk."

"How much farther?"

"Not much. Tel Aviv is a suburb of Jaffa." Avi sighed. "Twenty years ago, this was only sand dunes. Some Jews from Jaffa built little houses with gardens. And now look."

The lorry crawled through bustling streets, past hovels and new apartments, and through the Carmel Market, swarming with pushcarts, live chickens, and throngs of jostling housewives picking through stands packed with pots and pans, vegetables and shoes.

"The amphoriskos is on one of these pushcarts?"

"The shop we want is in a fancy neighborhood, a new hotel on the beach. Not much further." He maneuvered the lorry around large vans blocking the street, parked near the entrances of warehouses. "None of this was here four years ago. Since the Mufti called the general strike and the Arabs closed Jaffa Port, shipping has gone through Tel Aviv."

They turned onto Hayarkon Street near the port. Avi parked in an empty lot. They walked along the sand-covered sidewalk toward hotels that faced the beach. Near the harbor, construction workers in the shade of buildings ate lunch and napped.

"We've arrived during siesta," Lily said. "The shop will be closed."

"Not here."

People came and went from hotels. Some were dressed for town. Some, in broad-brimmed hats and sunglasses, wore bathing suits and had towels slung around their necks. Along the sand, bathers in bright woolen suits shouted and splashed, weaving among umbrellas, lounging in beach chairs. Girls and boys linked arms and strolled along the dunes; children filled buckets with sand; mothers, their skins tanned or angry red from the sun, pushed squalling babies in wicker prams.

Avi led Lily to a hotel with an imposing curved entrance. The ground floor was studded with shops and travel agencies.

"In here. Inside the hotel."

They went through the revolving door, out of the humidity and heat, into an air-conditioned lobby. "Oh my," Lily said. "How grand."

"The shop is along the corridor next to the newsstand." He looked down at his shorts and sandals. "We don't look rich enough for a place like this. They'll probably ask us to leave."

From the outside, the shop looked like an elegant room in the house of a private collector, with deep leather chairs, a Per-

sian carpet. Mahogany breakfronts with softly lit shelves lined
the walls. A buzzer sounded when they opened the door. The
muted strains of a Bach concerto lingered over the dark, polished wood of the cabinets.

A tall man with a goatee came out from the back of the
shop. He eyed Avi and Lily and pursed his lips. "The newsstand
is next door."

"We're looking for an amphoriskos," Lily said.

"You're a collector?"

"Of course."

"I have something that would interest you." He opened a
drawer and brought out a small velvet box. "An intaglio that
belonged to a queen." He opened the box and held a small gold
ring with a carved stone up to the light. "Aphrodite." He looked
Lily up and down. "A portrait of you," he said and bowed.

"I collect glass."

"Ah." He reached for an iridescent long-necked vial from
one of the shelves. "From the tomb of a prince." He held the
vial carefully between two fingers and turned it so that it shim-
mered silver, blue, and green, with a myriad of colors. "Beautiful, yes? It once held the tears of the prince's beloved. She wept
into it at his funeral."

"Too common," Lily said. "I'm looking for something special. In sand-core glass."

"Those are rare and expensive. It would cost at least two
hundred pounds."

"You have one?"

"An Arab brought one in a few weeks ago. He pretended
that it came from an excavation. It was a fake." He inclined his
head with modest pride. "I can tell at a glance."

"What excavation? Where was he from?"

"Told me some bizarre story he concocted. I didn't pay much
attention. They're all the same."

"Did he have anything else?"

"He had a decanter with him."

"A decanter?"

"You're interested? You want to see it?"

"Please."

He disappeared into the back of the shop and emerged a few minutes later. He held out a Judean-type decanter from the eighth century BCE, like one she found in a tomb at Tel al-Kharub.

"And the amphoriskos?"

The man eyed her quizzically and hesitated. "I told you it was a fake. I didn't buy it."

"You expect the Arab to come back?"

"Not likely. I never saw him before."

"Too bad." Lily turned to go.

The man bowed and clasped her hand. "The intaglio would look beautiful on your finger." He held her wrist and bowed again, kissing the air above her hand. "*Küss die Hand, Gnädige Frau.*"

She pulled her arm away. "We have to go."

"If I find such an amphoriskos, I shall call," he said. "Just give me your address. . . ."

"I'm at the hotel. Leaving this afternoon." She reached for the door of the shop and opened it. The buzzer sounded.

Out in the street again, Lily squinted in the bright sun. "I think Abu Musa was here. That decanter looks like the one he tried to sell to Judah at the King David. I think it's from Tel al-Kharub."

"You want to go back into the shop? Maybe he can tell us more."

Lily shook her head. "We came here for nothing. That man's a charlatan."

"It's all right. We're on holiday." Avi linked his arm in hers. "We'll go *spatziering*. It's what everyone does in Tel Aviv."

"I suppose," Lily said. "When in Rome, do like the Rumanians."

They strolled up Allenby Street toward Mograby Square.

"Tel Aviv has all the modern conveniences," Avi said with a wave of his arm toward the confusion of traffic, the cacophony of horns and angry drivers stalled behind a farmer churning down the middle of the road in a tractor. "Cinemas, pedestrians who cross the street in the face of traffic, modern shops with fashionable clothing."

A man in black slacks and a straw hat hurried past. He carried a briefcase. The corner of the case knocked against Avi's leg. Avi glared after the man, bent down and rubbed his shin. "It even has men who think they're too important to be polite, who carry briefcases that hold nothing but their lunch."

"How do you know they carry lunch? How do you know they don't carry bombs?"

"Tel Aviv already had a bomb this month."

"Bombs are rationed? Only one to a city?"

Avi bent down and rubbed his leg again. "I wish that were so."

"Could be poison," Lily said. "Your leg feel numb?"

"Poison?"

"I read in the paper that sometimes a needle in the corner of a briefcase . . . Oh, forget it. Why would anyone want to kill you?"

"That day outside the King David, when someone took a shot at us?"

"They were after Abu Musa," Lily said.

"Now I'm not so sure." He took a few limping steps. "If anything happens to me, would you miss me?"

"Very much," Lily said. "You joined the *Irgun*, didn't you?"

"Would you remember me forever?"

"Forever," Lily said.

"And light a candle for me every year?"

"Every year."

He rubbed his leg again and looked up at Lily, his eyes clouded with an unknown grief. He straightened up, took her arm and started laughing. "I was kidding. Really." He smiled. "We're on holiday."

"Where are we?"

"Allenby Street, the Rue de la Paix of the Middle East. We'll sit and watch the riffraff pass our table at a sidewalk café."

Behind him, a dark green car darted around vehicles and started a new wave of impatient shouts and curses. The driver seemed to be a young Arab; the passenger looked exactly like Henderson.

"Was that Jamal?" Lily said.

"Where?"

"In the green car."

Avi squinted at the car, already halfway to the next corner. "What would Jamal be doing in a Jaguar? In Tel Aviv, no less."

"Maybe I was wrong." But it was Henderson. Lily was certain. Who else drove a Jaguar in Palestine?

They sauntered arm in arm, keeping to the curb and out of the way of the tables scattered in their path. Avi stopped now and then to inspect a café, looking for some nuance that Lily couldn't decipher. To her, one café looked much like another. Small white tables and chairs spilled out onto the sidewalk, and umbrellas advertised Cinzano.

"Here we are," Avi said after inspecting at least half a dozen. "This year's fashionable café. Everyone comes here."

"Everyone?" Lily asked.

"Even Einstein. He was here the other day."

"He's in Princeton."

"Max Einstein. The waiter." He pulled out a chair for her.

Men in open-collared shirts read newspapers, women nodded their heads under floppy hats. People at the tables smiled, talked, leaned back in their chairs, watched passersby, brandished cigarettes in the air. Men leaned back in their chairs to stare at Avi and scan Lily from head to toe.

"They're famous for their dobish torte. You want coffee? I'll be back in a minute," Avi said.

"You want me to go in with you?"

Avi smiled at her, bowed and pulled out a chair for her. "Please, madam. Pretend we're on a date. Wait here. I'll bring it out to you."

Lily watched the man and woman at the next table, who leaned toward each other, talking softly, the woman in a dress with a broad belt and a halter top, her white gloves next to her on the table. The man placed his hand over hers and squeezed her fingers. The woman hunched her bare shoulders, said something to him in a low voice, and smiled. They glanced at Lily. She looked away, embarrassed, at the street heavy with traffic then at Avi inside the cafe.

He was standing at the bakery counter, pointing to pastries in the case.

Lily noticed a dark-haired man inside the shop, paying for pastries. He seemed to jostle Avi and then ran out the door. He darted in and out of the tables on the sidewalk, dropped his bag of pastries near Lily's table, and rushed off down the street.

Lily called after him. He didn't turn around. She called again, picked up the bag of pastries, and started to run after him.

He had reached the corner when a sudden clap of noise enveloped her with a rush of air, pressed against her head, reverberated against her chest.

Then silence.

A numbness in her ears.

She looked back at the café. Glass erupted toward the tables, the frame of the window shivered, wood splintered, plaster burst and ricocheted. The café ceiling sagged and fell, dangling wires, collapsing like a tired sigh.

Again and again. Wave after wave of heat and silence throbbed against her. Glass from the window marked with red splotches. Hot blasts of wind. Bits of cake exploding from the bakery.

Avi? Where was Avi?

Sights and sounds pulsating with fire, with darkness, with noise too loud to be heard.

"My gloves," said the woman at the next table. Aimless. Helpless. Turning around and around. The man clutched her chair and blinked.

I must find Avi.

"All those cakes," a woman with a piece of glass wedged in her back was saying in a plaintive, flat voice. "All those cakes. Cakes are everywhere." Her dress had large white buttons with big red spots.

"I must find Avi," Lily told her.

Flames erupted in the shop, flowed like water along the floor, up the walls. Pieces of lath hung by loose nails and ruptured into an inferno. Chairs burst into tinder. Avi's foot stuck out from beneath a fallen table. It twitched and kicked. Lily moved forward. Fire licked his sandal, caught at the leather. The shop flooded with flame and smoke.

"In the courtyard," Lily said to the woman next to her, "the woman was clutching her child. I found a severed arm at Tel al-Kharub. Kate did. And broken pots under a pile of mud-brick."

"You saw that?" the woman with the bloody back said, and fell against her.

Lily propped her on the table. "I must get Avi. I must." She moved toward the shop. Heat from the fire, the terrible smell of burning, beat against her in waves. She peered through fallen beams and buckled walls. "I must get Avi."

A heavy arm grabbed her and pulled her back.

"I must get Avi."

"You must get out of here."

It was Henderson.

TWENTY-SIX

LILY STARED IN FRONT OF HER at the glossy polished wood of the dashboard, at a bug flattened against the windshield, at an incomprehensible range of dials and knobs in front of Henderson. They had already rushed past the clock tower of the Jaffa souk.

Nothing was right. Henderson drove from where the passenger seat should be, his face an implacable mask.

"I'm on the driver's side." Lily said.

Henderson kept his eyes on the road. "Jaguar. Right-wheel drive."

"Where are you taking me?"

"Jerusalem."

Why am I in this car? How did I get here?

Stay calm.

"We have to go back." She tried to sound as reasonable as possible. "We have to get Avi."

"He's dead." Henderson's tone was cold and brusque.

"You don't seem to understand." She spoke slowly, as if to a child. "He went inside to buy a cake. He'll look for me when he comes out."

"He's not coming out." He smiled at that.

"You're not frightening me," she told him. "You've been in my nightmares before."

This time he didn't smile. His jaw began to work. "You're awake."

"Oh, God," she said and pressed her palms against her face, felt the hollow below her check bones, the curve of her brow. She held her hands over her eyes to combat waves of nausea, to block out the sight of Avi caught under the debris of the café, the witless stare of the woman with the bloody back, the smell of burnt cloth and hair, of gelegnite, and the cloying odor of scorched sugar.

The road climbed through olive groves. She lurched with the motion of the car as it swiveled around hairpin turns.

Try to sound casual. Just make conversation.

"I saw you driving down Allenby Road," Lily said.

"Feeling better?" Henderson asked.

She ran her fingers along the burled wood of the dash and the shining chrome.

"Don't do that," he said.

"What are all these dials?"

He pointed to the one nearest her. "Throttle." His hand moved to the knob below it "Choke."

He stepped on the gas. The needles on the dials wavered as the car lunged forward. "Motor mount's still loose." He grunted. "Damn. Someday I'll turn a corner and the motor will go in the opposite direction."

"You were with Jamal." She said, still conversational.

"The Arab who took you home from the German colony?" The side of his face twitched. "Your friend Jamal," Henderson paused, "had an accident."

"Where is he? What happened?"

Henderson glanced at her through narrowed eyes. "Terrible accident." He spoke slowly, as if he savored each word. "He fell into a pit. Impaled on a stake in the bottom of a pit." His voice was oily and resonant.

"How—?"

"Carelessness. It could happen to anyone." He looked over at Lily again and his right hand reached inside his jacket. "Could happen to you."

"I don't understand. He said he had to work at the hospital in Jerusalem."

"Never got there."

"He's dead?" Lily's fingers grew cold. She felt the blood drain from her face. "What were you doing in Tel Aviv?"

"Why were *you* in Tel Aviv?"

"Looking for the amphoriskos."

He slowed the car and withdrew his hand from his jacket. "Find it?"

She shook her head.

He dropped his hand into his lap. He slowed as they drove through Ramleh and concentrated on the road clogged with children ducking between bicycles and donkeys, women trudging under heavy loads from the market, men smoking and talking.

The dead donkey that she and Avi had seen this morning still lay in the ditch, its stomach distended, its odor a leitmotif that carried in the wind with the buzz and murmur of the street sounds. Henderson was steering with both hands now. "Stinking country."

He wiped his forehead with his right hand, patted the bulge on his jacket. The car wavered. The powerful motor whined as they left the town and began to climb.

Lily thought of the first time she had seen Henderson, the day of the riots in front of the King David. KH. Keith Henderson.

Was that his real name? And was he from Cincinnati?

Lily had been in Cincinnati as a child. Her father had taken her on a tour of Harriet Beecher Stowe house. Anyone from Cincinnati would know the house.

"You remember Eliza?" Lily said. "She jumped from one clump of ice to another, as though they were stepping stones. Does the river freeze in winter?"

"What are you talking about? What river?"

"The one in Cincinnati. I forget the name."

He glanced at her, then looked back at the road. "Ohio."

At least he knows the name of the river.

"Who's Eliza?" he asked.

"You know. Uncle Tom."

"You have relatives in Cincinnati?"

"Everyone knows Uncle Tom," Lily said.

"Never met him."

He's not an American. Who is he?

They had passed Latrun. They approached Bab al-Wad and the pathetic clump of saplings struggling to grow in the rocky soil. Avi had called it the forest of Jerusalem.

Lily stared at Henderson, watching his impassive face. His hands held the steering wheel lightly, and he drove as though nothing had happened. He had killed Jamal. And Avi. He didn't even know Avi, and he killed him.

Angry tears burned in her eyes. Henderson's the one who rouses them to frenzy, the one who pays them to kill.

And the amphoriskos. Why did he want it?

"They're looking for a man named Karl," Henderson had said that night at the King David.

She scanned his jutting jaw, his burning eyes, and in her mind she heard Sir William's reedy voice droning, "I met Konrad Henlein. He has a brother Karl." Sir William, spilling his soup on the table, repeating, "Your young man . . . family resemblances, like pottery types . . . a nose here, an angle of the jaw there."

Karl. Of course, Karl, that must be his name.

"Karl," she said out loud, and he turned.

"What did you say?"

That was a mistake. "You remind me of someone named Karl."

"I told you. I don't know anyone named Karl."

"I meant Karl Marx." He glared at her. His face was stony.

"The man with the lamp shop on Jaffa Road," she added quickly. "I left my desk lamp to be fixed."

She flinched in the acid wash of his eyes. The muscles around his powerful jaw churned.

He kills for a living. He'll kill me too. As easily as he'd kill a fly, as easily as he'd kill a cat.

His eyes slashed at her. He put his hand in his jacket pocket again.

The car swerved around the curve. "You should have believed me," he said, his jaw still working. "Too bad. I liked you."

The road was narrow here. Barely wide enough for two cars. The car wound around the edge of the precipice. Lily looked down at plowed fields and terraces far below. "Beautiful view," he said. "We'll step out so you can appreciate it."

Henderson had one hand on the wheel. His eyes shifted from Lily to the road and back again.

The car swayed toward the sheer drop of the cliff edge. Henderson yanked the wheel back sharply.

A thump sounded from under the hood. The car veered.

Henderson turned toward the sound. "Shit."

Almost by instinct, Lily hoisted herself up, with one knee on the seat, and pulled out the throttle. She grasped the steering wheel. She shoved it hard to the right, heard a jarring noise, felt the jolt of impact. The car hurtled into the wall of the cliff.

The dashboard crumpled and showered her with broken glass. A numbing pain shot through her leg. Henderson's head jerked back and forth through the windshield.

He slumped in the seat, his face bloody with cuts.

She tried to move. Pain throbbed in her leg, wedged between the crumpled remains of the seat and the crushed dashboard.

"Oh, God."

She closed her eyes and still saw Henderson's bloody face imprinted on the exploding café, the fallen beams and twisted rods, the flare of the fire, the woman with glass in her back, Avi's twitching foot.

Lily heard the sound of a car coming around the curve toward her.

She began to sob uncontrollably.

TWENTY-SEVEN

A CREAM-COLORED BENTLEY with Eliot at the wheel purred into sight and slowed. Dame Margaret peered through the windshield.

"Hold on," Eliot called out and stopped the car. He hurried toward Lily, his sandals slapping the road.

Lily tried to move again. A sheet of pain ran down her left leg. "I'm pinned."

Eliot pulled at the shattered door of the Jaguar. "Stuck." His face flushed with effort.

He placed one hand on the window, braced a foot against the fender and yanked again until the door rasped open. A hinge clanked on the ground. Eliot tugged once more. The door fell loose, tumbling from his grasp onto the road.

"Try moving now."

Lily strained. Another stab of pain thrust through her. She scraped her bottom teeth against her upper lip and shook her head.

Dame Margaret leaned out the open window of the Bentley. "What about him?"

Eliot glanced at Henderson. "He's not going anywhere."

The wide brim of Dame Margaret's hat flipped back and forth. "We'll take care of him later." She reached up to steady the hat.

Eliot turned back to Lily. He struggled to lift the dashboard, nudging it just enough to relieve the pressure on Lily's thigh. "Try again." Beads of sweat glistened on his forehead.

"I can't." Lily licked her lip and caught a glimpse of her ashen face in the mirror. "I think my leg is broken."

He indicated the dash. "Put your hand under there," he directed and slid Lily along the seat, mumbling, "Carefully. Carefully."

Lily winced.

He lifted her out of the car. Lily cringed with each jarring motion.

"Hold on, girl." His voice rasped with exertion. "We'll make it, girl."

Panting, he hoisted Lily to the Bentley. Dame Margaret stood by the opened door of the back seat, leaning on a stadia rod. "All I could find in the boot. Give me your belt."

Dame Margaret gently raised Lily's foot with both hands, rested the broken leg on the seat, and used Eliot's belt to lash the stadia rod to Lily's leg. "We'll be in hospital in no time," she said and stroked Lily's arm.

"What about Henderson?" Lily asked.

Dame Margaret straightened up. She rubbed the small of her back with both hands and looked back at the Jaguar. "His name is Henlein." Her voice was glacial and deliberate. "He told you he's Henderson?"

Eliot strode to the driver's side of the Jaguar, reached through the window and put a finger on Henderson's wrist.

Not Henderson, Lily reminded herself. Henlein.

"Pulse is faint. But there."

Dame Margaret stood next to him. She tilted Henderson/ Henlein's head back against the seat, pulled at his eyelids, took a handkerchief from her sleeve and dangled the corner in front of his nose. Almost imperceptibly, it wavered with his breath.

"Still alive."

She shrugged. Eliot and Dame Margaret exchanged glances.

A sudden gust of wind lifted the brim of Dame Margaret's hat and carried it off. Eliot and Dame Margaret watched it waft back and forth, dancing in the wind past the rocks at the edge of the cliff, across the ruins of the Kastel, as it sailed into the valley below. They glanced at each other again and nodded.

Dame Margaret tucked the handkerchief back into her sleeve while Eliot scurried to the other side of the Jaguar. Together, one on each side of the car, they pushed it backwards, leaning their weight into it. Slowly, it moved away from the cliff face toward the center of the road.

Lily watched Henderson's head sway with the impact, watched a thin trace of blood seep from his mouth, heard a faint moan.

Eliot and Dame Margaret didn't seem to notice. Both were frowning, intent on shoving the car across the road.

"He's alive," Lily said. Were they deaf? Lily shifted in her seat, felt the stab of pain in her leg and gasped. "What are you doing?"

The car crept toward the embankment. Eliot grunted. "Nothing, really."

And they continued to push the car.

Dame Margaret's face was crimson. "This is a dangerous curve." She halted, panting, and pushed back her hair. The handkerchief fell from her sleeve and fluttered across the road. "Slippery in the rain."

"It isn't raining," Eliot told her.

"But it could be." Dame Margaret pushed against the car again.

"Why are you doing that?" Lily asked, starting to rise. A spasm in her leg threw her back on the seat.

"Cars skid off this cliff all the time." A streak of perspiration stained the back of Eliot's shirt.

"Stop it," Lily said.

Eliot's face reddened with exertion and the Jaguar moved to the edge of the cliff.

Eliot and Dame Margaret gave the car a final thrust and watched it tumble. The clang of metal struck against the rocky slope, dust billowing with blow after blow as it shattered down the hillside, hood over trunk, until it came to rest.

Then silence.

"You killed him," Lily cried. "Just like that. You killed him."

"I certainly hope so." Dame Margaret wiped her hands against her dress. "Poetic justice. The attaché before Henderson went off the road at the Kastel." She pointed down the valley. "Right here."

"It won't do any good." Eliot went back to where the car door lay on the asphalt. "Henlein will be replaced."

"What have you done?" Lily shouted. "Are you mad?"

"We gained time." Eliot moved back to the door of the Jaguar lying on the road. "It will be days before he's missed. Maybe a week."

Dame Margaret nodded in agreement. "Then they have to train his replacement."

"Delayed them for two weeks, a month at the outside." Eliot's voice was hoarse with his struggle to hoist the remnant of the car with both of his hands. He bent under its weight. As he carried it to the edge of the cliff, the hinge clattered onto the road.

"Wind and weather permitting," he said between breaths, "we only saved twenty, maybe thirty lives."

He heaved the door over the precipice, retrieved the hinge, and still panting, tossed it into the canyon. Dame Margaret watched it clang to rest.

"*Inshalla*. God willing," she said. She picked up the other door hinge, threw it after the door, and wiped her hands against each other with a cheerful slap.

Dame Margaret returned to the Bentley with a satisfied smirk on her face, then turned to Lily with a puzzled look. "What were you doing in the car with that man?"

"The fire," Lily said, "the explosion—he pulled me away."

"You were in the café that was bombed."

Lily nodded and closed her eyes. "And Avi."

"We know. We've been following you since you left Jaffa," Eliot said.

"I didn't see you."

"Take heart," Dame Margaret said to Lily. "We'll have you at hospital in the blink of a sheep's eye."

They started up the incline toward Jerusalem and drove over the tire tracks that ran across the road into the cliff wall. "Won't the police notice the skid marks?" Lily asked. "They go in the wrong direction."

Eliot turned slightly. "Not for days. Besides, there's no connection to us. We've all been in the southern Shephelah at Zakariya today. We surveyed the archaeological site, measured the walls, checked the fortress. That's how you broke your leg. Didn't you? You fell off the tower. Didn't you?"

"But—"

"It's an important site. Probably ancient Azakah. Next year we may excavate there. Won't we?"

"I—"

"You're on the senior staff. You remember, don't you?"

"I suppose," Lily said.

"Next time," Dame Margaret wagged her finger at Lily, "be more careful."

Eliot slowed as they went around the next curve. "She's doing all right, considering," he said to Dame Margaret.

"Considering what?"

* * *

Each nick and bulge in the road, each jolt, sent a shock of pain up Lily's leg.

"Only a little farther," Eliot said. "We're coming into Jerusalem."

Rafi will take care of it, Lily repeated to herself, closed her eyes and licked her lips again. "I want to go to Strauss Hospital. On Chancellor Road."

"Strauss it is."

Lily tried to smile through cracked lips.

Dame Margaret tilted her head out the window, wiping at her forehead with the back of her hand. "Hot today." Her hair blew across her face and she pushed it back, narrowing her eyes against the wind.

They slowed for a barrier that blocked Jaffa Road just past the entrance to the city. "Now what?"

Eliot braked. "Another bomb?" he asked the policeman who directed traffic to the right and left with broad sweeps of his arm.

"This time a bus. On Jaffa road." The policeman gestured to the right. "Have to detour."

"Left," Lily said.

Only a little way to go.

The blare of an ambulance horn keened behind them. Eliot pulled to the side of the road. The ambulance bellowed again and continued along the Street of the Prophets in the direction of Rothschild Hospital, rocking the Bentley as it passed. Clouds of dust swirled in its wake, obscuring the red Star of David painted on its side.

Another red-starred ambulance whined behind it and turned onto Ethiopia Street.

They followed it to the emergency entrance of Strauss Hospital.

"We need some help here," Eliot called to the orderlies who were lifting a stretcher onto a gurney.

A nurse in starched white emerged from the hospital, pushing an empty wheelchair. She peered into the back of the Bentley. "Another victim? Broken leg?"

Eliot helped transfer Lily into the chair and smoothed her skirt over her knees. "They'll fix you in a jiffy," he said. "You'll be all right now," and returned to the Bentley.

* * *

The hospital smelled of antiseptic and sour flesh.

"I want to see Doctor Landon," Lily told the nurse over the moans and sobs and voices on the edge of hysteria that permeated the crowded waiting room.

The nurse didn't answer, continued to push the chair with one hand, and raised the other above her head. "Anglit. English." She pointed down to Lily with a flick of the wrist.

Another nurse, this one in a blue uniform, snaked through the bevy of wheelchairs, gurneys, and benches toward Lily. "It's a *balagan* here today. A madhouse."

"I want to see Dr. Landon."

"All in good time." The blue one adjusted the wooden leg rest of the wheelchair and carefully lifted Lily's leg. "You weren't the only one on the bus."

"I wasn't—" Lily took in her breath and wet her lip again. Where's Rafi?

"First we put you in the queue for Xray," the blue nurse said, parked the chair next to a table, and disappeared behind some swinging doors.

Lily looked around, at a man who held a bloodstained arm in an improvised sling, at a woman who pressed a gory piece of gauze to her eye, at a child sobbing against the shoulder of a stolid woman who stared straight ahead.

They could all be dying. I only have a broken leg.

Someone slammed against her chair and a spike of pain ran up her leg. Surprisingly, the wheelchair moved. Her leg throbbed; her head eddied with nausea.

Where was Rafi? Please, Rafi.

Lily reached for the table to pull the chair out of traffic. She closed her eyes while the murmur of voices washed over her, individual inflections lost in a whirlpool of sound. Her head jerked forward. Startled, she opened her eyes again to watch for Rafi from her roost at the side of the table.

An orderly pushed a cart through double doors at the opposite end of the room. Lily caught a glimpse of Rafi at the end of a long, sloping corridor.

Tentatively, Lily pushed away from the table. She reached backward, clutching at the large wheels of the chair, and rolled herself, inch by inch, across the room toward the double doors.

The room wavered in front of her. Perspiration ran down her spine.

The doors opened again. She saw Rafi, intent on Xrays that hung in front of light-boxes lining the hallway.

She pushed herself past the doors and into the corridor.

A pink lady carrying a tray brushed past Lily, bouncing against the chair. It caromed against the wall. From the opposite direction, an attendant grasping a stainless steel pitcher rushed toward them, while Lily struggled to shove away from the wall.

The attendant and pink lady collided. The tray and the pitcher clattered to the floor.

Lily's wheelchair slid away from the wall.

"Cleanup," the attendant called.

A girl with a bucket and mop appeared from a side room. The attendant pointed to a widening puddle of tea that swept down the hall. The girl dabbed at it and tossed the soapy contents of the bucket onto the terrazzo floor before she mopped.

The wheelchair gathered speed. Lily skidded through the slippery layer of soapsuds, careening toward Rafi.

"Look out," someone shouted.

The sharp pain of impact was sudden and unexpected. Rafi, reaching toward the chair, was knocked off balance.

A flash of blue flared out of his pocket and crashed to the stone floor. Lily looked down at the shatter of broken glass.

It was the amphoriskos, splintered into a hundred tiny shards, lying next to Rafi's foot.

A tiny roll of film spun away from It, rotating down the corridor.

Lily licked her lip again. Then she passed out.

TWENTY-EIGHT

LILY HEARD MURMURING around her, and muffled voices that seemed to come from another room. Her mother sat among weeds on the rotted steps of a shuttered house. Dead leaves swirled around her. Lily's mother looked up, her face shattered with grief, her eyes uncomprehending and swollen. "It's all gone, you know. All gone." Crimson rivulets seeped through the fingers of her mother's clenched hand. "You see. Gone."

"What are you holding?" Lily asked, and gently opened her mother's clenched fist to find blue splinters of shattered glass smudged with blood.

"We must go to the hospital now," Lily told her

"You came at last," her mother said to a private ghost behind a broken window. "At last."

* * *

"Coming around at last," Rafi's voice was saying.

Lily's leg, encased in a massive cast, throbbed. She lay under a burden of sheets, heavy and crisp with starch.

She opened her eyes to see Rafi leaning over her, his face so close that she felt his breath on her cheek.

"Go away." She closed her eyes again.

"Are you in pain?"

Silence engulfed her and ticked around the room, covering the table beside her, the dresser, the chair next to the bed.

"I don't want to see you," she said after a while. "I don't want to see anyone."

When she opened her eyes, Rafi still leaned over her. She felt a flush of anger and turned her head away. A pepper tree nodded and bowed in the window.

"Avi's dead." The words caught in her throat.

"I know." Rafi took in his breath. Something about his voice made her look at him. The rims of his eyes were moist and tinged with red.

Behind him, a candle sputtered in a glass on the corner of the dresser. Rafi followed her glance. "I lit it for Avi. Hope you don't mind."

"I promised him," Lily said.

"Why was he in Tel Aviv?" Rafi asked.

"We went to find the amphoriskos." Lily fingered the sheets. "The amphoriskos," she repeated. "Don't you understand what you've done?" She felt a void, deep as a chasm, in her core. "I trusted you. I believed you."

"You can still trust me."

"I trusted Eastbourne too."

"And now you don't? What do you know about him?"

"You lied to me. You had the amphoriskos all along."

"I found it in the house in Sebastiye," Rafi said. "During the wedding. Abu Musa must have stolen it when Eastbourne was killed."

"You know about Eastbourne? For all I know, you killed Abu Musa too," she said, and for a moment, the horror of the thought stuck in her head. An angry tear spilled down her cheek.

"I'm sorry. I'm awfully sorry about the amphoriskos. But we needed it."

"We?"

"Eastbourne hid the film inside the amphoriskos. That's why he was bringing it to Jerusalem."

"Why didn't you give it to me when you found it?"

"It was evidence. I couldn't get out the film. The inside of the vial was rough. Sand core glass, you said. The neck was narrow and the film stuck. I needed a long-nosed tweezers from the lab to get it out."

"You carried it around in your pocket."

"I came in to develop the film in the hospital darkroom. Have to use a water bath to control the temperature because of the sensitivity of the film. There was no time. The bomb on the bus, one trauma after another."

He reached toward her, his hand poised to stroke her cheek.

"Get away from me." She turned away and looked out the window. "What did you expect to find in the film? And who is 'we'?"

"I've been working with Henderson. He's here. He's waiting for the film."

A stab of fear numbed her. "Here?" The bough of the pepper tree shook as if to warn her. "He's alive?"

"Of course he's alive."

She tried to get out of the bed. The movement jarred her leg and the pain shot through her body.

Rafi adjusted the covers. "You look uncomfortable. Too warm? In pain?" He held out a glass of water and two pills that glistened in his hand.

"What's in the pills?"

"Just something to take away the pain."

She looked toward the other bed in the room. It was empty. The pills were a nauseous green. "I don't need them."

"I'll leave them here." He put the pills and water on the nightstand. "In case."

The only thing to do is bluff it out. "It was foolish of me to be so clumsy." She tried to smile.

"Something's fishy." Rafi sat down on the chair next to the bed.

"What do you mean, fishy?"

"For one thing, I don't think you broke your leg falling off a tower."

"What makes you say that?"

"Your femur has a spiral fracture, not a transverse fracture."

"What's the difference?"

"If you broke it in a fall, you'd most likely have a transverse fracture—straight across—unless you got yourself tangled. But you don't. Your leg twisted. I've seen breaks like that from automobile accidents."

He knew. Henderson told him. They're both in this together and I have to get out of here.

She tried to sit up, to swing her leg over the edge of the bed. The sudden clap of pain made her gasp.

"Sit back. I'll get what you need."

I must get help. The call button for the nurse was pinned to the pillow. Lily reached for it and fell back panting.

"You *are* in pain." Rafi picked up the water and pills again.

"No, no." She pulled up the covers, as if she could hide under them. "I have to go to the bathroom."

"Let me help you."

"It's all right. I'll wait."

"You weren't at an archaeological site," he said. "You were in Tel Aviv with Avi."

"How do you know?"

"You just told me."

A light knock sounded at the door. Henderson?

A small bald man in a summer suit stood at the door. He held three roses wrapped in green wax paper. "I'd like to speak to you." He waggled the flowers and came into the room. "If you're up to it."

Who is this man? "What do you want?"

Two of them. Somehow, I have to get out of here.

"I tried to contact you earlier," the stranger said to Lily. "When you phoned me at the consulate, I was in Haifa. I expected you to call back."

"Haifa?"

"Clearing customs. I had just arrived a few days earlier. Wasn't settled in at the consulate yet. And I wasn't sure how to reach you."

"I called you at the consulate?"

"This is Henderson," Rafi said. The man bowed again. "Colonel Keith Henderson. He's attaché at the American consulate."

Lily felt a surge of relief, and then a jab of anger. "Your name really is Henderson?" How can I be sure? "You don't—"

"I had a lot to organize when I arrived. But I knew you were in good hands with Dr. Landon. He said he'd watch out for you."

"He told you that?"

"I understand that we're responsible for breakage of an artifact accidentally removed from your archaeological site. We'd be glad to reimburse the excavation."

"The amphoriskos. Dr. Landon told me you needed it. I don't understand why."

"Nothing to be concerned about. Had to do with some maps. The originals had been damaged—altered."

Rafi glanced in Lily's direction.

"Photocopies of the maps were inside the vial," Henderson said.

"She's exhausted," Rafi told him. "Can you come back later?"

The little man looked from Lily to Rafi and back again. "I'll let you get some rest now. We can talk more tomorrow." He put the flowers on the nightstand and left.

Next to the bed, Rafi picked up the bouquet. "I'll get these in water." He started out the door.

"Rafi?"

He turned back to her.

"I think I'll take those pills now."

He handed her the glass. "They'll make you a little sleepy."

She swallowed the pills, and he leaned down to kiss her forehead. She turned away to the window again. Red peppercorns dangled in the lacy leaves like drops of blood. The pepper tree shook and curtsied back and forth, back and forth in the wind. She watched the delicate pattern of the branches dip and bow, back and forth, back and forth, until her eyes grew heavy.

* * *

Her father held the blue glass vial delicately between thumb and forefinger. "This little bottle," he was saying, "is a talisman. It guards your life."

She reached for it, and he held it away from her, up to the light. "It diverts danger, takes the blows itself and shatters. Then the danger is past."

"Is that what happened, father?" She held out her hand to him, and he disappeared.

* * *

She opened her eyes to see Sir William and Lady Fendley seated next to her bed, watching her.

"You've had a bit of a bother," Lady Fendley said. "Didn't mean to disturb you."

"This last month—" Lily said.

Sir William took her hand. "I know. It's like when I first came to Alexandria, long, long ago," he said. "Nationalism is as bad as religion. I used to think they were a good thing, God and country and all that. Now I don't know."

A nurse bustled into the room, carrying a vase of flowers. "Visiting hours are over." She put the vase on the dresser. Rafi waited in the doorway. "Doctor wants to examine you."

Sir William turned to go. He leaned on his wife's arm, saw Rafi near the door, and turned back to Lily. "Don't let him bully you. Don't let him tell you that archaeology is just an excuse for self-indulgent adventure, the world's most expensive team sport. We are in the business of inventing memories. A necessity in the modern world. We are as necessary as water." Sir William waved at Lily, wiggling the fingers of his free hand. "Ta ta," he said.

Lily turned her face to the window.

"You still angry with me?" Rafi asked.

"Of course."

He came closer to the bed. "You don't understand."

"Oh, but I do," Lily told him. "It reminds me of a story."

"Please . . ."

"You want to hear the story?"

"Not really."

"A scorpion and a duck were on the banks of the Jordan."

"I know the story," Rafi said. "I know what you're going to say. But the whole thing is more complicated than you think."

"The scorpion said to the duck, 'I need to get to the other side of the river. Will you carry me on your back?'"

"I had to get hold of the plans before Henlein," Rafi said.

"And the duck answered, 'Certainly not. If you get on my back, you'll sting me. That's the nature of scorpions.'"

"It wasn't what you think," Rafi told her. "You told me you wanted to find Abu Musa."

"So the scorpion said," Lily continued, "'I can't swim. If I sting you, you'll sink and I'll drown.'" Lily pushed the button to raise the back of the bed and ignored the twinge in her leg it caused. She was enjoying this. No wonder Rafi had a story for everything. "When they reached the middle of the river, the scorpion stung the duck. As they were sinking, the dying duck said to the scorpion, 'But you gave me your word.' And the drowning scorpion said—"

Rafi finished it for her. "'How could you believe me? This is the Middle East.'" He reached out a hand to adjust her coverlet. "Did I ever say I was telling you the truth? I've always been honest about lying. It's a matter of principle."

"That's the nature of scorpions."

Rafi flashed her a tentative smile and spread his fingers. "You're pretty sneaky yourself, you know." He reached into his pocket and took out a piece of paper. "The note you left in the journal."

"You're the one who took the note? Who looked at the maps?"

"You're the one who changed them."

He leaned over her and brought his lips close to her forehead. "By the way," he murmured, "where are the coordinates of the original map?"

"Go away."

"I can't go away," Rafi said. "Too much has happened between us."

Were they were all linked together—conquerors and madmen, the Hitlers and el Husseinis and Henleins, who gorged on hatred and moved people around like chess pieces? The Eastbournes and Hendersons and Dame Margarets, who played at intrigue like fractious children, convinced that they were making history? Even Rafi? Weariness overwhelmed her.

"I can't forgive you for the amphoriskos. You lied to me. You had it with you in Netanya."

"It isn't me you can't forgive. You can't forgive yourself."

"Forgive myself? You took the amphoriskos. It fell from your pocket."

"It's more than that. You told me you never said goodbye to your father. You think you could have stopped him if he told you?"

"Maybe.

"That's a terrible burden for a ten-year-old."

"I thought the amphoriskos was his message to me, to tell me goodbye." All she could remember was the last sight of her father, when the door opened to the closet under the stairs.

"And the amphoriskos broke. Maybe that was the message. To break with the past."

Restless, she fingered the sheets and drew her hand across her forehead. "Maybe . . ." she said, but her voice choked.

Why hadn't she remembered the laughter and smiles and limitless love of her father, the marzipan automobile hidden under her napkin, sitting on his shoulder to watch the Rose Parade?

Tears clouded her eyes and started down her cheek.

Rafi brushed them aside.

She turned her face away. He sat on the edge of the bed, and she turned back to him.

"You must hate me," he said.

Her eyes began to sting. "Not really."

If I start to cry now, I'll never stop. She felt warm tears on the back of her hand, the fold of the sheets. She felt a heaving in her throat and sobbed without end as she leaned against Rafi's shoulder.

"It's time to say goodbye now," he said.

Tears kept coming. She hid her face in the curve of his neck, and he kissed her neck, her cheek, her lips.

"Time to say goodbye," she echoed.

TWENTY-NINE

RAFI CALLED EVERY MORNING after Lily came home from the hospital.

Each time he called, Lily felt a wash of excitement and leaned into his voice. And each time, after she hung up, misgivings eddied through her. She would walk back to her room, the words "he lied, he lied," thrumming in her head, still angry at his deception, fearful that someday, he too, would be gone. As her father had done, leaving nothing behind but empty rooms.

"I'll have ten days to woo you on the way home," Rafi had said that morning. "Taxi will be there at two," he reminded her. "Be ready or we'll miss the boat."

Lily closed the trunk filled with field notes, pottery and artifacts from the tombs at Kharub. Her leg still bothered her when she was tired. That too will pass, Rafi had told her.

She had just finished packing when Rafi came upstairs with the porter. He looked at the trunks and suitcases stacked on the floor.

"All this?" he asked. "It won't fit in your cabin, much less the taxi. I have a few bags, too."

"Only the Gladstone bag goes in the cabin. The trunks go in the hold."

The porter, heavy and sad-eyed, wore a shirt that was too small and gaped between the buttons, exposing smudged portions of a sweat-dampened undershirt.

Rafi helped lift one of the trunks. "What do you have in here? Lead pellets?"

The porter bent forward with a grunt while Rafi helped secure the load on his back with a tumpline.

"Books. Papers. Artifacts. The weight of history."

The porter staggered into the hall, and Lily heard the trunk clatter between the wall and the banister all the way down the stairs.

"You go ahead and say your good-byes," Rafi said. "I'll stow the baggage in the taxi."

Lily went into the garden. Dame Margaret was there, ensconced behind an open *Palestine Post*. Only the feather of her hat could be seen, wagging in the wind.

The headline covered half a page. *PEACE IN OUR TIME.* Lily sat down across from the newspaper. *CRISIS AVERTED.*

"Good morning," said Dame Margaret. "There's going to be a war." She was still hidden behind the paper. "I came to say goodbye."

"Now that it's over," Lily said, "I wanted to tell you that I'm glad we became friends."

"It isn't over. It's hardly begun. Austria and Czechoslovakia are just the beginning. Poland may be next. Hitler's already talking about violation of Germans' rights there." Dame Margaret lowered the paper.

Arrays of sparrow hawks, one formation after another, soared overhead, sailing on the wind, dipping and gliding across the sky like vast *corps de ballets*.

Lily watched them. "Where are they going?"

Dame Margaret looked up. "Somewhere in Africa." She folded the paper and put it on the table. "We leave tomorrow for Mesopotamia," she said. "Just for the digging season. Until the rain sets in."

"What will you do if war breaks out?"

"It won't. Britain isn't ready for war yet. It will be at least a year. First we have to get all our ducks in a row. There'll be more concessions. The Mandate will have to accede to Arab demands to stop Jewish immigration."

"Why?"

"The Chinese sages say that every battle is won before a war begins. Victory is based on deception, my dear. The winners are those who can turn harmony into chaos, certainty into confusion."

An involuntary shudder surged through Lily. "That's horrible."

"More horrible than we ever imagined, thanks to the miracle of modern science." Dame Margaret shook her feather. "Before it's over, we'll all be collaborators, steeped in silence and guilt."

Dame Margaret folded her hands and hesitated before she spoke again. "Good luck to you and your young man. I'm sorry about Eastbourne."

"You mean about his defection?"

"I'm sorry that he was killed," said Dame Margaret, smiling. "Always remember that it was the work of unknown bandits. He was warned so often about traveling on the Jerusalem-Hebron road."

"And Henderson?"

"You mean Henlein?"

Lily nodded.

"He seems to have left the country. No one has seen him for over six weeks."

Dame Margaret's feather still wavered in the breeze as Lily went into the Common room to say goodbye to Sir William.

The old man, seated in the big black chair, looked smaller and more frail than ever. He glanced up at her. "You're going home to write your dissertation?"

"Yes."

"About the graves at Tel al-Kharub?"

Lily nodded. "Perhaps you should go back to England. It's no longer safe here."

"There's nowhere else to hide," said Sir William. "I shan't see you again, you know."

Lily bent down to kiss him. She brushed against his dry cheek and touched his crackled skin.

"After this, archaeology will never be the same to you. When I was young, I wandered the streets of Alexandria through snapping fires and thought only of Caesar and the sack of the city, delighted at the chance to witness the recreation of a great event. Then I saw their eyes, and their fear."

"You understand then," Lily said. "I can't escape into the bloodless deaths of the past any longer." Just layers of charcoal and burnt beams, charred bones and shattered jars.

"It's not just data." The woman cowering in a gutted court-yard at Tel al-Kharub; the dead with wounded arms and smashed heads, shoveled into an ancient trench like sticks of broken wood. Now they had names—names like Avi and Eastbourne, like Dr. Stern, and even Abu Musa.

Will I be like this someday, lost in a chair, recounting tales of the violent days in Jerusalem?

Tears welled up in her eyes and she left, going through the hall and out the door to the waiting taxi.

Lily hesitated for a private moment of goodbye to Avi, to Jamal, and even the corrupt Abu Musa. Just one more layer in the archaeology of Palestine, Eastbourne had said.

Rafi stood by the car. He had already stowed bags in the trunk and the front passenger seat. Suitcases filled the floor of

the cab and occupied the back seat. "I don't know if there's
room for us with all this baggage."

I'm bringing home more than baggage, Lily thought, and
leaving more than keepsakes behind. "That's all right," Lily
said. "We'll sit on top."

She climbed in, mounting the running board and the suitcases as if they were stairs. "We'll manage," she said. "I'm Lily
Sampson, girl archaeologist," and she reached out her hand to
help Rafi into the cab.

ACKNOWLEDGMENTS

My THANKS GO TO Linda McFadden, Cathy DeMayo and Sally Scalzo, who read draft after draft with keen insight and endurance; to Don Sheppard, Terri Eselun, and Toy King, who nursed the book through the first rough draft, and cured it of the purple passive; to Barbara Collins Rosenberg, who gave me sage counsel and encouragement; to Buffalo Boots Tiemann, for advice on the development of the Minox and its uses in the years just prior to the outbreak of WWII.

The ostraka mentioned in Chapter 3 are modified versions of those found at Lachish in Israel that refer to the invasions of the Assyrian army under King Sennacherib (Torczuner, L.I., et. al., *The Lachish Letters*, Oxford, 1938).

Most of all, I would like to thank Anita and Jordan Miller and the staff at Academy Chicago Publishers for their work on the book and their patience and support.

Aileen G. Baron
August, 2002

GLOSSARY

kefiya .... head scarf
fellahin .... farmers
finjan .... coffee pot
sherut .... jitney cab
hamsin .... desert wind
souk .... market
fiq .... a greeting
kova tembel .... "an idiot's hat"
habibi .... darling
mezuzah .... a religious amulet